WAGEREASY

WagerEasy

TOM FARRELL

WagerEasy©2021 Tom Farrell
ISBN: 978-1-7365932-0-2

Editing by Steve Parolini
Copy Editing by Susan Brooks
Cover Design by NovakIllustration.com
Typesetting by NovelNinjutsu.com

www.tomfarrellbooks.com

1

After exiting the Dan Ryan, Liz drove several blocks north then circled back to avoid a certain part of Chicago I wouldn't drive a tank through, especially at night. The neighborhood was once a prime industrial area and now a favorite hangout for winos and gangs. Rows of broken factory windows were dark and empty like tombstones. Weeds grew out of cracks in the front steps.

Liz, my uncle's old partner from the homicide division, still hadn't told my Uncle Mike and me why she'd invited us along to the murder scene. She hadn't requested our assistance once since my uncle retired more than a year ago. Uncle Mike had brought me along on cases when he was still working, and I believed he and Liz had come to respect my opinion.

We parked and walked toward one of the vacant factory buildings. The street was lit up with flashing lights of emergency vehicles stacked three-deep. In the blowing snow, it took a while to navigate a path through the police barricade and the emergency personnel, but everyone knew Liz was in charge and let her pass. Uncle Mike and I followed.

"Hey, Mike, Mike O'Connell." One of the uniforms called to my uncle and came over. "I was one of the first on the scene. Look at my hand." He held his hand out straight, his fingers trembling. "I thought I'd seen it all."

"A bad one, Murph?" Uncle Mike asked.

"Yup. You're not coming out of retirement are you Mike?" Murphy looked under the brim of his snow-covered hat toward me. "Talk your uncle out of it, Eddie."

Liz focused her deep-set blue eyes on Murphy from the top step. "I'll look forward to your written report, Officer Murphy."

Murphy shrugged and muttered under his breath while another officer a few steps away laughed.

"One of these days you'll learn when to keep your mouth shut," Uncle Mike told him with a clap on the back.

Murphy's face reddened but he managed to smile. "Thanks, Mike. Good luck on this one."

We stopped inside the lobby of the once-proud American factory where Liz could get an update from her team. On the wall behind a counter hung the remnants of a time clock that invited us to punch in. Across the room, open elevator shafts exposed cable hanging down. In another corner lay more steel cable coiled like a snake. Wind whistled from the upper floors and down the shafts.

Liz and her team led us into an expansive room two stories high and a couple of football fields in length. Walls had been demolished and chunks of concrete were stacked around the perimeter. Skeletal metal fixtures still clung to support beams and made me wonder what they once manufactured here.

In the middle of the room, the police had set up halogen lights focused upon the victim as if to stage the murder scene. At first, I couldn't believe my eyes. The victim was strung up by ropes in a spread-eagle, star-shaped design—a mad artist's conception of pain. The blackened area of the crotch and nearby blowtorch explained the smell. I tried to catch a gust of fresh air through the broken windows to avoid the stench.

A bullet to the neck had ended the man's ordeal and might be evidence of a need to rush at the end. The body tilted forward at about a forty-five-degree angle, giving me an impression the figure might take flight.

My eyes drifted to the ropes that suspended him in midair, one extended upward over a beam that ran the length of the structure. The ropes were knotted around the broken rebar that grew out of broken concrete. The rust that ringed each prong of twisted rebar told me the partial demolition had occurred long ago.

The knots were nothing a ship's mate or even a Boy Scout would take pride in. The rope was wrapped and knotted as if more than one person had done the work. Maybe the ankles had been tied before the wrists to anchor the victim. Then the ropes around the chest had been pulled to draw the victim upwards into a helpless position. Other ropes strung across the neck and body provided a spider web effect.

If Michelangelo had been a murderer, this might be the result.

Two other bodies lay off to the side as silent witnesses. From this distance, I couldn't make out their faces. The blowtorch at the feet of the outstretched victim was left behind as Exhibit A.

As the photographers finished up, other experts moved about the scene with hushed words, businesslike, stepping lightly between the bodies and the pools of blood, stopping periodically to peer up at the figure. Their collective attitude was one of reverence.

I had a zillion questions in my head and wanted to examine the suspended body more closely, view the other two prone bodies, and start to put it all together. Walk inside the cave-like interior where water dripped from the ceiling and search for more clues. Yet, I also wanted a moment to study the production. To try to understand the lengths a person or persons would go to wreak such havoc.

The victim's ripped slacks were made of fine cloth. His black leather shoes had been shined to a high sheen. The white dress shirt, ripped and bloodied, ironed and pressed. I even spotted a cufflink that glistened in the sharp white light around one wrist.

It took willpower to avoid staring at the man's crotch, the blackened area that produced the horrid stench of burned flesh and complemented the scream that lingered upon the face. I was compelled to imagine how the blowtorch flames produced such a blood-curdling reaction. Wind whistled through the remnants of the old factory.

Had Liz invited us because she knew we did investigative jobs for Burrascano, the gambling boss? A case years ago had involved a blowtorch. Maybe she thought the scene before us was mob-related and hoped my uncle could confirm it or supply some information. I didn't believe the answer would be so simple. The complicated nature of the tapestry before me demanded more.

I stared once more at the side of the victim's face, a rubbery mask. The figure appeared other-worldly—skin made of wax for a carnival show. If the snarling scream could be unimagined, the terror wiped from the eyes, there were characteristics I found familiar. There was something about the eyes.

I stepped around Uncle Mike for a better look.

I knew this man.

The revelation startled me, and I almost blurted it out. I bit down on my anger. I wanted to cut him down and put an end to the show.

There were police all around. Liz stood only a few feet away. She'd ask how I knew this man and that question would lead to more questions. What did I know? Was I holding something back? Could I have prevented this? None of that made sense, because they knew me, and knew I would never get involved in something like this, but those were the thoughts that rifled through my head.

I hadn't seen him in a couple of years. I didn't even know his last name. The police would grab the man's wallet once they deconstructed the scene and his identification would lead to his address, his job, and more information than I could provide.

The smart move would be to keep silent, let the pros carry out their duties. I was merely a spectator, a bartender with a start-up PI business, and a gambling debt.

One of the crew, a woman in a white coat, came over and asked Liz if she could join them. Other personnel had come into the room and started working as if it were another pain-in-the-ass workday. Liz left and issued orders. The level of noise increased across the dark, once-empty floor. The factory had come to life again to process murder.

Uncle Mike nudged me. "I don't miss those days. Liz has to supervise and be sure nobody screws up. Procedures got to be followed to a 'T.' In a high-profile case like this, Internal Affairs and downtown will be all over your ass. You got rookies who pick up something they shouldn't. You're responsible for everybody doing what they're supposed to do."

The way his feet took a false step behind his old partner told me he wanted back in the game. He had never spoken of it, but it was clear the way he'd been hustled out of the department after a confidential Internal Affairs inquiry had left a sour taste that still lingered.

"At first I thought you and Liz were going to walk arm and arm down memory lane to handle one more big case," I said. "Now, I'm not so sure. Why do you think Liz brought us along?"

Uncle Mike placed the stub of an unlit stogie into the corner of his mouth. "Don't get cute, Eddie. She doesn't need anyone's help to handle a case. Liz wants my input, that's all."

"She thinks it's a mob killing and wants you to confirm it."

Uncle Mike grunted. "Maybe. Why not? I'd do the same thing if I was in her place. But she also knows I can't walk up to Burrascano and expect to get straight answers. Even Joey L,

God rest his soul, wouldn't turn rat for me or anyone. You know that."

"It looks like a mob killing to me. Or maybe some gang."

"Right. Somebody's sending a message."

"You think it has anything to do with the change in the gambling laws?"

Uncle Mike shrugged. "Could be. Could be drugs. A turf war. We'll know a lot more when they tell us who this guy is."

I kept my voice steady. "You remember that skinny guy who came by the bar and asked you all kinds of stuff about horse owners?"

"No."

"He heard you used to own a couple of racehorses and he had a whole list of owners to ask you about? He thought if he knew more about each owner, he'd get a feel for what a trainer might do with a horse in a certain situation. He wanted the whole picture."

Uncle Mike turned to look at me. His stone face, the cop face, returned. "That was a long time ago."

"We called him the Leech."

"Right. Always pumping people for information. Whatever happened to him?"

I caught my breath and pointed a finger toward the man suspended in midair. "That's him."

"What?"

"Don't say anything. Liz will find out soon enough." I checked around to be sure no one could overhear. "You think I want her pumping me for information? I don't know shit. I haven't seen him in a couple of years."

"What the hell's he doing–"

I almost raised my voice. "Pretty fucked up, isn't it?"

"You're sure?"

"Yeah, I'm sure."

"You hung out with him at the track?"

"For years. Smartest fucker I ever met. You know that big Pick Six I won?"

"Right. Santa Anita simulcast?"

"We pooled our money. He picked one of the longshots. We won a lot of other bets, too."

"If he's so smart, what's he doing up there with a burned-out crotch?"

"Beats me."

"Was he in the habit of borrowing from the wrong people?"

"No way."

"Doing drugs? Dealing?"

I shook my head.

"You don't know shit."

Everyone called him the Leech, but I called him Jimmy. I never learned his last name, and he didn't know mine. You don't exchange personal information at the track. Strange how the people we hardly know can be the ones we're most connected to.

We argued over sports and horses. He always liked the up-and-coming horse or team while I preferred the proven, class entry. The money seemed secondary to him because he'd played for higher stakes.

Jimmy and I were partners at the track the same way Liz and Uncle Mike were partners. What the fuck happened? I stared up at Jimmy's face as the paramedics eased him down to the floor. We'd taken different roads.

Or maybe I'd taken the same road, but didn't know it. We were alike in many ways.

"I don't know shit." You lose touch with people and you wonder why. Things happen; things you could've possibly done something about.

In the shadows, Uncle Mike rolled the unlit cigar between his lips. "Jeesus. Let's keep this between us for now. See where all this leads."

2

THE NEXT DAY, UNCLE MIKE AND I DROVE WEST TO MEET
Liz at Jimmy's apartment building and get updated on the
official murder investigation. Despite our years at the track,
Jimmy had never invited me over to his place and, now that I
thought about it, I'd never invited him over to mine. We didn't
talk about life outside the track. Only a track bum understands
another track bum.

It had been a long night. I learned Jimmy's last name—
Golding. His face, contorted into a gruesome mask, came back
to haunt me. The struggle my old friend must've endured as he
tried to escape the flames was impossible to fathom. I learned
he worked at WagerEasy, a British sports betting conglomerate,
and the other two victims worked with him.

At first, I wondered if Jimmy's job had allowed him to
graduate to some high-rise condo on Lake Shore Drive, but the
address Uncle Mike gave me turned out to be a quiet corner in

Cicero only several miles from Thornton Racetrack. From the look of the apartment building, Jimmy maintained a modest lifestyle. I hadn't been a regular at the track the past couple of years, but I wasn't a stranger either, and I hadn't spotted him for some time. Maybe he signed on with WagerEasy for big money; a free agent snapped up for his natural talent and gambling savvy.

I found it difficult to picture the Jimmy I knew—the Leech—working a nine-to-five job. He drove a rusted-out twenty-year-old Chevy and wore the same faded Levi's and Bulls T-shirt every day, except in the winter when he'd switch to flannel shirts.

Jimmy cared only about winning. The races were run exclusively for him and if he didn't meet the challenge, it would amount to a personal insult to his core being.

Jimmy was proud of his "Leech" moniker. When he pumped people for information, he let them know his nickname, shrug and explained how it was his weakness. People would nod and give him information because his approach seemed official. Later, people would find him and ask him questions or yell out over the bar noise, "Hey, Leech, what did you hear about the last workout by the favorite?" or "Hey, Leech, what do you know about the injury status of the Bears left tackle?"

Jimmy became a repository for information around the track. Data came off the top of his head or from one of the notebooks he carried around when he recited the clocker's comments about a workout or an opinion on a football player's trick knee. You always got more information than you asked for; Jimmy rewarded any show of intellectual curiosity.

I frequently told him he should've had his own column in the *Daily Racing Form* and he'd always say they didn't pay enough, which made me wonder about the amount of money he was winning.

We were the kings of the racetrack and I didn't learn his full name until last night when they zipped up the body bag.

WagerEasy must've paid him big money to change course. Had he met a woman? No, Jimmy wasn't the dating type or the marrying type. He was a track bum. Hell, I had the same strain of track virus running through my veins.

Maybe that was why I had such a tough time with marriage number one and why the straight and narrow path to a PI business and regular income revolted me. I'd rather tend bar at my uncle's tavern and shoot the shit with the regulars I'd known all my life, while placing a few wagers, than plan a career.

I needed to know what mission or motive had stirred things up for Jimmy. Maybe the job at WagerEasy was so closely related to the track life that he'd been able to surrender to the nine-to-five world. Or maybe WagerEasy offered the chance for a track bum like Jimmy to see inside other intersecting gambling worlds and gather even more information. Jimmy had a thirst for information that could not be quenched. If only I'd seen Jimmy lately, caught up with him, and had lunch and talked, I wouldn't be left wondering and cussing myself out.

I almost felt more compelled to find the answers to all these sporting life questions than I did the answers about his murder. Then the horrific image returned. Jimmy strung up inside that vacant factory, caught in a web of ropes, a silent scream roaring from deep inside. I had to find out what happened. Justice came first, or whatever passed for justice these days.

Uncle Mike pulled on his coat and opened the truck door. "You ever been here before?"

The red brick apartment house had probably been an opulent address in the twenties. Upon closer examination, it looked its age with overgrown vegetation, broken screens, and faded curtains.

"No."

Uncle Mike moved his bulk out of the truck to the curb. "It would be nice if you knew something useful, other than what horse he would've liked in the third at Thornton."

I should've taken a deeper interest. But maybe that's what death teaches us. I slammed the door. I didn't need another life lesson.

Uncle Mike stood outside the truck and waited for me. "I should tell you. I heard from Burrascano."

"About the murders?" My heart beat a few ticks faster. "What did he say? Does he want to meet?"

"Yeah."

"You going to tell Liz?" I wondered if there were rules about finding a killer on behalf of a mob boss and a duty to confide that fact to the lead police detective. If there were, I didn't know where to find them. But Uncle Mike would want to be fair to his old partner.

He started up the sidewalk. "I don't know yet. Maybe Burrascano wants to meet for something else. Maybe some other murder."

I walked beside him and slipped on old crusty snow beyond the shoveled path. "What about the fact that I knew

Jimmy Golding? Should we tell Liz?" Holding back hit me with a sense of betrayal and made me sick to my stomach.

"Hold off. Let's see what's going on."

Uncle Mike wasn't happy that Liz hadn't called him to talk about the investigation and maybe that's why he was being cautious. "Why do you think she hasn't returned your call?"

My uncle's face went through several gyrations that suggested a range of anger and frustration. His heavy jowls fluttered and the creases across his forehead constricted into a scowl. "Something's going on."

I wanted to ask what the hell he meant by that but followed him inside. We walked up the creaky old stairs that had bolstered decades of tenants and, based on the scratches in the walls and woodwork, a stream of moving companies. The door to Jimmy's apartment was the only one open. Sometimes neighbors treated a cop visit like an open house meet-up, but not here.

Liz came out and met us in the short hallway that led into the living room. "There's not much to see. Somebody tried to break in the back door but must've been scared off because Golding's laptop was still here. We took it into custody, but there's not much else. You can look around if you like."

"Thanks," I said.

"Sorry I didn't get back to you, Mike," Liz said. "I've been pretty busy. You know how it is."

Uncle Mike nodded but didn't say anything.

"Jimmy Golding was getting paid half a million a year and lived in a dump like this," Liz said. "Go figure."

Half a million? Jimmy Golding, the Leech, had cashed in on the track after all. Sports betting hadn't even been declared legal in the state.

Liz escorted us into the living room and her partner joined us. Augie Saboski was a few inches shorter than me with close-cropped black hair. The black pants, white shirt, dark blue sports coat, and lack of a smile told me he was a straight-shooter. We hadn't gotten the chance to talk much at the murder scene last night.

His tight smile and red face told me he was pissed. He asked to talk with Liz in the hallway. Saboski obviously didn't like strangers trespassing on his territory.

Uncle Mike stayed planted inside the living room while I began to roam. Unlike my place, Jimmy's apartment had high ceilings and antique light fixtures. Battered old blinds hung across the windows. Funky old flower wallpaper had faded to a dull beige color. The living room was connected to a dining room and then a small kitchen. A door led out of the kitchen and down the back stairs.

I checked out the scratches on the back door around the deadbolt. A couple of deep gouges in the right places. They were the work of a professional. I doubted if the intruder had been scared off.

Why break in and not take the laptop? The media speculated that the murders were due to a drug deal gone bad. Maybe the burglar had been looking for drugs. But the Jimmy I knew never sold or used drugs.

I found nothing but a stack of TV dinners in the freezer. Enough to keep you alive until you could get to the diner the next day. The spare bedroom held exercise equipment blanketed in dust. The closet in the main bedroom had a row of new dress shoes and a few new suits and sports coats. Jimmy had stepped it up in the fashion department.

But a two-bedroom was still a two-bedroom and there wasn't much else to see. Jimmy led a Spartan life. No pictures of family, no posters, no pets. Not even a plant. He was able to focus one-hundred percent on the horses, sports, or his job.

And half-a-mil a year. Yeah, I was jealous even though he had nothing. Maybe it was having nothing that made me jealous. A chance to concentrate on one thing and one thing only and be a success. He had full discipline and focus. No girlfriends who made demands. The chance to be at the forefront of a groundbreaking company like WagerEasy in the soon-to-be nationwide legal gambling industry.

How can you be jealous of a murdered man? That thought brought me back to reality. I wandered over to the desk that sat in one corner of the dining room and began to inspect a clutter of envelopes. Most were bills. They had been marked and would be bagged as part of the investigation. That meant they'd been opened by Jimmy. The lack of clutter inside the apartment made me think something must be missing. Something I needed to examine.

I glanced over to Uncle Mike. Liz had returned. The way they smiled and laughed told me that Uncle Mike hadn't yet told her about Burrascano's meeting request. Uncle Mike had always stood up for Liz, and she'd done the same for him during the Internal Affairs inquiry. Liz and her husband, Wayne, were holiday regulars at my uncle's house. Now, Wayne was in hospice.

One of the envelopes caught my attention. It was from a company called Parlay Partners. In gaudy red lettering splashed across the envelope, it promised the highest percentage of winners in pro football. It was a tout service. Jimmy would never pay for advice. He prided himself on his handicapping expertise and ability to gather his own information. Yet the envelope had been opened and the contents seemed to be missing.

Uncle Mike called me over. The three of us huddled in the living room. I expected he was about to tell Liz that Burrascano wanted to meet with us and that I knew Jimmy from the track.

Instead, Liz spoke up. "I'm glad you both could stop by. I wanted to tell you before you heard about it. It's the reason I haven't returned your calls, Mike. Sorry."

"That's okay," Uncle Mike said. I knew he was lying. There were all kinds of things he wanted to know—the forensics report, the possible clues left at the scene, and if any wino stumbling around the skid row neighborhood at the time of the murders had been sober enough to witness anything.

I had questions as well. What did they find on the bodies? Were there any drugs in Jimmy's system?

Liz forced a smile. "I can't tell you why or what I've heard because I don't want to put any of us in an uncomfortable situation."

"Uncomfortable situation" was code for some conflict that could get her or Mike in trouble with Internal Affairs and cost them their pensions. Liz didn't have much time left, maybe a year before retirement, and she was counting the days.

Liz placed a hand on Uncle Mike's wide shoulder. "You know how these things go, Mike. Everything points in one direction. I've got to question Burrascano."

"What?" Uncle Mike took a step back.

"Sorry, Mike. I'm under a lot of pressure on this one."

We were benched. We wouldn't be a part of Liz's investigation. She must know our secret—that Uncle Mike and I had a "complicated" relationship with Burrascano. Maybe she was afraid our secret wasn't much of a secret anymore.

It could be a new procedure and Liz was nervous about her upcoming retirement. Or, it could be the work of her partner, Saboski.

"But I need a favor, Mike," Liz said. "I've tried to contact Burrascano, but no luck. I don't want him to take a convenient vacation to Florida. It will only hurt him."

"You want me to talk to him?" Uncle Mike asked. "You want me to persuade the guy?"

Liz nodded and lowered her gaze. She had invited us to the murder scene to absorb all the gory details so there'd be no way Uncle Mike could deny her request. Typical homicide detectives playing the long game. Although he'd never admit it, I'm sure Uncle Mike admired her strategy.

Uncle Mike placed his hands on his hips. "Well, that's just great. Eddie and I get shut out, and you ask me for a favor."

"I know, I know. Do it for me, Mike. It's not the department. It's the feds."

It left me and Uncle Mike without a legit way into the Jimmy Golding investigation. But we'd find another way. I needed to find out what Liz was talking about when she said, "everything points in one direction."

We'd meet with Burrascano.

3

When Burrascano requested a meeting, it meant the same day and he picked the place. This time it was Thornton Racetrack. Uncle Mike and I showed up during the third race as instructed.

For a Wednesday night, it was a decent crowd for the harness track, but if it was O'Connell's Tavern, I'd pronounce the place "dead." The bartender had enough time to read a magazine between orders.

The escalator to the upper grandstands had been roped off and the doors to the stairway were locked. Only three ticket windows were manned. The smell of burgers wafted from the grill, but no customers stood in line.

Thornton had tried to get legislation to allow slot machines and casino games to increase purses and attract more horsemen. But every attempt to increase revenue had been rejected, and left Thornton to fight a losing the battle against well-financed out of state tracks. Add to that the competition from Illinois casinos and barroom video gambling machines, and the crumbling one-hundred-year-old racetrack had only one possible future—the wrecking ball.

Uncle Mike and I walked outside through the glass doors to the apron that fronted the finish line and looked out upon the lighted tote board. Horses and drivers warmed up down the backstretch in preparation for the next race.

The announcer's voice echoed across the infield acreage. "Only four minutes. Better hurry."

I caught the smell of horse manure mixed with the stench of the nearby oil refinery. "Hurry for what?"

"To get back inside out of the cold weather. Jeesus." Uncle Mike flipped the pages of the harness program. "Anything jump out at you on this race?"

"I can't focus on the horses. You don't have any clue why Burrascano wants to meet?" I kept my voice low. Except for a couple of kids near a picnic table, the wide area was vacant.

"We're supposed to look like we're playing the horses," Uncle Mike said.

It was the same brushoff he'd given me on the way over. Of course, I didn't expect the crime boss to discuss his intentions over the phone, but I couldn't help but speculate. The Blowtorch Murders, as Jimmy's murder and the shootings of the other two employees were now called, had received banner headlines in the newspapers and on the internet. The murders of white men in the highly segregated south side neighborhood had caught the media's attention.

It must've been a drug deal gone bad, the media said. That got under my skin. Jimmy tortured and murdered then wrongly accused of a drug deal.

Liz had said that everything pointed to Burrascano. Maybe it was the blowtorch. "Any idea why Liz wants to set up a meeting with Burrascano?"

"Maybe it's better if I don't know."

"Burrascano stands to lose when companies like WagerEasy move in, right?"

Uncle Mike pulled out a stogie and a lighter. "When it's all legalized?"

"God knows the state of Illinois, a walking bankruptcy, will legalize."

"Right. Legalization of sports betting, pot, and anything else they can think of." Smoke from his cigar billowed across the white-dirt track. "What's Burrascano going to do? Kill them all one by one? That's nuts."

"Burrascano must want to meet about Jimmy's murder. Are we going to work a case in competition with Liz?"

Uncle Mike looked down at his program. "No. I've got to tell you, Eddie, and you can decide if you want to go in with me or not, but the way Liz talked—"

"What? Of course, I'm going in. Jimmy was a good friend."

"Liz would never say 'everything points in one direction.' We never started a case thinking that way."

"Right. I never know where an investigation will take me."

"I think Liz wants our help. She just can't ask for it."

I didn't need another reason to take this job for Jimmy, but I was glad we could help Liz at the same time. "How much does Liz know about us?"

"She knows more about our jobs than she admits. These guys who work for Burrascano have big mouths. You think they don't talk about us out on the street? That a former homicide detective solves murders for them? What they don't talk about is the fact Burrascano has agreed to turn the killers we find over to the police. 'Justice' isn't in their vocabulary. But Liz can put two and two together."

I tried to soak this in. Even old partners didn't tell each other everything.

Uncle Mike tapped my arm with his folded program. "C'mon, let's get a bet down. If Liz didn't want me to work the case for Burrascano, she would've told me."

"This was so easy when Joey L was alive." Our old friend in the mob, the one who had brought us down the path to these detective jobs for Burrascano, had been murdered in Vegas last year. Joey L insisted we charge for our services as a matter of respect, and we'd done so, but our fee was reasonable. Without Joey L, we'd be walking a tightrope without a net.

"Yeah," Uncle Mike grunted. "He looked out for us."

I followed Uncle Mike back inside. Sometimes Joey L told Uncle Mike, "this judge is on the take," or "we know that cop." Uncle Mike never betrayed such a confidence but would find other ways to have a case reassigned from that particular judge or get the cop transferred. Corruption was ingrained in Chicago. The lines had become blurred. Maybe that's why Uncle Mike had such a tough time sleeping. When I was growing up living at my uncle's house, I'd hear him walking the halls late at night and find him asleep in an easy chair in the morning.

Some of the players walked out for the start of the race as we joined others running to make last-minute wagers at the windows. The small crowd seemed to swarm in every direction as the announcer shook things up. "Only one minute."

I could put down a couple bucks on the race in case there were cops around. I had noticed guys near the entrance that were over-dressed for the harness races, but maybe they were Burrascano's men.

On our way through the momentary chaos, a short, thin man with a White Sox cap pulled down low over his eyes, stepped up to us. "Follow me. The Man is waiting for you."

He walked more than a few steps ahead of us, so a casual observer or a cop might conclude that Uncle Mike and I weren't with him. It would appear that we were headed toward the grill at the far end of the cavernous room or maybe to the restrooms around the corner. Instead, we bypassed the restrooms and ducked through a door to the Jockey Club.

On the way up the narrow three flights of stairs to the club, Uncle Mike had to stop to catch his breath. "I'm not as young as I used to be. Maybe I should've taken the elevator."

"How's the leg?"

"Not bad. Where's our friend?"

The guy with the Sox cap had disappeared up the stairs. "He's the shy type."

When we made it to the top, I barely recognized the Jockey Club. It was dark and most of the tables and chairs from the exclusive dining space had been removed. The wood surface of the long bar and the stage still glimmered from the light that found its way through the far windows from the track.

Once, when I was a teenager, I came up here the night before the Thornton Derby. Waiters in white coats carried trays of prime rib, a three-piece combo played on stage, and couples danced.

"Let's check the private suite," Uncle Mike pointed to a room at the far end of the bar.

The door was ajar.

4

WHEN WE WALKED INSIDE THE PRIVATE SUITE OF THE
Jockey Club, a man in a pinstripe suit and silk tie greeted us. It
was Vic DiNatale. We were not on good terms. He didn't look
any happier to meet us, but we shook hands to keep up
appearances.

"Mike, Eddie," DiNatale said. A phony smile was plastered
on his face, his gold bridgework flashing. He didn't like outsiders
taking care of business for the Outfit and he especially didn't
like me or my uncle. "How are you?"

"Vic," Uncle Mike said. "Didn't expect you. Where's
Rosario?"

"Mr. Burrascano will be back in a second." DiNatale
straightened his tie. "He had to hit the head. How you guys
been? Eddie, I haven't seen you since Vegas."

"We meet again." I wondered where DiNatale stood in
the line of succession. From the intensity of his cologne, I
figured he'd moved up several notches.

Rosario Burrascano walked into the suite from the private restroom. I was shocked but did my best not to show it. He was only a shell of the man I knew. He was stooped over, his face ashen, and his gray suit hung loose around his shoulders. The times I'd met him before, he reminded me of a Wall Street titan.

"Mike, good to see you again." Burrascano hobbled back to his chair at the round table with DiNatale's help. "Eddie, glad you could make it." The voice of the gambling boss trembled.

We exchanged greetings and shook hands all around. DiNatale and I settled into chairs a few feet away from the table where Burrascano and Uncle Mike sat.

"How many guys you got working downstairs?" Uncle Mike asked. "I think there are more of your guys than racing fans."

"Even here, security is a concern." Burrascano coughed and cleared his throat. "Sometimes I feel the way this track looks."

"I nearly tripped on broken tile by the bar outside," Uncle Mike said.

DiNatale and I gave a short laugh and then studied each other. He probably didn't approve of my jeans and flannel shirt.

"Yes. They've let the place go," Burrascano said.

"Used to be there was a line to get into the clubhouse," Uncle Mike said.

The pained expression on Burrascano's face reminded me how much he disliked small talk. In his world, small talk was a sign of weakness.

"We okay in here?" Uncle Mike asked.

A smile lit up Burrascano's face. "My guys are smart as shit, Mike. They went over it with all their tech stuff. Isn't that right, Vic?"

"I watched them personally," DiNatale said, sitting up a bit straighter.

Uncle Mike looked down at the track. "You don't have any hot tips tonight do you?"

Burrascano waived a thin, bony hand. "Naw. It's small potatoes anymore. I let the young bucks handle it."

Uncle Mike took out a cigar. "Okay if I light up?"

Burrascano nodded. "No problem. I hoped you would. Remember us and Joey L here? Those were the days."

Uncle Mike had prepared me for the cigar. It was a custom to smoke whenever he and Burrascano met.

"Get him an ashtray, Vic," Burrascano said.

I masked a smile as DiNatale jumped to fetch an ashtray.

"Eddie and I were talking about Joey L earlier. A great man," Uncle Mike said.

"And a great friend," Burrascano said, nodding toward DiNatale when he placed the ashtray on the table.

Uncle Mike and I had solved the murder of Joey L in Vegas. It repaid a personal debt we owed him.

"Okay," Uncle Mike said. "What's it about?"

Burrascano leaned in close across the table. I had to listen hard to hear his muffled voice. "I'm under a lot of pressure on the Blowtorch Murders."

"Yeah. My old partner, Liz, is handling the case. You know that right?"

Burrascano nodded.

Uncle Mike took a thoughtful puff on the cigar. "She needs to interview you."

"What? Interview me? You've got to be kidding. Fuck the cops."

"You know how that will look."

"I'm telling you right now. I didn't order these murders."

"Then what's the problem?" Uncle Mike spread his hands on the table. "You answer a few questions about where you were that night and it's over."

"You think I operate alone?"

There were other bosses. They depended on each other and the basic rule of the Outfit prohibited a chat with police detectives under any circumstances.

"This one is different," Uncle Mike argued with no edge to his voice. "Those other guys will understand. If you didn't order it, who did?"

"Good question. That's what I need you to find out."

It was what I wanted to hear.

Uncle Mike puffed on the cigar and rubbed the palm of his hand across his bald head as if he expected Burrascano to say this all along. "How about the people who did the deed? Any leads?"

"None."

"What do the cops have? They must have something to call you in."

Burrascano studied the end of my uncle's lit cigar. "You're the ex-cop, you tell me."

"That kind of attitude will get us nowhere."

DiNatale looked up from the floor and then at me. Maybe Uncle Mike had gotten too close to the line.

"You're right." Burrascano turned and looked down at the tote board. "What are the fucking odds? The world is such a fucked-up place." He turned back to face Uncle Mike. "I was there. Vic, too. We were doing a deal with this poor bastard, Golding, the Leech."

"What?" I stood. I couldn't help myself.

DiNatale shot me a "what the fuck" look. I sat back down.

"You were there?" Uncle Mike stuttered. "What deal? With WagerEasy?"

Burrascano didn't look toward me. He stared down at his hands. "We planned to close the deal with WagerEasy that the Leech set up. WagerEasy gets the names of the high rollers. It gives them a leg up on their competitors."

It was pure genius by Jimmy. If WagerEasy could get first crack at the high rollers, they'd dominate the sports betting market. Tons of people placed sports bets, but only a chosen few bet big money and could afford to lose big money. Vegas casinos had fought over these high rollers for years, and now that Illinois was about to go legal, the same pitched battle would be fought here.

"How did you get your hands on the names of the bookies' high rollers?" Uncle Mike asked.

Burrascano smiled. "These bookies act like their high rollers are a trade secret for fuck sake. But who do their customers run to when they need ready cash? Us. We know our debtors better than our wives. Why not sell the list—get ahead of all this? Things will change."

Uncle Mike nodded as if the capitalistic reasoning made perfect sense, then he scratched the tip of his broad chin. "Let me get this straight. The mob had a deal to sell its list of high rollers to WagerEasy, a British company? What the—"

"We found him strung up." Burrascano didn't show a trace of emotion. "Me, and Vic, and our driver."

I glanced at DiNatale. The mob enforcer didn't flinch. A blowtorch was probably his stock in trade.

"It was terrible, just terrible," Burrascano continued. "I'd negotiated with the young man, the Leech. We'd give them a list in return for a sweet down payment and a cut of the losses by the high rollers. The Leech was a straight-shooter."

"You heard I was there last night with Liz?" Uncle Mike asked.

"Yeah, I heard," Burrascano said.

Uncle Mike was right. There were no secrets.

"It was a frame-up?" Uncle Mike asked.

Burrascano's face reddened. "It was fucked up. The minute we saw the guy hanging there in the ropes with the burned-out crotch, we heard sirens. Fortunately, Vic had an emergency escape route ready."

I glanced sideways. DiNatale's hands balled into fists.

"What about the other two?" Uncle Mike asked.

"They couldn't tell us nothing," Burrascano said. "They were already dead."

"Anything else?"

"We were only inside a minute or two. My driver had to carry me out for fuck sake."

"Shit." Uncle Mike puffed hard on the cigar. "Maybe you left evidence at the scene. Maybe that's what the cops have. And you want me to find out who set you up and killed Golding?"

"I'm more concerned with who set me up. But, yes, those who did the actual handiwork would be helpful."

I filed away Burrascano's suspicion—that the guys who killed Jimmy at the factory were underlings, most likely hired by someone else.

"Who else was with you?" Uncle Mike asked.

"I told you. Only Vic and my driver."

Sometimes Uncle Mike asked the same question again. He didn't take notes.

"That's all?" Uncle Mike probed.

"A lookout car outside."

"If I ask you lots of details, I'm doing it for a reason, and you should know it. I want to trip you up. Because if you did it and you're hiring me as cover . . ."

It would be a good trick. Hire Uncle Mike so he could tell Liz that Burrascano had nothing to do with the murders.

"It wasn't me. I won't vouch for anyone else. The deal with the Leech wasn't popular with a lot of people."

"I'll need names," Uncle Mike said. "But you can't expect me to hold off the cops. I'll need some time."

"I'll take a convenient trip—"

"You know how that will look. It will only make things worse."

"Once the publicity dies down—"

"Nope." Uncle Mike shook his head. "I need you around. I need your sources, your input. And don't think I'm working with Liz or the cops. In fact, she made it clear I'm not a part of it. But I've got loyalties, too. Just like you."

"Fuck them. They've made up their mind."

"Not Liz. She'll give you a fair shake," Uncle Mike said.

"You want me to answer her questions? Tell her I was framed?"

"Not easy. But if they have something on you, you need to give your side of things. The feds—"

"Liz is getting pressure too?" Burrascano needed us more than ever. "The publicity is a concern, Mike. We don't want to scare off our good customers. Not now. Not until a deal is done. Or longer."

Uncle Mike stood and walked toward the window and looked down at the track. I took his hesitation as a ploy to negotiate. "I won't take the job unless you do the interview with Liz."

"The cops want a scapegoat."

"C'mon, Rosario. You've got lawyers. They can help you get through this. You want WagerEasy to point the finger at you? It makes sense, doesn't it? They've got a publicity department and they're probably saying how Golding had gone off the rails and was doing drugs. They'll say how they don't know anything about any deal and, if you let time go by, they'll shred any evidence of a deal. That's how you end up as the scapegoat. By doing nothing."

DiNatale and I looked at each other. Maybe *we* should be taking notes.

"The feds already have a hand in these murders." Uncle Mike sat back down. "They can't wait for an excuse to take the case away from Liz. How did you, and DiNatale, and a lookout car happen to slip away? The usual procedure is to set up a perimeter and post a squad car at certain exit routes around the scene. Maybe they've got a cop who saw something. Don't expect me to tell you what they've got. And maybe your sources aren't as good as you think. You need your lawyers to poke around."

Burrascano scratched at his ear and yawned. "What the fuck. You think I'd go into an interrogation room like a fucking gangbanger?" He smiled in a way that made my blood run cold.

Uncle Mike reached over toward the ashtray and tapped ash from the cigar. "The best thing you've got going for you right now is that Liz is handling the investigation. She'll do a thorough job. She'll meet you at your house, a coffee shop, or even out here at the track. She's not like others. The department has tried to clean up its act, but you know it's not a hundred percent. They might assign the case to a different detective. Some asshole with a grudge. Why not take care of business now, while Liz is handling it? Do it. Do it for me as a favor."

Burrascano studied Uncle Mike and then he nodded slowly as if thinking through things. It seemed that the word "favor" worked some sort of magic. "Fine. If you do me the favor in return and find out who set me up. For the usual fee, of course."

"Deal," Uncle Mike stood, cringing from his bad leg, and shook Burrascano's hand.

DiNatale's clenched jaw made me want to request a contingency clause. If Burrascano passed away, the deal should be called off.

5

AT THREE A.M., I DROVE PAST JIMMY'S APARTMENT. AN EMPTY squad car sat out front and there appeared to be a light on in the apartment. Liz believed somebody had tried to break into Jimmy's apartment, but since the laptop had been taken by the police, she assumed there was nothing else left of value. No reason for Liz to post a uniform inside.

I turned a block away from the apartment and drove down the alley and pulled into a spot behind a garage, where I'd have a good view of the back of Jimmy's building. There was no squad car parked in back and no sign of activity.

I turned off the engine and snow began to accumulate on the windshield. Snow flurries always meant sparse crowds at the track but could provide the meeting's best payoffs. I'd look over Jimmy's shoulder at his chicken-scratch comments in the margins of the racing program. He was the master artisan and I was the eternal apprentice.

I decided to wait. Maybe an insomniac would spot my vehicle and call the police. If a patrol car came by in the next fifteen minutes, I had a story ready. I was a PI on a stakeout, and my uncle was Mike O'Connell, the retired homicide detective. That should do it. But what if it didn't? What if Liz heard about it?

Liz would say, *"What the hell, Eddie. I invite you over to Golding's apartment, but that's not good enough for you? You break in? What the hell?"*

I had to come up with another story, something plausible. As I sat and froze, I tried to think.

I cracked open a window and the cold seeped into the car. A few snow flurries swirled beneath a single street-light near the end of the alley.

Earlier tonight, when I'd visited Jimmy's apartment with Uncle Mike, I got a good look down the back stairs and the back ally. As expected, there were no security cameras. Later, I told myself it would be easy. That the job was in my wheelhouse, a piece of cake. There'd be no need to bring in Uncle Mike and explain my reasons. Then I let the fear creep back in with the cold.

If I told Liz what I was looking for and why, she'd find the stuff and take it into custody. No way Jimmy's stuff should languish in a police evidence locker. Still, I needed to come up with that story to explain my presence to Liz, if needed.

A light came on over the back porch of the house at the end of the alley. My heart began to pound.

The Blowtorch Murders had become a symbol of police incompetence and the media buzz hadn't shown any sign of dying down. Seventy-five unsolved shootings over a summer weekend were bad enough, but three white guys murdered in a vacant factory on the south side? If I was caught, maybe Liz wouldn't be able to help me. My old connection to Jimmy Golding at the track would be discovered and I'd qualify as a suspect.

A siren could be heard several blocks away and I waited. Then the porch light went out. Maybe it had a sensor and a cat had triggered it.

If only I still smoked, time would go faster. The police siren faded. Stillness returned.

I could tell Liz that I believed the burglars who tried to break into Jimmy's apartment would return. What if they hadn't found what they were looking for? I could say that a gambler like Jimmy probably flashed a bankroll and the intruder wanted to dig through more hiding places inside the apartment. My stakeout at night was part of a public service. I went over my excuse several times and it seemed to hold up.

I pulled down on the black stocking cap, checked the tools in my pockets, and got out. The frozen gravel beneath my feet didn't crunch but the bits of ice granules did. I stepped carefully and tried not to slip. I crossed a side street to the alley that led up to Jimmy's place, acting like I was another guy walking home late from the bars, while at the same time checking for a curtain rustling in a window or the pinpoint light of a cigarette from a late-night smoker.

The missing clutter inside the apartment. I should've thought of it earlier. Where were the stacks of racing programs? Jimmy had mentioned his foxhole to me several times. How he had no choice but to retreat to the basement storage area to work. How he lost himself in the races late at night while his newlywed neighbors rocked out, smoked and drank, then fought and fucked through the night.

If the tenants got a hint that I was about to break into their basement storage space, they'd think I intended to abscond with their crown jewels and come running out into the frigid cold with kitchen knives. I knew what kind of mildew hole I'd find. Moldy furniture that had to be stored for a decade before it could be thrown out. But this kind of hole was the perfect escape for a guy like Jimmy. The ideal spot to sit and handicap.

I slipped in behind the overflowing dumpster at the bottom of the back stairs and got a whiff of the stench. A few yards across the landing, the door to the storage area had more iron draped across it than a shuttered liquor store on skid row. The fist-sized padlock secured a heavy chain the size of a boa constrictor. Iron mesh wrapped the small side window inside and out. A rusty deadbolt ensured the storage junk would be as secure as a vault of Wall Street bonds.

Before I attempted to play Houdini, I waited. I thought I heard the back stairs creak above. Thought I heard a late-night commercial. An infomercial about how to make zillions investing in real estate.

No sound of a door. Perhaps the creaking was my imagination.

I took off my gloves and pulled out my tools. I could pick that padlock in my sleep. But the chain wanted to rattle in the night and might alert the guy taking notes on how to make zillions. Despite the lack of light, I wrestled the rusty snake to the ground. Then the deadbolt popped in response to one of my tools.

I stepped inside and pulled out my penlight. Jimmy's locked cage was easy to find and even easier to unlock. The foxhole was lined with stacks of racing programs. Had Liz and Saboski bothered to inspect this place? Maybe. But they wouldn't find anything useful. My story for Liz about Jimmy's hidden bankroll wouldn't help me now.

A lamp and a beat-up old recliner and a coffee cup with solidified muck in the bottom occupied the space. In one corner a fan was directed at the recliner and in the other corner a space heater. Against one wall of the chicken-wire cage sat a four-foot-high bookcase crammed with stacks of well-used books on handicapping. Some I recognized, and some I didn't. A dated computer desk that probably once held the laptop Liz took into custody was positioned beside the recliner.

Jimmy would need the internet to watch video replays of races and do other research. But he couldn't question people at the track with a handheld device or laptop and expect to receive answers. That kind of information was passed along in whispers in return for favors, if at all. Jimmy had been forced to remain old-school and make hand-written notes. I checked the cardboard box—it contained Jimmy's latest stack of spiral notebooks.

I hauled the box outside and locked the cage. Outside the vault, I redid the deadbolt and then draped the heavy boa chain and secured it with the padlock. I felt like a thief in the night. Like I was stealing a part of Jimmy. The good part.

As I walked down the alley with the heavy box, trying not to slip on the ice, I also felt like a fool. No one would understand why I took this late-night risk. It was why I'd tried to come up with a story for Liz, and why I hadn't told Uncle Mike about my planned break-in. Only those of us who'd spent long hours sweating over races and sporting events knew what kind of treasure a handicapper's old notes might contain.

6

THE THURSDAY NIGHT CROWD AT O'CONNELL'S TAVERN was a welcome sight. Neither Uncle Mike nor I could afford to abandon our day job since murder cases for Burrascano were sporadic at best. Uncle Mike continued to handle his duties as owner of O'Connell's, and I continued to manage the bar and work as a bartender. It wouldn't be easy to juggle all these responsibilities, but we'd do it for Jimmy and to give Liz an assist.

Five minutes until happy hour expired. The rush for a refill kept me and my staff jumping. A first-timer to O'Connell's Tavern would think the crowd had braved the blowing snow and slick streets to catch the Thursday night football game, but I knew better. They were here to see Oscar Colasso.

Oscar, our local bookie, had ingested a huge dose of courage now that everyone from the governor to the mayor touted legalization of sports betting in the state. Oscar's Thursday night visits became an instant hit at our bar, but I hated everything about them.

O'Connell's was a neighborhood bar that tried to be half-sports bar and half-restaurant, but I had to admit, we weren't all that serious about the food. Located at the end of the block on a busy corner, O'Connell's had become a hub for groups to meet-up before or after a meal at one of the fine restaurants within walking distance.

A few minutes after six, happy hour ended and the lull in the action allowed me to return to my old friend, Marini, a sportswriter. He was a short guy so he leaned in over the bar, beer foam hanging on his scraggly beard like frost. I bent down to hear him over the noise of the crowd and classic rock playing on the jukebox.

Stats and inside information rolled off his tongue as fast as the mayor's promises. He informed me that simply because we hated the Packers was no reason not to bet on them tonight. My eyes glazed over after a minute of his detailed argument and left me thinking about tonight's game. Maybe I should get a bet down. Put all this knowledge Marini picked up around the sports department to use. I'd glanced at Jimmy's notebooks this morning and the details he considered for any horse race or sporting event made a mockery of my handicapping. It made me think of my recent bets placed with Oscar.

I'd gone on a losing streak and owed money. Not for the first time. Oscar and I had come to an agreement on a reasonable payment arrangement and interest rate. The last time he hadn't been so charitable, turning my obligation over to a mob-connected guy who charged an ungodly rate.

Of course, Oscar wasn't a philanthropist. When he agreed to my payment plan, he wasn't thinking about my welfare, he was thinking about O'Connell's Tavern. I didn't own the place, my uncle did, and if Uncle Mike found out about my debt, he'd blackball Oscar for life. Oscar needed our customers' business and his newfound platform and counted on my support.

I wasn't proud of the debt. Around the bar, I'd become known for winning at the horses. Why I let myself get pulled back into betting football, I'll never know. A football fan thinks it's easy. How hard can it be?

The minute I dipped my toe back in the action, I'd be thinking about a serious wager. A bet made without enough research would be dead money. Jimmy's notebooks reminded me of the level of study and time required to win, and right now time was in short supply. I had to get a handle on Jimmy's box of stuff. Not only were there the notebooks with handicapping notes, there were business records of WagerEasy. I'd need to inventory these items and see if any of them might be relevant to our investigation.

The last thing I wanted to see tonight was Oscar's smug smile. The idea that Oscar held a degree of power over me produced a rancid brew of self-loathing and anger.

The same sour mash extended to my present finances. My current job status as bartender and bar manager didn't cut it. Uncle Mike's old partner, Liz, had given me a lead on investigative work with a criminal lawyer downtown, and I was scheduled to meet with the attorney tomorrow morning. I hoped to use it to jumpstart my private detective business.

Until I could turn a steady buck as a private detective, I'd need to keep my current gig. Uncle Mike and I also had a meeting set tonight with DiNatale and another contact from the gambling world to get started on the Jimmy investigation for Burrascano. A bet on tonight's game didn't enter into the equation.

A group of three guys and a woman swarmed into the bar. Two of the guys were regular customers and usually hung out together. I didn't know the striking young woman with shoulder-length blond hair, but I did know the third guy. Kubala would be looking for trouble.

It had been more than six months ago at a bar downtown. One of those quick fights I get into sometimes. Kubala had gotten the worst of it. The ugly smile on his face told me he was thinking rematch. He'd reportedly done time in prison for an assortment of felonies.

Kubala was a few inches shorter than me, forty pounds heavier, and had put in some time in the weight room since we last met.

He smirked as he took a draft beer and a shot of bourbon from me. "Eddie O'Connell, I heard you worked here. We've got some catching up to do." He turned and walked away before I could respond.

The young woman took her beer and offered a hand across the bar. "Nice to meet you, Eddie. I'm Tara Reilly."

I welcomed her to O'Connell's. I wanted to ask her why she was with these three guys, but I didn't want to sound like a schmuck, so I settled for small talk. We talked about the frigid weather and the crowd and then she excused herself to join her two friends and Kubala.

Most new customers to O'Connell's didn't shake hands with the bartender unless they were buzzed. Her clear blue eyes told me she wasn't.

High cheekbones, clear complexion, a charming smile, and confidence, she had it all. Was she involved with one of the two regulars? Neither one acted like it and Kubala was out of the question. It was an odd group. The three of them slipped through the crowd at the bar and walked toward the pool room in back to join Kubala.

I settled across from Marini and he asked if I knew when Oscar was scheduled to arrive. I told him I wasn't Oscar's personal secretary and asked what he thought about the over/under.

Before Marini could respond, Mr. Urbanski, the old chief of police for one of the surrounding suburban towns, signaled me with his empty. I grabbed another longneck Old Style from the cooler and strode over.

His eighty-year-old watery eyes focused in on me. "Eddie, you look more like your uncle every day."

I laughed. My uncle was overweight, bald, and retired, while I stayed in shape at the gym and sparred in the ring. I was also about five inches taller at six-foot-three and still had my hair. Mr. Urbanski made the same comment every night.

I offered my usual response to the running joke. "You're right. Every day I look in the mirror and feel that much smarter."

Mr. Urbanski smiled and returned to the pre-game show that played on one of the many flat screens mounted around the bar. He'd been a regular ever since my uncle bought into the place. Back then, Uncle Mike still worked homicide at the Chicago Police Department, so other cops adopted the bar as their designated watering hole. A contingent of public servants and newspaper people soon followed.

In my late teens, I worked in the basement stockroom and kitchen. I'd spend time on the stairs listening to the stories at the bar, reading books, or studying the racing program. Since my uncle had also invested in a racehorse, he'd brought me along, and I'd become a fan of the track.

Things weren't always easy back then. My mother had died and my father had called in sick when it came to parental duties. I was welcomed into my aunt and uncle's family, but that didn't mean I always fit in. The stockroom job, the books, and the track were a refuge.

I followed Mr. Urbanski's gaze to the flat screen. There was still time to get money down on the Packers.

People stood at the tables by the front door and shouted to others. I looked to the front door to see what the commotion was about. Oscar Colasso threw off his coat, and gloves, and waved to his loyal fans. He came toward the bar, stopping to shake hands with customers like a politician. He was well over three-hundred pounds, a short, round ball of a man with a red face and toothy smile. His bodyguards stayed by the front door.

People parted to make a path for Oscar. He walked up to the space we'd cleared and heaved his satchel onto the bar. Then his round, short body scaled one of the empty stools with Marini's help.

A bead of sweat dribbled down Oscar's fat cheek from the exertion. He took a swig of the beer but didn't bother to thank me for it. Then he swiveled around to face the crowd.

People had left their booths, and chairs, and pressed in close. The crowd was a mix from the neighborhood. It included older folks close to Mr. Urbanski's age, college-aged kids who slipped out back to smoke and puke, and middle-aged, hard-working people trying to make ends meet. Others had sold their home to take advantage of gentrification but still came back to their old neighborhood bar.

Oscar made sure he had everyone's undivided attention. "Well, you football fans really got into my shorts."

The crowd roared their approval as if the fat bookie was a stand-up comedian.

Oscar reached over and clapped Marini on the shoulder. "What happened to you, Marini? You were dialed in this week."

Marini promised more winners. Somebody offered Oscar a slice of pizza. The bookie got comfortable and greeted people by name.

"Okay," Oscar said, opening the latch on the satchel and pulling out several sheets of paper. "We might as well get started." He put on a pair of reading glasses that slipped to the end of his pudgy nose.

Oscar gnawed at the pepperoni pizza. You'd have thought it was fourth down for the Bears with thirty seconds left. It was that kind of silence.

Shouts erupted from the pool room. Kubala let loose with a loud string of off-color cusswords and threats that signaled trouble. The crowd around the bar froze.

I walked to the end of the bar then stopped and listened. The loud voices had quickly subsided, so I decided to let it go. Oscar shrugged and shuffled papers. The crowd turned its attention back to Oscar.

The bookie hesitated a moment as he perused a piece of paper. Like a game show host, he seemed to revel in the limelight. "Okay, I've got a winner of the four-game parlay. Or, should I say winners? Betty and Marge, where are you?"

A roar rose up as two middle-aged women in oversized sweaters passed through the adoring crowd. Betty and Marge played a twenty-dollar, four-game parlay card every week of the football season, despite raising six kids between them as single parents.

The double-sawbuck wasn't a casual investment for the pair. They surveyed the so-called experts at O'Connell's on what team was a lock and what team was in a downward spiral. The ladies would listen and take notes and then study and hash over their picks. Neither of them knew much about football, but they knew whose opinion to value and who to bet against. I wondered if they had the Packers or the Seahawks tonight.

Oscar retrieved one of the pay envelopes out of his satchel, pulled out the cash, and flashed it around in front of Betty and Marge. He counted out the bills on the bar. The way he studied each of the twenty-dollar bills made me think of a squirrel counting nuts. Then I remembered he was in the recycling business.

But Oscar never showed up on Tuesday night when the bills cycled back to pay losses. He'd send one of his goons to collect. I wished I had a video of that scene to remind the crowd.

Oscar stacked the bills and flashed the cash. "That's the third time you've taken me this year." He glanced back at me and the others as if to say, *"If they can win, so can you."*

Betty explained in a trembling voice that she and Marge were saving up for a trip to Vegas because Marge was a huge fan of Celine. The crowd ate it up.

"You know this will all change with legalization," Marini said.

Oscar talked through a mouthful of pizza. "You're such an asshole, Marini."

"You could try honest work selling used cars," somebody called out.

Everybody laughed, including Oscar. He didn't mind a ribbing when he was the center of attention.

Others suggested additional career choices that might fit Oscar's skill set—math teacher, alderman, sports broadcaster.

"I hear that once it's legal, so many people will be playing that both legal and illegal books will be busier than ever," I said.

Oscar's eyebrows knitted and he glared at me. "Eddie, what about you? You haven't played for a while."

"I'll stick to the horses." But my words rang hollow. Everyone it seemed had money on the Thursday night game.

"I can see why," Marini said, "That Pick Six Eddie won paid more than I make in a year. The harness meet just opened at Thornton Racetrack. Eddie will clean up."

It'd been a long time since I won that Pick Six.

Oscar shook his head in a sign of disgust. "C'mon, the horses are a pain in the neck. Football is simple. It has injury reports. Only a trainer knows if his horse is in top condition."

The crowd nodded in unison and turned its attention to me.

"The sports channel tells everybody everything. You got to study the horses. My handicapping gives me an edge," I said. It wasn't the whole truth. Sports betting required all the inside information a sportswriter or anyone else could dig up.

"Forget about your edge. I service lots of bars. All my winners are right here." Oscar slapped the bar.

The crowd roared but then it grew quiet in anticipation of my response. They seemed to love the fact I was on the hot seat.

"With the vig, on straight bets, you need to win fifty-three to sixty percent of the time to be a winner on sports," I said. Sometimes I wished I'd listened to myself.

"Even Betty and Marge win. They'll get to Vegas, I'm sure of it. They know how to set a limit on their wagers," Oscar said. "You won't get anywhere with your attitude."

The crowd roared again. A limit on the amount wagered— something I'd failed to do. Maybe Oscar planned to hold me up as an example of the bettor who could not exercise proper money management.

Oscar pointed a finger. "Eddie, you stand here every day with every football game on all these flat screens, and you don't have any action?"

He accused me of being either antisocial or anti-sports. Neither one brought a bartender any friends in a sports bar.

"You know what happens when a player runs out of bounds on the five-yard line at the end of the game, instead of scoring to beat the spread?" I asked. "I laugh my ass off."

The crowd applauded my zinger then stopped. Shouts and threats from the pool room drowned out Led Zeppelin on the jukebox. Kubala unleashed the same string of cusswords. This time I couldn't ignore them.

I hustled down the hall and ducked under the hanging sports pennants. The pop of a fist on flesh and a groan. Other sounds I expected to hear in the boxing gym. Then another stream of cussing from Kubala.

I knew what I'd find—Kubala causing trouble. The crowd hustled behind me, the same way they'd gathered around me that one summer night a few years back.

It was the night I'd been forced to square off against a retired Bears linebacker. I'm not sure how the fight started—people said he asked for it. The facts had grown hazy over time and didn't seem to matter. What I do recall was how a switch inside me flipped.

No way I'd back down from Kubala. There was no time to call the police. I had to protect my customers—even those two clowns and Tara Reilly, the blonde, who'd made the mistake of hanging with Kubala.

I reached the entrance to the pool room in back. "What the hell is going on?"

Kubala stood over one of the guys and nodded toward me with a shit-eating grin. "Look who's here—Eddie O'Connell, the bartender."

The guy on the floor moaned and rubbed his jaw. His friend and Tara Reilly huddled together on the other side of the table, pool cues in hand.

I asked the man on the floor if he was okay. He mumbled something about a broken jaw. He was half Kubala's size.

"Pussy," Kubala told the man.

"Get the fuck out, Kubala," I said.

Kubala slapped a fist into the palm of his other hand. "Fuck you, I haven't finished my drink. I'm owed money."

"Get out. You're drunk," I said.

"A few drinks don't bother me." Kubala took a step closer. "Plus, I'm not done teaching these two boys a lesson."

"You started this for no reason," Tara Reilly said.

"Shut up," Kubala said.

"I said you'll have to leave—now," I repeated.

"No," Kubala shook his head. "Why don't we go outside?"

There wasn't enough room to maneuver inside the pool room. Outside would play into my hands. The guy needed to be taught a lesson. My Golden Gloves trophy had qualified me for felony charges the last time. I got off with probation thanks to a decent record and influence from Uncle Mike's friends. But this time?

Somebody tapped me on the shoulder, but I didn't take my eyes off Kubala.

"What the heck is this?" It was Uncle Mike.

"The asshole wants to fight," I said. The words sounded like they came from somebody else. All my thoughts were on the alley out back, my first steps, and first punch.

"Jeesus Christ," Uncle Mike pointed at Kubala. "Didn't you hear what Eddie did to that poor pissant from the Bears?"

"Fuck you, old man," Kubala said.

My license to be a private investigator. That mist they call your future. None of it mattered.

"You idiots bring this goon here?" Uncle Mike looked first at the man on the floor and then his friend.

The two guys looked at each other. O'Connell's was their home turf, the place they'd hung out since they were old enough to produce fake IDs.

"This is between me and the bartender," Kubala said.

Kubala needed to be taken apart piece by piece.

"C'mon," I said to Kubala. "You'll get what you want." I'd dance out of his way, let him throw a few wild punches, and then shoot a few jabs. When he was off-balance, I'd move in with a combination.

The crowd stepped back and a curtain of silence dropped on the scene. Their frightened eyes gleamed at me with anticipation. Maybe with Uncle Mike present, they didn't think it'd ever happen. But it was happening. Tonight.

Uncle Mike grabbed my arm. "Make it quick. Our appointment is waiting outside."

But Uncle Mike's reverse psychology wasn't working on Kubala or me.

"C'mon, Kubala. Time for the rematch." I turned away and stepped back into the crowd to go outside.

An ear-splitting noise like that of a shattered baseball bat tore into the eerie silence. It wasn't the sound of a gun, thank

God. More like a floor beam beneath the old tavern had cracked under the weight of the crowd. I spun back around.

Tara Reilly held one end of a splintered pool cue with two hands. She was staring down at Kubala who was out cold on the floor.

7

UNCLE MIKE AND I WERE OUTSIDE O'CONNELL'S TAVERN walking toward DiNatale's limo when my uncle turned toward me. "Wow. I didn't see that coming. That's one tough lady."

"Damn right." After Tara Reilly clubbed Kubala with the butt end of the pool cue, we'd gotten Kubala into an ambulance. While he was being worked on by the paramedics, he swore he'd get me and Tara.

"You get her name?" Uncle Mike asked

"You bet. I got her name and address. We'll need to send a patrol car over to her house tonight." Tara Reilly didn't ask for protection. The way she'd shrugged off the incident made me think she'd been clubbing bullies with pool cues her entire life. But she didn't know Kubala. Of course, I'd gotten Tara Reilly's phone number for another reason. I planned to ask her out.

Uncle Mike and I had made Tara Reilly's case with the detective. The statements of a hundred of O'Connell Tavern regulars were more than sufficient to argue self-defense on Tara's behalf.

Uncle Mike blinked in the snow whipping sideways from the wind. "The asshole will make good on his promise of revenge?"

"Damn right. When Kubala gets back on his feet, he'll come after her. I fought him once and tonight he wanted a rematch. Being knocked out by Tara while his back was turned will drive him up the wall." He'd come after me as well. I needed to be ready.

"Why can't these things happen at some other bar?" Uncle Mike picked up the pace. "Let's get in the limo. I'll call the precinct and get somebody on it."

Uncle Mike could still get favors from the department when he needed them. Loyalties ran deep and Mike O'Connell had helped a lot of officers on the way up the ladder.

I shuffled thoughts of Kubala aside.

The driver got out and opened the passenger door of the limo for us. Uncle Mike went first but stopped at the door.

"Hey, where's your boss?" Uncle Mike asked the driver.

The driver explained that DiNatale was at a club downtown, and the driver had been instructed to take us there. "Plenty of champagne in back," he added.

"I should've guessed," Uncle Mike said under his breath and then turned to the diver. "We'll drive down ourselves. I've got other commitments tonight. Give me the name of the club."

The black leather insides of the limo looked inviting on a night like this and a glass of champagne wouldn't hurt my mood. Instead, I'd be the one driving Uncle Mike's truck downtown on the slick city streets.

After I scraped the ice off the windshield and back window, I got into the truck filled with a cloud of Uncle Mike's cigar smoke. "What other commitments have you got?"

"Commitments to privacy," Uncle Mike scratched the gray hair at his temple, his eyes focused on the end of his cigar.

I got it. Since when had I dropped my guard when it came to DiNatale? The guy probably had the limo wired to record our conversation. Maybe we'd say something he could take to Burrascano to get us fired, or, at the very least, he'd learn about our ongoing investigation into Jimmy's murder.

I took Halsted south out of the Lincoln Park neighborhood. The club the driver had given us was located in Old Town on the near north side of Chicago. Traffic was heavy and slow. After Uncle Mike made the call to the precinct about the Kubala situation and protection for Tara Reilly, I asked him if he'd gotten in touch with Liz to set up the interview with Burrascano.

"It took a while. You know Wayne is in hospice now."

"I heard. That sucks." The cool and efficient way Liz handled police procedures at Jimmy's murder scene the other night, almost made me forget about Liz's troubles at home.

"Liz told me she'd handle things with Burrascano going forward. Can you believe that? I'm on the outside looking in."

"Right. Any idea where or when?" I imagined Burrascano sitting down with a detective to answer questions. The whole idea of it seemed incredible. The upcoming change in the gambling laws brought about strange things.

"Not yet. Liz gave you that referral to Helen St. Clair? They're old friends dating back to when they were at St. Agnes."

Uncle Mike was reminding me to treat Helen St. Clair like royalty because of Liz. Uncle Mike's three daughters got married and moved out of Illinois so sometimes it seemed he treated Liz like a fourth daughter.

Uncle Mike didn't need this investigation for Burrascano. He should be playing cards with the boys and enjoying retirement. But by taking on the investigation my uncle was looking out for his old partner, Liz. Plus, he had a thing about killers. He still kept copies of old police files in the basement of O'Connell's and could be found digging into cold cases at closing time.

"I'm scheduled to meet with Ms. St. Clair tomorrow. She mentioned it was an assault case." She'd also mentioned to me that time was running short before trial. If I was going to handle it in time, I should plan to work exclusively on that case instead of running down leads on Jimmy's case, but my old friend had priority.

"St. Clair give you the client's name?"

"Yeah. Asked if I might have a conflict and I told her 'no.' Yuri Provost is the client."

"Son-of-a-bitch." Uncle Mike slapped the dashboard. "We've been trying to catch up with that scumbag for years. Operates a car theft ring out on the west side. That's a big-time case. Liz's old friend has really graduated to the big leagues. I wonder why Yuri's boys wouldn't take care of any rough stuff? Yuri's too careful to get snagged on a bullshit assault charge."

"Self-defense. An argument in a restaurant downtown with an upstanding executive, and I guess Yuri couldn't resist. Punches were exchanged, but the exec got the worst of it. Maybe the guy will wise up and be a no-show at trial, but in the meantime, it will be my job to dig up somebody to testify how it was righteous." Yuri Provost's fate would hinge on what I could discover in a few days. A sudden case of nerves made my stomach churn.

"Witnesses have a way of not remembering. They don't forget to complain or call in when a cop screws up, though. Watch your backside, Eddie. Yuri is a badass with a finger in a lot of pies."

The case would be a start to my private detective business.

Uncle Mike puffed on the cigar and smoke trailed out through a crack in the window. "I heard more about this guy, Travis Sloan."

He was the guy we planned to meet with DiNatale tonight. According to Burrascano, Sloan, a onetime Dallas street thug, had proven himself. What started as a small bookie shop had grown. First, he consolidated his gambling ring in the Dallas-Fort Worth area then slowly expanded in every direction. He took over small towns, roadhouses, and took other bookies under his wing. Then he moved on to Houston.

Sloan knew how to organize, keep people in line, and seize opportunities. After Houston, he shored up his southern flank by moving on San Antonio and El Paso, became an expert on border stuff, and played footsie with the cartels. Burrascano's friends in New Orleans were getting nervous.

Now he was moving up the Mississippi like a channel catfish. When Burrascano told the story about Sloan, I had glanced at DiNatale. I could tell he appreciated the enterprising nature of the gambling ringleader.

Why Burrascano didn't simply eliminate Sloan eluded me. I guessed that Burrascano needed to know if Sloan killed Jimmy and tried to frame him because Sloan might be backed by another faction.

"He owns a huge ranch about fifty miles north of Dallas," Uncle Mike said. "They say that's where the bodies are buried. A lot of those small-time bookies refused to sell."

"Sloan would have good reason to kill Jimmy," I said. A deal by Burrascano to sell the exclusive list of high rollers to WagerEasy would leave the illegal black-market bookies high and dry. Sloan wanted to consolidate those illegal bookies into a force that could combat legalization and, at the same time, line his own pockets. He'd have the motive to kill Jimmy in order to stop the deal from going forward.

"Plus, the brutality of Jimmy's killing fits his M.O.," Uncle Mike said. "Sloan gave the okay on the legislation to throw the tribal casinos out of Texas even though he had a big piece of those casinos behind the scenes."

"That's one ruthless bastard." Money usually trumped everything with these guys. Breaking that rule made Sloan uniquely dangerous.

"Right. Money doesn't mean as much to him as empire building and he's here in Chicago for that reason."

I pulled into the valet station at the club in Old Town. We told the head bouncer out front that we were there to see DiNatale and, after a quick phone call, we were ushered inside. The joint was packed despite the rotten weather. Electronic music spun by a DJ threatened to pierce my eardrums. A massive disco ball reflected flashing lights above a dance floor crammed with gyrating figures. It wasn't my kind of joint.

In a private suite on the second floor, we found DiNatale and Sloan with bottle service and four young women with tight black dresses and long legs who made a show of ignoring our entrance.

Sloan and DiNatale uncoupled themselves from their dates and stood to greet us. Six-foot-four, Sloan wore snakeskin cowboy boots, a western shirt, and a four-inch-wide gold belt buckle. His cowboy hat sat on the table. Sloan and DiNatale were of the same generation in their fifties, but that was where the similarities ended. DiNatale wore a dark suit and purple silk tie and took charge of the introductions. He told the women to go powder their noses and then "get your asses back."

Sloan gave Uncle Mike a wide grin. "Vic here has been telling me that you're The Man in this city. Says you know the politicians, the police, and everybody else who matters."

Sloan made a point of ignoring me and I didn't take offense. Our plan with Burrascano was simple. Uncle Mike would take on the position of Sloan's consultant and see what he could find out. Meanwhile, Burrascano would keep Sloan close. DiNatale would make sure of that.

"That's right," Uncle Mike said. "If I don't know them, then they don't matter."

"He told me you're a retired homicide detective, but says I got nothing to worry about. Is that right?"

"No, you've got plenty to worry about if murder is committed," Uncle Mike told him.

"That's what I want to hear." Sloan slapped Uncle Mike on the back. "Won't be no need for that kind of thing no how. Just want to get to know a few politicians and let our lobbyists talk to them all fair and square."

"Then I'm your man."

DiNatale turned to me while Uncle Mike and Sloan exchanged small talk. "Heard that you decided not to take my limo. You've got other commitments tonight, Eddie?"

"Just a few things to go over with Liz about the investigation," I lied. Nothing I liked better than keeping DiNatale off-balance. "Of course, I can't go into it and Uncle Mike would deny we even have a meeting with Liz."

DiNatale frowned. "Too bad. This is the hottest club in town. No need to introduce you to the ladies when they get back."

Sloan named a number of political hacks, some of whom I'd never heard of before. I thought I knew all our resident bloodsuckers. Uncle Mike responded with revealing and humorous details about each one of them. The way DiNatale watched Sloan showed me that every move the Texas gambling ring entrepreneur made in Chicago would be reported to Burrascano.

"Damn. Let's have a drink to my new consultant. Vic, you guys know how to pick them," Sloan said. "Which one of these bottles do you take a hankering to, Mike?"

I was watching Sloan, too. He was playing a game with Burrascano, and we were the designated chess pieces.

8

THE NEXT DAY, I MADE IT WITH FIVE MINUTES TO SPARE TO my appointment as a private investigator. Helen St. Clair's law office was located in an ancient, narrow three-story office building on the far south end of the Loop. According to the lobby's directory, the building housed a number of law firms, accountants, and small businesses. From the vacant look of the place, the small businesses were out of business.

Her office was at the end of the hall on the top floor. The receptionist sat at a station with a high, rounded, art-deco-style desk that might've served as the building's lunch counter fifty years ago. The office lobby was littered with battered chairs and a small coffee table with dog-eared copies of *Reader's Digest* stacked in the dust. A haze of cigarette smoke hung in the room. I began to wonder if I should ask for a portion of my modest fees upfront.

The phone didn't stop ringing. A petite woman with her black hair pulled back in a tight bun, stabbed at the phone with her middle finger. The nameplate attached to the lunch counter identified the woman as "Miss Spiegleman."

"Good morning, Miss Spiegleman, I'm Eddie O'Connell," I said.

She flipped a page of the appointment book. "You're her ten o'clock?" To the phone, she said, "Can you please hold?" Then back to me, "You're the new investigator?"

I nodded. There was a single business card in a holder on the desk. I grabbed it and she gave me a sharp glance as if the cards weren't free.

"Have a seat," she said. "And for future reference, I'm not 'Miss Spiegleman.'" She punched another line with a vengeance. "Please hold." She punched again. "Please hold."

By now, most of the city had been placed on hold. Purely out of reflex and courtesy, I asked, "You're married?"

She shot me a sour look. "No. Miss Spiegleman hasn't been here for ten years. Ms. St. Clair doesn't order new nameplates because people don't last long. I'm a temp."

With the declaration of her temp status, an expression that could only be described as complete and utter relief swept across her face. A woman's shouts echoed from the back of the office.

The temp picked up a small spiral note pad and ran around the lunch counter and down the hall. I walked across scuffed brown tile and sat in one of the straight-back chairs you might find in a cafeteria. A slight breeze off the lake must've found an open window because the smoke cloud drifted through the open door toward the elevators. The Green Line "L," a block away, screeched to a stop as I picked up one of the magazines.

———

It was twenty-five minutes before I got called into Helen St. Clair's office. The smoke was thicker here. There was a couch against one wall beneath a row of windows with the blinds pulled tight as if the light might kill whatever was meant to grow in this subterranean place. Her desk was covered in a mosaic of thick court pleadings, legal pads, phone message slips, and law books. A computer screen and keyboard sat on one corner of the desk and the phone at the other. A large ashtray filled with butts sat in front of Ms. St. Clair, who sat back in her chair and studied me as I entered the way she might study a potentially hostile witness.

Her silver hair was cut in a short bob. Her thick glasses had pointed frames connected to a silver chain that hung down around her neck. A black sweater had been thrown over her shoulders to shield her slight frame from the chill that crept through the open window.

Behind her, rows of framed diplomas and certificates lined the wall. Two chairs fronted the desk. One held a pile of files, the other was empty. I reached across the desk to shake hands, but she waved me away with the cigarette grasped tightly in her claw-like hand. I sat down in the empty chair.

"Finally, we meet," Helen St. Clair said. "I don't know if you know this but I've known you for a long time."

She sucked on the end of the cigarette and I could almost hear her lungs wheeze. The wrinkles around her leathery face coalesced around the cigarette's filter the way an old baseball mitt snags a groundball.

This job for Helen St. Clair, Esquire, felt like a huge drop-in class. The murder investigations I did with Uncle Mike made my duties for the attorney—questioning witnesses—seem on a par with those of a ticket seller punching out bets at Thornton Racetrack. Compelled to fill the awkward silence, I said, "Because of Liz?"

She nodded. "Liz and I have known each other—" She stopped and her beady eyes glanced upward as she gasped for air. "I don't know how many years. Since elementary school. The nuns made us tough. They went after Liz with a vengeance. They thought she might be nun material. Me? I got more than my daily share of thrashings, but they were well-deserved. You see, I was bursting with sin."

"Is that why you do criminal law?"

She laughed then cut it short as if afraid of hurting herself. "I guess the nuns didn't get to you. You've got a sense of humor. Yes, I can identify with the criminals. Liz and I have met for coffee for years. I'm her crutch and I guess she's mine. Of course, our conversations are limited. If we talked about our respective professions, a catfight would probably break out right there in the diner. You see, she finds them and arrests them, and then I help them walk. We do it over and over. You can understand that, can't you?"

"I didn't go to law school."

She laughed again and some of the smoke got twisted up in her lungs, and she had to hack it out. After the painful episode, she struggled for a lungful of oxygen and continued.

"Liz always said you were something. You know she and Mike have been partners in homicide for how long? Forever. She hated it when your uncle was forced to retire. Women like me—professional women—don't usually have much of a family life. I got divorced after a year. But Liz had a family. She's a rare bird. Poor Wayne and what he's going through. But I always thought that Liz had a hidden crush on your uncle."

It was true that Uncle Mike and Liz had a special relationship, but I wasn't in the mood for gossip. "I wouldn't know."

The phone intercom buzzed and the temp spoke. "Ms. St. Clair, Judge Andropolous is on the line."

"Tell him one minute." She turned to me. "Yes, you are the way Liz said."

Her meaning was clear. Liz had been her pipeline for years and knew everything Uncle Mike knew. All my secrets had probably been laid bare. St. Clair's sly smile confirmed it. It wasn't easy to meet someone you never met before only to find out they know everything there is to know about you.

St. Clair licked her wrinkled lips. "Tell me why you're here. I know you're out to build a business as a PI. But you're a smart kid. You could get a cushy job downtown, go to night school and work your way up. A PI can be tough work and doesn't pay much. There are no guarantees." She sat back and stared.

I didn't need a lecture. I dug up something to satisfy St. Clair's question. "It seems like interesting work. Plus, I got experience."

"I know all about your *experience*. You've been lucky, Eddie. You could be in prison sharing meals with somebody like our client, Yuri Provost. You know the kind. Scum. But Yuri is the kind of scum who helps pay the overhead around this dump. That way I can take pro bono cases for people the system wants to throw in prison. Innocent people who need looking after. Is that what you want? Work for scum or for people who can't pay?"

I stared back at her. She knew about the fight I had outside O'Connell's that one summer night. The fight with the Bears linebacker that left me in a legal quagmire. She knew how close I'd come to serious time. All I needed was a start. Something to give me credibility—a reference—and a chance to get other PI jobs.

I said, "I'll take my chances working for scum or people who don't pay."

"I heard you like to gamble."

"Sometimes."

The temp buzzed the office. "Ms. St. Clair. Judge Andropolous is still holding on one. You told me to tell you."

St. Clair talked back to the phone. "One minute." Then she turned to me. "Well, Eddie, I can't afford to gamble. When I walk into that courtroom, my reputation is on the line. Even scum like Yuri Provost deserves competent representation. With a record as long as both my arms, if convicted of aggravated battery, it will mean serious time. I've got to tell a story in the courtroom. Explain how the ass-kicking Yuri gave the victim was in self-defense. I need one witness, one witness, who I can rely on. One upstanding citizen who is unimpeachable, a church-going, clean-cut respectable asshole that no one will have any choice but to believe."

"Why would that kind of asshole witness be in a bar with Yuri Provost?"

She lit another cigarette. "Because he's humping the waitress, or owes money because he bet the mortgage on last week's football games, or got a flat tire out front and needs to use the telephone. Somebody who was in the wrong place at the wrong time. You've got the stomach for this type of work, don't you Eddie?"

Liz must've told her. No doubt about it. I could see it in St. Clair's beady eyes. My mother had been in the wrong place at the wrong time. St. Clair must know how my mother had been taken when I was only six-months-old. How my mother was pushing me in a stroller through the park on that crisp, fall day. How the murderer and rapist took her and left me there, her body dumped in a culvert a mile away.

Maybe Helen St. Clair Esquire also knew what legal precedent was used to free my mother's killer on a technicality after he had confessed. She was testing me.

"If the asshole witness was there in that bar and saw the fight, I'll find him," I said. "And then you'll have your affirmative defense for Yuri Provost. Now let me ask you something."

"Okay, Eddie. Go ahead." The cigarette hung from her lips as she pulled the sweater tight around her shoulders.

My mother's killer was the son of a downstate county official where it happened. When he was set free by the judge, he took off. Uncle Mike and Joey L took up the chase. "If Liz was murdered and her confessed killer got off on a technicality due to a crooked judge, what would *you* do?"

She plucked the cigarette and blew smoke toward the ceiling. "Yes, I know. It's not fair. I know all about you and you know nothing about me."

The temp buzzed. "Ms. St. Clair—"

"What?" the attorney shouted back.

"Judge Andropolous."

St. Clair picked up a two-inch-thick file off the desk and tossed it in my direction. "Look it over. Do us proud."

It was the file on Yuri Provost. "I'll take some notes and leave it at the front desk."

"And I need the name of the witness by Monday. That is if I can sweet talk the judge holding on the line."

"Monday?" That gave me today and the weekend and I still needed to follow the trail of Jimmy's killer before it got cold.

Her eyes turned soft and her mouth relaxed into a little girl's smile that might've greeted the nuns on the first day of school. Maybe she hadn't been trying to vet me with the third degree. Perhaps she'd actually been concerned about my welfare. "It should be plenty of time for someone with your talents," she said.

"You told me Yuri Provost is scum. What kind of scum?"

"The address is in the file. Go and meet our esteemed client. You'll find out what we deal with around here." She picked up the phone but her eyes didn't leave me. "Anthony, how are you? Sorry, you had to wait. It's been crazy."

9

After a quick review of the Yuri Provost file, I went to The Point Spread Restaurant where the beat down of Dr. Reynolds Blick, PhD. by Yuri Provost, had taken place. There were photos of Blick in the file. Close-ups of the stitches on his face. Detailed medical records of his complaints of internal symptoms.

The chain restaurant, where the altercation took place, was located along the Chicago River, close to the big hotels near Michigan Avenue that held conferences and supplied revenue for sales tax. Conventions and conferences were big business and Blick had been an attendee. The river had become the rediscovered gem of the city. Everyone wanted to feel safe along the river-walk and daydream of the Seine or the Danube. I thought of walking arm in arm with Tara Reilly on a summer evening.

I drove into a parking garage and walked over to the restaurant. Office buildings reached up into a cloud bank that promised more snow. A bitter wind off the lake forced most of the Friday lunch crowd to stay inside.

My questions to the bar's afternoon skeleton staff yielded nothing. Maybe the chain's corporate hierarchy had sent down an edict of silence. Or maybe the employees didn't want to get involved.

Finding the asshole who may have witnessed Blick's verbal threats and racial taunts to possibly persuade a jury to enter a non-guilty verdict by Monday wouldn't be easy. According to the file, I was the third investigator on the case and the bar's video had conveniently gone missing before the police arrived. The chance I'd run into a friendly bar regular was slim. It wasn't a neighborhood place like O'Connell's. The conference types and tourists that plagued the sterile sports bar were in town one weekend and then returned home to other parts of the country.

I decided to take St. Clair's advice and visit the client. The address in the file was in the North Lawndale neighborhood, so I called ahead and drove over. On the way, I continued to look in the rearview mirror. By now Kubala was up and around, and with a cop posted at Tara Reilly's house, I was Kubala's best option for revenge.

Yuri Provost's neighborhood was one of the epicenters of the problem referred to by the mayor as "gun violence." The gunmen, the factions, and splintered gangs, many in their teens and early twenties, needed to retaliate for any perceived insult and didn't care if their target stood in a crowd.

Bordered by Cicero to the west, the gang territory's streets were lined by snow-covered vacant lots from the MLK riots back in the sixties and a few surviving boarded-up Greystones. The city had paid little attention to this largely segregated part of the city, except to close schools and health clinics. Luckily, liquor stores and bars anchored the neighborhood. The number of people shot each weekend was reported in the morning papers like statistics in the sports section. The mayor's reaction had become as clichéd as the post-game comments of a team manager. To solve things, several battalions of police officers had been assigned to patrol this neighborhood and others, a war zone now commonly referred to as Chi-Raq. When the stats kept coming as reliably as the winter and summer, the chief of police threw up his hands and explained that his people could not be on every corner of every street, every hour of every day.

North Lawndale was the kind of place where Kubala could take his revenge on me with a drive-by shooting. The guy liked to brag about his accomplishments and demanded that no one disrespect him. It was part of a code Kubala had picked up in prison where he'd once slipped drugs into a guard's coffee. Another time he'd slashed an inmate's throat.

I parked in a lot across the street from Yuri Provost's body shop and salvage yard. Compared to the surrounding blocks, Yuri's business complex teemed with commercial life.

Inside Yuri's building, the receptionist led me into a spare office with a wood desk and boarded-up windows. A black man about six-foot-six emerged from the door behind the desk and demanded I stand for a frisk. I held up my arms.

73

He was clean-shaven, muscular with a heavy dose of cologne. I guessed ex-cop. I told him why I was there and he identified himself as one of Yuri's bodyguards.

He handled my .38 with respect. "Not smart to be out on these streets without one."

"Not smart to be out here period," I said.

He nodded. "Nice piece." He kept the gun as he stepped back behind the desk and sat down. He didn't smile as he pointed the gun at me. "I hear you got questions."

"I need to talk with Yuri Provost."

He smiled. "What? You don't like talking to me?"

I stared into the barrel of my own gun. Maybe it needed to be cleaned. "It will be Yuri doing time, not me."

His lips turned into a sour grin and his gaze drifted down behind the desk. Maybe an intercom.

He cleared his throat. "Ms. St. Clair said whatever the client says to you is confidential?"

Most people who tried to get in touch with the busy attorney were probably still on hold from this morning. It told me that Yuri had pull. Or maybe this case was more important to St. Clair than I thought.

"That's right," I said. "Unless you're contemplating a crime."

He came off the chair and the gun came at me like a fist then stopped midway. "We don't *con-tem-plate* nothing."

The Blue Line "L," one thin incidental link to downtown, screeched to a stop outside. I didn't take my eyes off him, stood very slow, and held out my hand. He seemed to be calculating lots of stuff in his mind then handed back the gun. He straightened like a cop and walked out the same door he'd come through.

I sat for five minutes and began to get pissed off at the drama. Uncle Mike had called me earlier about the Jimmy Golding murder. He planned to meet with one of Sloan's lobbyists later in the day and asked if I wanted to join him. Maybe we'd get a clearer picture of what Sloan wanted to accomplish. I told Uncle Mike that I'd meet him if I had time.

The door behind the desk opened halfway. A few seconds later, a black woman strode out, shut the door behind her, and stood at the desk. She was in her late forties or early fifties, short hair, black pants, and a black fleece zipped up to her chin. At least five-foot-ten, the stocky woman stood ramrod straight and stared through me like I was dirt. She made me think of an athlete prepared to take the field.

"You're my investigator?"

"Yeah."

"A pretty boy. And a white boy. My hotshot lawyer must think you can slip into all the right places."

I hadn't expected a woman. According to Uncle Mike, Yuri was big time and I'd assumed a man. But that's probably why she'd sought out St. Clair, Chicago's most reputable woman criminal lawyer. "I don't know what Ms. St. Clair thinks."

Her fingertips traced a path along the smooth black skin of her jawline. She inspected my face. "Okay, I'll bite. What do you want? Or did you come down here to pad your fee?"

"Look." I stayed seated. "I've got until Monday to find you a witness to back up your bullshit story—"

"Bullshit?"

"If I'm sitting in the jury box and I'm told some dumbfuck by the name of Blick from the sticks threatens you?" She didn't look like the type who could be threatened by anyone. But she'd never get the chance to say what she felt or thought because St. Clair would never put Yuri Provost on the stand. Not with her record for theft, assault, and attempted murder.

Her lips tightened. "I don't take a racial slur from anyone. He also told me to take my Welfare Queen black ass back to the ghetto."

I didn't know if it was enough to justify a beating but lucky for me, I wouldn't be sitting in that jury box looking out at a crowd that would include the six-foot-six ex-cop and probably a host of other badasses. "What about the video?"

She folded her arms across her chest. "What video?"

"We don't have time for games. The video from The Point Spread is missing. What did you do with it?"

"Like I told the police—"

"What you told the police is irrelevant. I need to see that video to get a look at the faces of the people in the bar."

"Because it's missing, you assume I took it?"

"You're not stupid."

"Thanks."

"How can I find a witness without it? I'm the third investigator on this case."

"The first to come here."

"That's right."

She came around the desk, folded her arms, and leaned against the desk. "You got a set of balls."

It wasn't a compliment about my investigation skills. "Next time I'll send an email the cops can read."

For the first time, she smiled. "You didn't know Yuri Provost was a woman, did you? I saw the look on your face." She chuckled.

I nodded.

"My ex gave me my last name. People think they're dealing with the Russian mob." She shook her head and laughed to herself. "The Asian parents who adopted me named me 'Yuri' and raised me right. My father was an enforcer for yakuza. I learned not to take shit."

"Good to know."

"You know something else? That tape shows a black woman kicking some sense into a motherfucker." The smile disappeared. Her chin jutted out and her lips quivered. "A lot of people need a good ass-kicking, and they know it too."

"I only need one witness."

"Why don't you try credit card receipts and the wait staff?"

"I don't have time to track down people who may have been in town just for a two-day conference. I need somebody standing there who saw and heard what happened and can testify about this racist pig."

"White faces."

"You don't know that. People stand up and tell the truth." It was a rare event, but it could happen.

"Won't make no difference. The police want to close me down."

"Ms. St. Clair is the best." I wasn't sure it would matter. Yuri Provost faced six counts of aggravated battery, each with a sentence of six to thirty years in prison.

"She costs enough. The cops should work on the murders around here."

"This ass-kicking happened downtown."

She pointed an index finger at me. "That's right. What was I doing in a place like that? Why don't I stay down here in Chi-Raq where I belong?"

"What were you doing there? The food sucks." I'd been to The Point Spread chain.

"The police asked me that, too. I don't have a right to go into the city? I was meeting my brother. He works downtown. Okay?"

"Fine." I didn't believe her and according to the file, neither did the police. "I don't have time—"

"You got a busy schedule? Lots of big cases with all the right people up there on Michigan Avenue getting divorced? Not like out here on the west side where people line up to shoot each other. Those that survive get a prison sentence. What do you think the people here would have if not for me? They don't have nobody. At least nobody'd treat them right."

She bought the stolen cars. Churned them through her body shop and salvage yard across the street. She bought and fenced other stolen goods brought in by gangs. Maybe she was a knight in shining armor or maybe she was part of the problem, it wasn't my call.

"You have the video." It wasn't a question any longer.

"Sure, I got it. I made that boy squeal for his momma." She smiled again in a way that told me how she got where she was in life. "If the video gets in the wrong hands, I'm fucked.

A picture is worth a shitload. Why'd you think those videos go viral? The first thing I thought about that night."

The surveillance video would lack audio. It would slant the case in favor of the prosecution. Maybe there was a digital copy floating around in the bowels of the company's security system, but to date, neither side had served a subpoena. "Don't worry, I'll take care of the video."

"It's not me who will worry. See these boots?" She leaned back on the desk and held one foot up in the air and twisted her foot.

A sturdy black army boot laced up to the calf with a steel toe shined to a brilliant sheen reflected the harsh white light. She held her leg up without any effort. She was muscular and on edge.

"Let me tell you this," she said. "If that video turns up at trial or gets into the wrong hands or shows up on goddamn Fox News, I'm going to put these boots to use. And what I did to that hick will look like a French kiss compared to what I'll do to you."

"Also good to know. Now give me the video."

10

I used Uncle Mike's office at O'Connell's Tavern to examine Yuri's video. There were several views inside the restaurant, but only one clear view of the incident. It would take time to pinpoint faces and get a decent screenshot of a witness. I planned to work on it through the night if necessary.

Yuri and the executive, Reynolds Blick, had engaged in a heated verbal exchange. Then as each stood face to face, gesturing and shoving, Yuri kicked the man in the groin. When he went down, Yuri employed the balance of a ballet dancer, arms outstretched, one steel-toed boot jackhammering the balled-up body on the floor, in an ultimate ass-kicking tour de force.

The video was mesmerizing. Without sound, it appeared that Blick got more than he deserved. That Yuri had crossed the line of proper behavior into the crime of aggravated battery with the groin kick and then added several more counts of aggravated battery as she kicked him again and again. A case of self-defense didn't seem at all possible, but there had been pushing and shoving beforehand. Those alleged incendiary words uttered by Blick that Yuri had told me about might do the trick depending on the jury and St. Clair's trial skills, but it wasn't my job to reach for legal conclusions.

A man in the bar video seemed equally mesmerized by the scene. A man who'd witnessed the entire incident. Due to the late hour, not many people were present. I was able to isolate his face and obtain a decent frame that wasn't too grainy. As Yuri had said, it was a white face. And I couldn't wait to find the man and get his story and hope that what he had to say matched what Yuri had said about the racial taunts.

I was asking myself why anybody in their right mind would get into a fight with someone like Yuri Provost, take a beating, and then call the cops to swear out a complaint. The guy must have a death wish.

The file notes showed that Blick was attending a conference. A friend of mine, Lanikowski, was an event planner at one of the big hotels, and I got in touch with him before he left for the weekend.

"What's the name of the conference?" Lanikowski asked me.

"It was a sports betting tech conference at the Marriott." I gave him the date.

"I heard about it. That conference was swamped with techies from all kinds of Silicon Valley companies, lawyers, accountants, lobbyists, and foreign companies all looking to get a piece of the action. My company included. It's just the tip of the iceberg."

"I'll need to get a list of attendees if you can swing it," I said.

"Sure. But it'll cost you."

Since when did anyone get anything in Chicago without paying? "No problem."

"Hey, this private detective business of yours is taking off. Our company might be able to use you."

I wouldn't tell him it was my first job. "Good. Keep me in mind. What else do you know about this conference?"

Lanikowski loved to talk. He said there was lots of tech stuff, but the conference agenda also involved lobbying efforts to push sports betting legislation in various states. Big-name sports figures had given talks and signed autographs and schmoozed with the attendees. Booze had flowed like the Chicago River, and people got sloppy and out of control.

I thanked him for the information and Lanikowski said he'd make my request his top priority.

The fact that Blick was from out of town explained his willingness to press charges. He didn't know who he was dealing with. Somebody should tell him why Chicagoans didn't come forward and testify. Once the criminal proceedings were over, Yuri's boys would track Blick down and administer another generous dose of common sense.

I could contact Blick and try to enlighten the racist, but that would be a breach of ethics, and my first foray into the business of being a private dick would be a bust. Better to do what St. Clair instructed. I had the feeling my silence was expected, part of the justice game. Rake in a fee from Yuri so St. Clair could take pro bono cases for the disadvantaged, while Blick, the citizen-victim, faced a future filled with terror. What a system. But it seemed to work because the racist would get what he deserved.

Uncle Mike walked into the office. "I got a call from the precinct. They got a call from that woman's house."

"Tara Reilly?"

"Yeah. They said the call came from an old lady."

"Maybe it's Tara's mother. Anybody hurt?"

"No. But the woman is scared shitless," Uncle Mike said.

"We've got a few extra minutes. Where does she live?"

Uncle Mike fished a piece of paper from his shirt pocket. "It's not far. But I don't want to be late. I'm due to meet that lobbyist for Sloan at a hotel out by O'Hare."

I got up from behind the desk. "Don't worry. We'll make it quick."

———

The Reilly house was one of those fifty-year-old bi-level brick homes nestled amid manicured juniper bushes and mature trees; their branches intertwined over the street. In the summer the trees must create a shady canopy, but in November, the knobby fingers of the bare branches crisscrossed the steel-gray sky and left the sidewalks of the respectable neighborhood exposed.

The patrol car parked out front and the woman standing on the front stoop reminded me that crime could find its way anywhere. I pulled up behind the patrol car.

Officer Murphy was stationed in the patrol car in front of the house and approached our truck. "Hi Eddie," he called. "Got my transfer out of hell thanks to Mike."

I told him congratulations. The southside assignment where we found Jimmy did seem like hell. He and Uncle Mike caught up on precinct gossip as we walked up to the front door, where a woman stood on the cement landing.

Uncle Mike introduced us to the woman and asked if she was Clara Reilly.

She nodded as she pulled at the winter coat draped over her shoulders. "Nothing like this has happened before. This guy tried to kill us. He tried to run us off the road."

Clara Reilly reminded me of Uncle Mike's wife. She had my aunt's red hair gone gray, thin tight lips, apple cheeks, and rounded chin. A rosary hung from a breast pocket like a weapon of last resort.

Uncle Mike asked her a series of questions in an effort to calm her down. Where did it happen, what type of car was it, was their car damaged? Murphy pulled out a pad and took notes.

Clara Reilly did her best to answer the questions and told us no one was hurt. Then she lost it again. "My daughter, Tara, was driving. She says this is all about last night and that bar you own. What kind of people do you let into that place?"

I asked if we could talk to Tara to get the full story. It might save time and get us on the road and out of the cold. I could see my breath.

Clara looked at me as if I might not be important enough to handle her emergency. "What story? A maniac tried to run us off the road." Then she opened the front door and yelled for Tara.

Tara poked her head out the door and examined us with those blue eyes, a crooked smile playing on her lips. Murphy took a step back.

"Tara had to take the day off from work to drive me to the doctor, and her company doesn't like her to take time off," Clara said to Murphy as if that fact needed to be added for the record.

Tara pulled back a curtain of blonde hair. "Hi, Eddie. I heard stories about you last night. Maybe I shouldn't have hit that guy with the pool cue. I spoiled everybody's fun."

Yes, a fight with Kubala out in the back alley would've been fun for everyone. I could've sold tickets. But I didn't think Clara Reilly would appreciate levity. "The officer was out front. Why didn't you let him know you were going out?"

Murphy said, "I would've been glad to escort you and—"

Clara turned to Tara, "I told you—"

"I'm not going to be a captive in my own house," Tara said. "Mother, maybe we should go inside. The neighbors will think I'm dealing drugs."

"Oh, good Lord," Clara said, reaching for her rosary.

Tara looked at us. "C'mon, I made coffee."

We followed Tara into the house as if we'd all been invited to a contemporaneous party. Tara didn't seem to be fazed by the incident with Kubala. Not a single sign of nerves.

Uncle Mike refused coffee and the three of us stood in the entryway. Clara began to straighten pillows and throw-blankets, and picked up a stack of newspapers and took them into the kitchen. I noticed the old console television in the corner, the beat-up couch and recliner, and the coffee table covered with magazines and coffee cups. A worn trail along the faded carpet led from the living room toward the kitchen.

"You don't know the kind of guy you're dealing with," I told Tara while her mother was out of the room. "He's a psycho."

"The police can only do so much," Uncle Mike said. "If you don't want to cooperate—"

"Look, the only reason we asked Kubala to join us last night was because he said he knew Eddie and needed to see him." Tara hunched her shoulders. "There's a psycho on every corner. Deal with it."

"You just happened to run into Kubala?" I asked.

"One of my friends ran into him," she said. "The one with the broken jaw."

Clara walked back from the kitchen. "You were with this nut? Tara, what have I told you about strange men?"

"Please, mother," Tara said.

Uncle Mike asked Tara the same series of questions he'd asked her mother. This time he got the color and make of the vehicle and where it happened.

Tara folded her arms across her chest. "I was driving. He came up from behind and cut me off. We almost went down an embankment. I don't need a babysitter."

Uncle Mike and Murphy gathered what nuggets they could. Unfortunately, it was all fool's gold, no clear identification of Kubala or license number of the car. It was the kind of police report that got filed in the Fuck-It Bin, and everyone except Clara seemed to know it.

"I don't mean to scare you," I said. "But take advantage of the officer from now on and don't take any chances."

Tara smiled, exposing a row of perfect movie star pearly-whites and then her expression changed to one of puzzlement. "Wait a minute. Mom calls the police station and you two come running?" She leveled her gaze at me. "That doesn't happen. This guy —Kubala—must be something else, right? I mean really dangerous? You know what I said—about how I didn't want your help? Well, forget it. I do."

She had this way of arguing with herself that put her in control and at the same time put everyone at ease. I wasn't sure if it was an act or not, but it forced us all to laugh. There was an edge to her voice as well, and for a second I thought Kubala might be the one who needed to be forewarned.

"Good," I said. "Now you get it. Kubala is dangerous."

"Tara's a nut," Clara Reilly told us. "Forgive her."

11

I FINALLY GOT A NAME TO GO WITH THAT FACE IN THE YURI
video. I'd convinced my buddy, Lanikowski, the event
coordinator, to work with me on his day off. We had to bribe
one of the techies in charge of the conference. Conference
management had taken picture IDs to insure no one shared
another person's ID to enter the conference exhibit areas and
avoid payment of the exorbitant registration fees. Certain
conference attendees made their living in the black market and
didn't appreciate the photo requirement. In response, the
utmost privacy had been promised. To diminish the guilt
associated with breaking the promise, I had to negotiate a cash-
healthy bribe for the conference techie. St. Clair would
understand. It was how things worked in Chicago.

We grew blurry-eyed trying to match my grainy screenshot
of the face I'd isolated as a witness to the fight between Yuri
and Blick with one of the thousands of ID photos in the

conference database. After several hours, we were able to pinpoint the one face that matched my screenshot. A man named Garrett Walsh. A quick internet review of Walsh revealed some interesting stuff.

Walsh had worked for a sports channel. Even though I'd watched the network for years, I didn't recognize him. Maybe he worked behind the scenes as a producer or executive. The website said that Walsh had married an heiress and now worked in the private sector.

I'd dug a little deeper and found that Walsh had gone to work for WagerEasy. It made sense since there was an ongoing sports betting conference nearby. WagerEasy was where Jimmy had worked. If I could get Walsh to agree to testify to what he'd seen at the bar and the fight between Blick and Yuri, maybe I could also ask if he knew anything about Jimmy's role at the company. Get paid my PI fee while I fished for information on Jimmy. It would be more progress than Uncle Mike and I made yesterday talking to Sloan's lobbyist. The guy could talk and drink all night and not say anything meaningful about Sloan or his intentions.

The relationship between pro sports and sports betting had grown more cozy with each passing day since the Supreme Court decision. Gone was talk of "integrity of the game" and lawsuits, replaced by news of daily groundbreaking deals between the gambling sites and every sports team and league.

Walsh had played a prominent role at the sports betting conference. The schedule showed that he participated in several sessions and introduced a featured speaker.

I was able to obtain a home address for Garrett Walsh that led me to the northern suburb of Winnetka, home of some of the highest-priced real estate in Chicago. An exclusive enclave for the wealthy nestled beside Lake Michigan and not the kind of place where Kubala could follow me without being exposed. Traffic was light, but when I exited the expressway, I made a turn around a city block and waited. No car matching Kubala's vehicle came past.

It was happy hour on a Saturday night by the time I drove past Walsh's home. Typical for the neighborhood, it had at least ten bedrooms and a big front yard. A five-car garage, and tall trees without leaves, and lots of brick to keep away the Big Bad Wolf.

Luxury cars and SUVs lined the street out front, forcing me to park down near the lake. Heavy clouds hung over the water and high waves bit down on the vacant shore. The fast-approaching night forced me to hurry. As I walked through snow flurries, the snug scene inside the residence beckoned. Numerous people inside held drinks, a cocktail party in motion. I could almost hear the laughter and music and jingle of ice in the martini shaker.

I walked up and knocked. The face in the video opened the front door, a face ripened by laughter and drink. I think we were both startled. For me, because my screenshot had come to life, and for him, how to deal with an intruder who had failed to read the "No Solicitors" sign on the front door.

Walsh wore a white sweater with the arms draped around his shoulders and tied across his chest, a checkered shirt, and pressed jeans. His hair was groomed down to the millimeter and his teeth were television network white and perfect. He was at least sixty years old.

His smile disappeared. "Can I help you?"

"You're Garrett Walsh?"

"Yes, I'm Garrett Walsh." He nodded slowly and took a step back as if I might be a process server.

I introduced myself and told him who I worked for. "I just need to ask a couple of questions. You were in a sports bar downtown last May?" I tried my best to sound harmless.

His head tilted. "Why don't you call my office?"

"We need to talk." I didn't want to scare him off, but I didn't have much time. St. Clair needed a witness by Monday morning.

"Are you a cop or something?" He asked in a Boston accent.

"A private investigator. You witnessed a fight."

His eyes took another inventory. "No shit? You're an investigator? A private dick like Sam Spade?"

"Yeah." I assumed Sam Spade had a license and a track record as a PI, while I had neither.

He opened the door wide. "Well, come on in. Don't stand out there in the snow. You want a drink?"

His hospitality and change of demeanor threw me off guard. "Not right now, no."

"You're sure? I thought all you private dicks were heavy drinkers." He turned toward the big crowd in the oversized living room. "Hey, everybody," he called out. "You won't believe who showed up at the door."

I stepped inside and confronted a large framed photograph in the entryway of Walsh and, I assumed, his wife, smiling into the wind on a sailboat beneath a clear sky. In the expansive living room, heads turned in my direction. I felt underdressed for the occasion in my down jacket, jeans, and flannel shirt, a refugee from the racetrack.

"Come on in," he said. "They won't bite. You've got to meet everybody. What did you want again?"

"Who is it, Garrett?" A woman called out.

"Why don't we go into another room and talk?" I asked Walsh.

A guy at the grand piano stopped playing. A young woman in uniform stopped working the room with a cheese tray. Ladies with perfect hair and cocktail dresses looked my way. Men in sports coats stopped in mid-conversation and inspected me.

A statue in the corner of the room portrayed a thin, human-like figure, bent and beaten down. I felt like we had something in common. Fresh flowers on the glass coffee table. The smell of meat being cooked in the kitchen. A plush white rug I had not yet been allowed to step upon. Bartenders tended a temporary bar set up toward the back. Large windows provided a view of not only the front yard but extended one-hundred and eighty-degrees along the length of the room to the snow-covered patio and barbeque pit in the backyard.

"Can you believe it?" Walsh called out in an effort to suspend all the cocktail action. "Can you believe it—a private investigator."

People looked at each other and smiled. Then laughter rippled through the crowd of at least thirty people.

"Okay," Walsh said, holding up both hands like a conductor of an orchestra. "Who was it? It's a great practical joke but c'mon—"

Everyone looked at each other to see if the jokester would come forward.

I forced back anger and tried to sound professional. "Look, my name is Eddie O'Connell, and I work for a criminal attorney named Helen St. Clair. I'm not here to do a singing telegram or any of that shit. I'm here because you witnessed a fight at a sports bar last May—"

He spread his arms again to the crowd as if I might be part of a magic trick. "Can you believe this? Last May?"

People sat on white couches beneath paintings I might see in a museum if I ever went. They sipped their drinks carefully as if there was a prescribed limit. No one smoked. They strained to appear casual while I got pissed.

I said, "I'm working for attorney Helen St. Clair—"

"What did you say, young man?" A tall stylish woman in her late fifties, her blond hair cut short, wearing black slacks and a tight white sweater, walked up to me.

I repeated the name of my employer.

"What's it about, judge?" Somebody called out.

Chicago and its connections allowed people to network in unexpected ways. Maybe I could do a little networking of my own. "Do you know Helen St. Clair, your Honor?" I asked.

"Of course, I do. She's one of the most respected criminal attorneys in the city." She turned from the hushed crowd back to me. "What's it about?"

"It was a bar fight last May. Mr. Walsh wasn't a party to the fight or anything. He was a witness." I didn't want to say anything about the video.

The judge now had everyone's attention, including the party host, Garrett Walsh. "Garrett, do you recall seeing a fight?"

Walsh looked around at the faces. Yuri would have had me note they were all white faces. Walsh didn't seem to like the fact he'd bombed with his claim that I was a practical joke.

He hesitated. "Yes, I do."

"What happened?" The judge prompted.

"I don't know," Walsh stammered. "People argued and then a fight broke out. It was months ago."

The judge looked at me. "Well?"

"This one guy by the name of Reynolds Blick—"

"Why can't we do this at my office on Monday?" Walsh asked.

"Wait one second," the judge said, holding up her hand.

"We need to submit a name to the judge handling the case by nine a.m. Monday," I said.

"That's what I figured," the judge said. "Let's step into the foyer." She turned to face the crowd. "Show's over for now, people."

Walsh, the judge, and I stepped into the foyer. A short bald man stepped into the foyer with us.

"Okay, Stuart, you can stay, but be quiet while I get to the bottom of this," the judge told the man. "Now what happened?"

I didn't like the looks of Stuart so I decided to play it as straight as possible. I'd taken copies of the Yuri Provost file home to read and found a formal phrase within one of the pleadings filed by Ms. St. Clair. I decided that now was a good time to use it. "Ms. St. Clair's client, a black woman, was subjected to racial abuse by Mr. Blick," I said. "Blick told her she should get her Welfare Queen black ass back to the ghetto."

"What was she charged with?" the judge asked.

I regurgitated more of the Yuri Provost file and those pleadings. "Ms. Provost has lived her entire life on the west side of Chicago. She's seen shootings. Shootings of friends and relatives. She's been subjected to racial abuse her entire life and reacted the way a downtrodden person in that environment might react—she fought back. She defended herself and used the only means available. She kicked the racist."

"Aggravated battery?" The judge asked.

"A number of counts. When Blick refused to stay down, she kicked him again to protect herself from harm." I didn't add how Yuri did a Rockettes number on his face and torso.

The judge shook her head and turned to Stuart and Walsh. "Does this give you an idea of the kind of thing we're forced to deal with in the courts? So much is race-related. Years of bitterness. Who is this Blick?"

"He's from out of state and attended the same conference I attended," Walsh said.

"And you saw all this happen, Garrett?" the judge asked.

Walsh nodded. "Yeah, pretty much. There was a lot more yelling and cussing from both sides. Things escalated."

"It's bad enough we've got this racial time bomb in the city, we don't need outsiders coming in here lighting the fuse," the judge said. "Did you stick around and give a statement to the police? Why does this poor defendant need to have an investigator track you down at the eleventh hour?"

Walsh shrugged. "Hey, if I would've known they needed me . . . Nobody asked for any statement. It all seemed cut and dried. Now I remember—the police acted as if this woman, Provost, was wanted for something."

"Another simple case for the police. Too simple." The judge crossed her arms. "Black people get locked up and sent to prison far too often. You just stood by while they handcuffed her?"

Walsh shrugged again.

I told Walsh, Stuart, and the judge that I needed papers from St. Clair's office signed on Monday morning. I wished I had the papers with me, but the office staff told me they weren't allowed to prepare a blank affidavit in advance. The judge said that Walsh would be more than happy to cooperate. I was glad to hear that, but Walsh didn't appear enthusiastic.

Stuart spoke up for the first time and said he worked at a local news channel. "I'd like to follow up on the story." His upper lip glistened with sweat, and I wasn't sure I could trust him. His collar was frayed, and he'd obviously had one too many cocktails.

Who invited this guy to the party, I wondered? The last thing I wanted was a newshound digging into Yuri's criminal background, and her stolen car assembly line, especially after I'd just painted my client as the Joan of Arc of the west side.

"There are too many stories like this, where a black person is hauled off to jail without a complete investigation, and we need to enlighten viewers," Stuart said.

Stuart demanded my business card. I fished around in my pocket and handed him the last remaining card from the reception desk at St. Clair's office. Let the attorney handle the press. I didn't want to answer questions.

"We have one story after another that's negative coming out of the west side or south side of Chicago and we need a story like this that shows things from another angle," Stuart said.

I didn't need another angle. All I needed was one upright asshole who was a witness to a bar fight. The judge placed her hands on her hips and glared down at Stuart as if she might swat him like an annoying, buzzing insect.

Walsh shed his white sweater, and his face reddened. He looked like he couldn't wait to leave, but it was his house. WagerEasy had craved publicity to launch its sports betting offerings. Deal after deal had been announced in the media, yet Walsh seemed repulsed by Stuart's interest. I thought any publicity was good publicity. Walsh's reaction intrigued me. I wanted to dig for information on Jimmy Golding and WagerEasy while I was here.

"The Blowtorch Murders seems like another angle," I said.

Stuart nodded as if I'd read his mind. "That's right. We've all been talking about the Blowtorch Murders." The journalist, one of a dying breed, went on to say how "some people" thought the story of three white men murdered in a "certain neighborhood" had received too much attention. If the victims had been young gang members, nobody would care, and they'd have been added to the daily stats and forgotten. He asked me what I thought.

I could've told the judge and Stuart more about the Blowtorch Murders. About the elaborate construction of the murder scene. The eerie tomb-like vacant factory. The network of ropes weaved around Jimmy, and Exhibit A, the blowtorch.

"Ms. St. Clair would be the one to talk to," I told Stuart and the judge. I stepped over to Walsh whose ego appeared bruised and bloodied by the judge and the newshound. "Excuse me, Mr. Walsh, I'll need to bring by those documents—"

"Of course, of course." He motioned me toward the door. "Could you bring them by the office on Monday?"

We huddled alone beneath the picture of Walsh and his wife sailing into the sun. The mouse-like way he asked the question was a whole lot different from the guy I'd met when I walked in. Maybe Walsh wasn't at ease with the guests, and maybe he threw the party to impress them, and I'd cost him an invisible degree of status. I'd hit the guy up while he was down.

"I heard that those killed in the Blowtorch Murders worked at WagerEasy," I said. I wanted to ask Walsh about Jimmy's huge salary but held back. "I've read about a possible drug deal. Must be rough."

"Very difficult." He rubbed the back of his neck. "I'm getting a lot of heat from the home office in London."

"I could help. I've had experience in these cases, but it'd have to be undercover. I could take Jimmy Golding's place. Get answers for you." It would be a way to find out about Jimmy and why he was killed.

Walsh looked up at me and rubbed his chin. A thin smile crept across his face. He straightened his shoulders and pointed a finger at me. "In fact, I've been told to get a PI to help, but our lawyers haven't gotten back to me."

"I could get you references and information on fees." I didn't know exactly who I'd use as references besides Helen St. Clair. Uncle Mike wouldn't mean much since he was my uncle, and using Liz would be a major conflict.

"I'll need to get in touch with my people. I'll let you know." Walsh gave me a strange look. He seemed to evaluate me and hate my guts at the same time. Maybe he was the kind of guy who had everything in life and I was today's single obstacle. Or maybe he was in the habit of using people and I was made to order.

"Make it soon," I said. "I didn't want to say anything in front of Stuart, but I was at the crime scene with one of my contacts."

The look of shock on Walsh's face told me I'd get the job.

12

Sunday morning, I walked through O'Connell's Tavern to meet with my uncle. The bar was packed, typical for an upcoming Bears game. People had begun to congregate around each big screen. I checked in with Tim, one of my assistant managers.

"Everything's good," Tim said as he wiped down the bar. "Except for those guys at Table Four."

I'd noticed the group when I'd walked in. Table Four was over near the window in the corner, a spot usually reserved for newcomers or couples who wanted to be alone.

"What have they ordered?" I asked.

"They haven't, and they've been here for a while."

"Okay. I'll go over."

The most trouble I ever got on a Sunday morning was a Bloody Mary without enough green olives, so when I gave them a closer look, I was surprised. The five guys, several about my size, wore ball caps low over their foreheads and still wore their coats. Some of them had their hands in their pockets. They were on edge, looking out the window.

"Hi guys," I said. "Can we get you anything?"

Several of the men stared down at the table. The presumed leader, a beefy guy with his arms folded over his chest, looked up at me with a sneer. "The waitress has been by a few times. We're still deciding."

The menus were stacked on one end of the table. A couple of the guys chuckled but kept their heads down. I spotted a swastika tattoo on the side of one guy's neck. Around his ears, his head was shaved. The others also had shaved heads from what I could tell.

"Any questions I can answer?"

"We'll let you know."

I nodded and straightened the chairs at an empty table nearby.

"Hey, buddy," the leader said. "We said we're still looking. Okay?"

"Sure."

"It's a nice quiet place, let's keep it that way. Okay?"

"Fine." It was the kind of thing I had to put up with. A customer was always right even when he was an asshole.

I stepped over to the bar and told Tim that Table Four would let us know if they wanted anything. "Keep an eye on them. I'll be in the office if you need me."

On my way through the bar, I stopped to say hello to a few of the regulars. Through a window at the end of the bar, I noticed Liz's car turn out of the parking lot. I walked down the hall past the kitchen to the office and knocked on the office door, heard Uncle Mike yell to come in, and went inside.

"Hey, I just saw Liz—"

Uncle Mike had his feet up on the desk and the cigar in one corner of his mouth. He blew smoke through the ceiling ventilation fans. "She just stopped by to drop off this casserole dish for Maureen. Why?"

A familiar dish sat on the desk amongst the paperwork. "Hold on. These guys at a table up front might be trouble." I went back toward the door.

"What kind of trouble?"

"I don't know. I told Tim to keep an eye on them." I stepped out of the office into the hall where I could scan the bar. Table Four was empty. I walked up to the bar and checked with Tim.

I walked back into the office. "They took off."

"You never saw them before?"

"No. Didn't order anything. Looked like they were waiting."

"Think they're following Liz?"

"Could be. Skinheads with serious tattoos. Maybe a local chapter. They tried hard to keep themselves covered up."

"I'll call her." He explained things to Liz and ended the call with the comment that the fivesome wasn't interested in football which made them suspicious. Uncle Mike turned to me. "Liz appreciates the heads up. She'll call for backup."

"How's she doing?"

"I'm afraid things haven't changed much with Wayne."

"She say anything—"

"About her investigation? No. Eddie, we need to talk."

"Great." I didn't like the look on my uncle's face. Something was eating at him.

I took a deep breath as I sat down in the chair that fronted the desk. I had something to tell Uncle Mike too. "I've got a problem with this PI business of mine."

Uncle Mike dropped his feet to the floor and the old chair screeched. "What? Already? Didn't I tell you to watch your back with Yuri Provost?"

"No, that's not it. I think the Yuri Provost job has been handled. I've got a new client."

"Really?" He plucked the cigar from his mouth. "Who? Remember we got this job for Burrascano, too."

"The new client is WagerEasy," I said.

"What? How the hell—"

I had gotten the call from Walsh this morning. "My witness in the Yuri Provost case turned out to be Garrett Walsh, the regional manager of the WagerEasy office."

"Damn."

I explained how I found Walsh, about the sports betting conference, and my born talent to entertain at Winnetka cocktail parties. "I told Walsh that he needed a PI to look into the office drug problem and that I'd been at the crime scene. My job will be to step into Jimmy's shoes and find out what I can about his murder. Home office agreed that they needed to do an internal investigation. Probably to cover their ass."

He slapped the desk. "Goddamnit, that's great."

I didn't know if it was great. What if I showed up at WagerEasy tomorrow and Walsh gave me an embarrassed look, told me he'd been drunk and wasn't authorized to employ a PI? Or what if Walsh and I got into an argument over my role after a week and sent me packing? Then I'd come back to Uncle Mike to beg for my old job because I had to pay the rent and my secret gambling debt.

A smile crept over his face, and he shook his head. "You're right where we wanted you. Damn."

"Burrascano told us that WagerEasy was a possible suspect in Jimmy's murder."

"Yeah. He figured WagerEasy did the murders to frame his ass."

"Not a bad theory. That way they generate lots of bad publicity for the illegal bookies and force the high rollers to go legit."

"And they don't have to pay Burrascano a dime." Uncle Mike pointed the end of his cigar in my face. "You better keep your antennae out. Burrascano could be right. Walsh might be a wild card in all this. I mean, c'mon, Eddie. You're not exactly first choice for a billion-dollar company."

"Thanks a lot," I said.

"Did Walsh check your experience or do any due diligence?"

"He said he needed to call home office, and after that, he called this morning with the job offer. I don't know what 'due diligence' he may have done. I've got a feeling that my presence at the crime scene and connection to Liz got me through the front door."

What did I know about WagerEasy or Jimmy's job? Sure, I knew the Jimmy from the racetrack and could step into his handicapping shoes, but no doubt he'd morphed into a corporate type. I didn't have a batch of suits hanging in my closet and didn't know much about financials or corporate policies.

Jimmy had worked at WagerEasy for over a year. He'd probably thrown himself into the job with his usual one-hundred and ten-percent focus. Although his notebooks showed he continued to handicap, he probably wasn't the old Jimmy I knew. And if Jimmy was involved in a drug deal as rumored in the papers, then he was a completely different person from the one I'd known at the track.

"You think Walsh is up to something? You think that he knows about me?" I asked. Here I thought I was a genius detective who had Walsh, the judge, and Stuart, the newshound, eating out of the palm of my hand. If Walsh was smart enough to suspect me, I'd have a real challenge stepping into Jimmy's shoes at WagerEasy. Always lots of questions and loose ends in an investigation. Like a handicapping puzzle with a full field.

"It's tough to say what Walsh is trying to do. But watch yourself around him. What did you tell Walsh and the others about Yuri? Did you sugarcoat the whole ass-kicking thing?"

"I don't know what I was trying to do. Maybe I wanted to impress those rich bastards."

"It could be Walsh was impressed. Maybe the PI job for WagerEasy is on the up and up. But don't try that sugar-coating bullshit here at O'Connell's, they'll throw your ass out in the snow."

"I'd deserve it, too."

Uncle Mike pointed to a pre-game show on the small screen in the upper corner of his office. The replay showed a player that had been injured and was stumbling off the field with the assistance of a couple of trainers. "Here's a question for you. What if you were able to know when a player recovered from an injury? Say you were able to get all the info on each player—their blood pressure, oxygen level, and stuff—would that help you?"

"Help me place a bet?"

"Yeah."

"How would I get all that information?"

"I don't know. Medical reports. All the biochemistry at your fingertips."

"Did Liz talk to you about—"

"No," he shook his head. "Like I said, she just dropped off the dish. It's something I read about in one of those damn magazines."

My aunt had subscribed to a number of magazines to help the neighbor kids with their school funding. Usually, Uncle Mike complained about the magazines piling up on the coffee table, yet he read the fishing and sports issues from cover to cover. But I didn't think it was something he'd read in a magazine.

Uncle Mike had said that perhaps Liz wanted our help but couldn't ask for it. It wouldn't do much good for me to grill Uncle Mike about it. If he and Liz were working behind the scenes and didn't want to include me, it was only because they wanted to protect me. I'd play along for now, but maybe that's what he wanted to talk about. "When I came in, you said we needed to talk."

Uncle Mike sat forward in his desk chair and planted his elbows on the desk. "I saw that car out in front of my house today. You know, that green Dodge Challenger Tara Reilly told us about."

"Kubala?" Anger swelled in my chest. If I knew where the guy hung out, I'd run over there this minute and beat the shit out of him. "Fuck."

"Yeah. I knew you'd react like that. I didn't know how to tell you."

"Did he threaten you? Try to run you off the road?"

"No. Followed me here at a reasonable distance."

"What?" I didn't get it. What was Kubala's game?

"I've seen this shit over and over when I was on the force. Kubala wanted me to see him. Look, I can get a patrol car to sit out in front of my house, no big deal. But there's a bigger problem here."

"Like what?"

"Eddie, he's trying to bait you."

13

IT WASN'T TOUGH TO SET UP A MEETING WITH OSCAR Colasso. All I had to do was give him a call and tell him I'd made a killing at the track the night before and had a bundle of cash to make a partial payment on my gambling debt, and he hyperventilated over the phone while he tried to tell me where to meet him. He loved to get a payment.

I needed to pump Oscar for information about the sports betting industry. I only knew enough to be dangerous, and I didn't want to get laughed out of the office by my WagerEasy coworkers on my first day tomorrow. I would step into Jimmy's shoes but the coworkers wouldn't know that I was a PI planted by the company to uncover drug use. I had to gain as much information as possible.

I'd spent a good part of the night after work poring over Jimmy's box. His notebooks contained certain horses and games he planned to wager the next time they ran or played.

Some of the football games included small conference games. How had Jimmy found these teams, and why did he plan to bet them?

The business records in the box included employee records from a company called StatsRUs. The employees had previously worked various jobs that made them valuable candidates for the gambling world: a trainer of racehorses, a football coach, and a jockey agent to name a few. Financial statements of WagerEasy and StatsRUs had sunk to the bottom of the box. The detailed reports were outside my area of expertise, but I made a note to research StatsRUs.

There was also the deal between WagerEasy and Burrascano that Jimmy had negotiated. What factors led to this deal? The deal might reveal something about the motive behind Jimmy's murder.

Oscar asked to meet at a restaurant in Evanston on the north side. On the way over, I kept watch for Kubala's vehicle in the rearview mirror. His plan to bait me was probably simple. Get me pissed off enough to go looking for him, race into that dive bar where we had our last fight to be met by Kubala and a group of his armed friends.

Sure, I could call a few friends of my own and teach Kubala a lesson he wouldn't forget, but somebody might get killed, and it wouldn't accomplish a thing.

It meant I had to chill out. The strategy wouldn't work for long. Kubala wasn't about to let things lie, especially after his public humiliation at the hands of a blonde with a home-run swing. People talked about it every night. Someone suggested we frame the splintered pool cue over the bar with a picture of

Tara standing over the troublemaker she'd laid out, but Uncle Mike vetoed the idea. That kind of thing would get back to Kubala and only escalate our feud.

Of course, my "chill" logic came to fruition only after Uncle Mike talked me off the Kubala ledge. Then Uncle Mike and I worked on more practical matters like the next step in our Jimmy investigation. I would meet with Oscar, and Uncle Mike would meet a guy who worked for Travis Sloan, whose job involved meeting with illegal bookies. As a consultant for the empire builder, Uncle Mike would find out firsthand if Sloan was making progress expanding his gambling ring of black-market bookies in Chicago. It would also tell us if Sloan had fully accepted Burrascano's recommendation of Uncle Mike and how far Sloan would trust my uncle.

My meeting with Oscar was set up at Lloyd's, a comfort food restaurant on Dempster. I drove over and found a parking place in the front of the near-empty lot. Lloyd's was one of those places still trying to hang on to the past. It had gone through several name changes over the years—the Swiss Chalet, the Black Forest Smorgasbord, The Bavarian Inn—and then Lloyd, the owner, named it after himself. I stepped inside and was met by a hostess who wore a Swiss maid costume, probably a holdover from one of its past incarnations.

The place had wood beams that extended to the high-pitched ceiling. Despite the dark atmosphere, Oscar wasn't tough to find. Most of the tables and booths were empty except for a few tables of refugees from a nearby assisted living facility.

Oscar sat at a round table in the back with a panoramic photo of the Alps behind him on the wall. He looked innocent enough, the neighborhood bookie eating lunch. But he was more than that. He might pretend to be my buddy, but he had deep connections within the black market.

Oscar wore earphones. I figured he was listening to the Bears play-by-play, because, God forbid, there wasn't a TV in the place. The piped-in music was some morbid crooner from the fifties, Perry Como, or Vic Damone, or one of those. The seniors smiled and bobbed their heads to the tune, and I got nervous about the fat zero balance in my retirement fund.

I'd needed to make this quick. Pump Oscar for info and then get back to the Bears game. They'd been on a roll this season and everyone was stoked. The entire city was tuned in. I also needed to get back to O'Connell's to help out behind the bar and set up the work schedule with Tim. Then I could get back to Jimmy's notebooks.

Oscar waved me over. He didn't stand but he did take out the earbuds and we shook hands. I sat down.

Oscar smothered one of the hot rolls with butter. "You might want to think about adding one or two of these menu items to O'Connell's."

"What are you doing in this mausoleum? The Bears were in the red zone. Did they score?"

He held up a hand. "You're an asshole, O'Connell. No football."

"What?"

"This is my 'go-to' place. Show a little class, will you? Tell me you got my cash. Don't spoil my meal."

"Your 'go-to' place?" It had been painful to drain the last of my cash reserves that I now had tucked in my pocket, and I wasn't going to hand it over until I got some answers.

The waitress brought an appetizer-sized plate of something swimming in brown gravy, and set it before Oscar, and told him it was hot.

Oscar went quiet and studied the dish. Maybe he was saying a prayer to a gastro God. "These are the best Swedish meatballs in town." Vic Damone or Perry Como chimed in with the question, "Isn't it romantic?" Oscar swirled a meatball in the gravy and popped it into his mouth.

The waitress, who fidgeted beside the table, asked Oscar if it was the way he liked it. He chewed slowly, gravitating to a higher state of grace.

The waitress asked what I wanted and I told her coffee, but that I wanted to see the menu. I didn't have time to order food, yet I always did price comparisons on menu items for O'Connell's.

"How much money you take in on the Bears?" I asked.

"Please, O'Connell. Not here."

I got it. Oscar probably had a ton of money on the Bears, and he couldn't stand to watch the game. Lloyd's was a way for Oscar to self-quarantine, a self-imposed exile. How much did he stand to lose if the Bears won and won big?

"What are you listening to then?" I had to get Oscar talking about something other than food.

"It's a book on tape. You probably wouldn't know about books. Your generation doesn't read."

"I've read a few. Try me."

Oscar talked while chewing. "A bio of Robert Mondavi."

"The wine guy?"

"Yeah. There's a ton of money to be made off those fucking vines. One of these days, O'Connell. When you and a whole lot of others get done paying me what you owe, I'll get me a vineyard."

It took all my poker talents to keep from cracking up. I imagined Oscar's short, round body waddling through rows of vines. "I didn't know you liked wine."

Oscar sipped from his glass of milk. "I don't. It's vile shit. But all you got to do is hire a crew for nothing and sit back and watch the sun do its magic. I'm telling you—"

"The other night at the bar, Marini brought up legalization of sports betting."

"Sure, what about it?"

"We talked about me playing the horses and you argued on behalf of sports betting." I recalled Oscar's expression when the subject came up. He was worried about legalization.

Oscar pulled a hot bun from the basket and mopped up the gravy off the plate. "Making it legal won't change nothing."

"Bullshit."

He chuckled. "You're a perfect example. People who like to gamble need instant credit. Like you."

"We've got credit cards." It was a weak argument. My cards were maxed out.

"These legit companies like WagerEasy will be subject to taxes. Illinois has to dig out of its hole somehow. They'll give you shit odds, you watch." Oscar sat back from the table and took a deep breath. "Now where's that cash payment you were talking about?"

"I still don't see it, Oscar. People like to be legit."

"Shit, O'Connell. You think my customers want to run out in a blizzard to a sportsbook and stand in line? You saw them the other night. They love me. I hand them cash."

It sounded like a speech Oscar had memorized. There wasn't any underlying emotion. If we were playing poker, I'd know he was bluffing. Oscar had to be hiding something. The fact he was in exile at Lloyd's with the geriatric crew while the Bears covered again, told me things weren't perfect in his world. Dreaming of vineyards while Vic Damone sang his heart out, confirmed it.

The waitress brought a small pie-shaped dish to Oscar. "The puffed pastry chicken pot pie," she announced. "I hope it meets with your approval."

Oscar bent over the dish and knifed the flaky pastry. Steam escaped to his waiting nostrils and he nodded happily. "Wunderbar."

The waitress smiled then turned to me. "Here is the menu, sir. Your coffee is almost ready. I haven't forgotten."

"Thanks." I had to get Oscar to open up, and I knew just how to do it. "I start at WagerEasy tomorrow."

Oscar stopped in mid-chew. "What?" He dropped his fork. "What the fuck? Damn, O'Connell. How did you get that job?"

I thought that would get his attention. The bookie would want to know everything he could about his legit competitor. I gave him a story I'd made up about Uncle Mike and his connections and my wealth of knowledge at the local racetracks.

"I'll tell you," Oscar said, stabbing his fork into the heart of the puffed pastry, "WagerEasy does scare me. I'm going to need to pick your brain when you're up to speed."

"Why is that?"

Oscar speared a chunk of chicken. "Things are moving fast. Too fast. I thought the pro leagues would drag things out in the courts and state houses. Instead, I read about deals every day. Pro hockey and basketball did a deal with a giant corporation that owns Vegas casinos. A Fantasy site did a deal with a racetrack in New Jersey to open a sportsbook. Five states followed New Jersey and legalized. The floodgates have opened."

"You just said you weren't worried." I didn't make it an accusation; I made my voice soft and calm like a psychiatrist trying to get to the source of the trauma.

"You'd have to be an idiot not to be worried. Fuck. My buddy in New Jersey is losing his ass. You know what the state did legal in four months? Six-hundred-million in handle. That money gets sucked right out of the black market."

Oscar's fears showed what was at stake. Why Jimmy had made a deal on behalf of WagerEasy with Burrascano and how people ended up murdered. The coming sports betting tsunami was gathering steam out there in the ocean where we couldn't see it and would soon crash on shore and swamp us.

"What about Illinois?"

"I could wake up tomorrow and Springfield would've put the rubber stamp on it. But what my friend in Jersey talks about is 'in-play' wagering. It's going to kill him. Kill all of us. Fuck. At least I won't have to think about the Bears on Sunday anymore."

"In-play?" I had heard about it, but I wanted to hear his opinion of it.

"It's the rage in Europe, and they're betting soccer. Imagine football with all the time outs. It gives the bettor time to play. You bet on what will happen next. You're part of the action. You bet on if the team will score on the next drive or if the guy will make the field goal. All kinds of stuff."

"You have a computer site."

Oscar pushed the pot pie to the corner of the table and knotted his chubby fingers. "Do I look like a computer nerd to you, O'Connell? Fuck me. This takes real money. It's a mobile app where the customer streams the game and odds come up on each wager. You got to be on top of everything happening in every game or you're fucked. A quarterback gets whacked in the head. Everybody knows the team won't score on the next drive, and you better be on top of it. But what if it's a receiver or running back? How many games are being played right now on Sunday afternoon? Throw in the college games. Sharp bettors playing big money are on top of lots of games."

"But all that will take time," I said.

Oscar belched. "Don't be an asshole. These greedy-ass legislators all see what Jersey is doing. Sports franchises want people watching games. More viewers means more money, and more streaming, and more computer platforms with stats at your fingertips. These mobile apps and the in-play shit will go through the roof. I'm a little guy and WagerEasy is like Walmart."

"What will you do?"

"Good question. There's shit going on that makes me seriously think about getting out."

One of the seniors, an old man, shuffled past toward the restroom. Oscar watched him and the two exchanged a smile and a wave. Maybe they were both regulars.

"What kind of shit are we talking about here?" I asked.

Oscar leaned across the table. "A guy out of Reno. Finds these games to play. Little college games. The guy makes big money."

"A fix?" I thought about Jimmy's notebooks and his notations on small college games.

"We don't know. There's no common denominator. No crooked ref or certain teams. There's no rhyme or reason. A friend of mine needed to lay off some of his action. I got burned, too. A bunch of us are tracking the Reno guy. He knows how to keep his identity hidden, but we'll find the asshole. You watch."

I didn't know exactly how it worked, because I couldn't afford to bet big money, but I knew that bookies took action from other bookies to reduce the risk and share the wealth. If a guy put a hundred-grand down on a game, a bookie wanted to keep him as a customer but didn't want to take the full hit if the guy won. Keeping the customer for the long haul was what counted. Because sooner rather than later the customer would lose.

When bookies spotted strange bets for big money, it raised red flags. For years, the bookies in the black market had been the safety valve that kept games honest. Who would ferret out these problems in the future? Some government regulator?

The waitress set another plate in front of Oscar and whispered in a sultry voice, "The Hungarian short ribs."

Oscar's eyes widened. "It's all about the short ribs, O'Connell."

I stared at the tender meat soaked in dark brown gravy. The rich aroma of the beef made my stomach churn with hunger.

The waitress set down my cup of coffee and asked if I wanted anything else. I told her no thanks. She slipped the separate check near my elbow.

Oscar pulled his napkin up to his collar and began to dig into the short ribs.

I sipped the coffee and the acid cut into my empty stomach. "I hear there's a guy who wants to network all the bookies."

The fork with Oscar's first bite stopped midway to his mouth. "You're not taking your action to somebody else, are you? Is that why you haven't played lately? You shut me out?"

"No, Oscar. Nothing like that. It's just something I heard."

"It better be. After I extended you credit and put my ass on the line. Don't forget that. Your uncle will kick my ass out of O'Connell's if he finds out. The last thing I need right now."

"Don't worry. It's our secret."

Oscar slipped a chunk of meat dripping with gravy between his lips and his eyes closed in reverence. Perry Como or Vic Damone made it clear love was here to stay.

When he came out of his trance, Oscar pointed his fork at me. "You're talking about Travis Sloan, right? Out of Dallas? Sure, I know him. I'll meet with him and hear him out. But I already know he's dangerous. I might pay the Outfit's street tax, but I stay away from guys like Sloan."

He didn't always stay away. When Oscar stood to profit, he'd partnered up with the mob. He'd sold my prior gambling debt to the mob, but I guess that was more ancient history we wouldn't discuss.

"I'd like to know what Travis Sloan says," I said.

"Let's do that. Then you can tell me about WagerEasy."

Uncle Mike would be dealing with a killer while I sat in a safe office at WagerEasy. It wasn't right. Jimmy was *my* friend.

I pulled out my cash. "I won't ask for a receipt." I tried not to think of the sports bets that I'd lost that cost me this hard-earned cash.

"You know me. My figures are never off." Oscar stopped eating and studied my packet of cash. "Used to be when one of my customers paid on a debt like you're doing right now, everything would seem worthwhile. I trusted my customers and they trusted me. Everything worked. It was a beautiful business."

I stood. "I've got to get going."

"You don't want pie?"

14

WHAT DID I EXPECT, A VERSION OF A VEGAS SPORTSBOOK? Maybe. At least, I expected the offices of WagerEasy to have glitz and glamour. Flat screens mounted at every critical juncture televising sporting events from around the world. Electronic boards lit up like those on the NY Stock Exchange that would reflect the second-by-second fluctuations in the odds. In my imagination, I threw in a few cocktail waitresses, music, intermittent announcements of betting opportunities, beer vendors, and crowd reaction as if it were O'Connell's on a Sunday morning. But there was none of that. Instead, what I found at WagerEasy was another drab Monday morning workplace.

I sat in the outer lobby awaiting "Mr. Walsh" who would "see me shortly." All I could see past the lobby was a row of offices along the windows for those in charge and the typical warren of cubicles within the inner space.

I'd chosen to dress conservatively since the offices were downtown and certain offices were less casual than others. I wore dark slacks and a blue button-down shirt with an old tie. It took me three or four tries to get the knot right, but it was the first day on the job, and I didn't want to come across as a hungover private dick from a fifties noir picture.

"Mr. O'Connell," the WagerEasy receptionist said, "Mr. Walsh will see you now."

I followed her to the corner office. People talked on phones inside their cubicles, hunched over, some of the phrases heated. About forty people were employed in the approximate fifteen thousand square-foot space from what I could see. None of the talk seemed related to a sporting event or the point spread on the Monday night game.

Walsh was on the phone when I entered his luxurious domain. He held up one finger to signal me to wait. I took a seat in front of the desk.

Walsh said, "Okay, that's good with me," over and over in his Boston accent into the phone, one eye on me along with a slight smile as if we were all members of the same club.

The office held a modest conference table, lots of wood shelves with what appeared to be sailing trophies, and to my right, through a couple of skyscrapers, a limited view of Lake Michigan. The portion of the lake I was able to glimpse churned in anger beneath dark November clouds and winter wind.

I'd gotten a good dose of the wind on the way over from St. Clair's office earlier that morning when I picked up the papers for Walsh to sign. None of my fellow commuters, each wrapped up in Chicago warrior coats and scarves and stocking caps, had a smile on their face. It was only six blocks but I'd shared their misery.

Walsh's phone conversation became heated, and he swiveled in his chair toward the window with his back to me.

"Think of it as a way to deliver data, an awesome amount of data," Walsh said. "We'll drown them in data. Think of 5G, A.I., all that stuff. Our proprietary, in-house technology will deliver a shitload of data. Let them swim in data."

It seemed Walsh had forgotten I was there. I thought of Jimmy's notebooks, the data hand-written and scribbled into passages that took time to decipher.

"I'm telling you it's just the beginning," Walsh said. "We've got the coach on board. We'll have ABD. The first ones to build it and secure it will win. We'll be tech gods."

Maybe WagerEasy was involved in more than a race to secure high rollers. It was also a race for technology and the flow of data.

Walsh hung up and then swiveled back to face me.

"Which coach came on board?" I asked. Maybe it was the same coach from the employee records in Jimmy's box.

"Never mind. Well . . . Eddie." It seemed he had to make an effort to recall my name. "Glad you could make it down."

Not exactly the welcome I'd hoped for. I wanted the warm handshake, the slap on the back. "I'm ready to start."

"That's what I wanted to talk about." He sat back in his leather chair and played with a pen between his long fingers as if his deep thoughts were connected to his fingertips.

"I brought the paperwork." I unzipped the leather carryall and pulled out the documents from St. Clair's office. Court papers that would explain to the court what Walsh witnessed that night and that Walsh accepted service of a subpoena to appear.

He said nothing, reached for the paperwork and studied each page. A corner of his lip curled upward in a sign of something objectionable within the documents. I began to get a sick feeling in the pit of my stomach.

After a few minutes, he tossed them across the desk. "I can't sign these." He got up and began to pace before the windows, turned his back to me, and rubbed the back of his perfectly coiffed head as he looked down at the cityscape.

I said nothing since his body language seemed to indicate he meant to explain things.

Finally, he turned and said, "Blick is not just anyone. He holds an important position in the industry and although he's a small fry in the grand scheme of things, these petty bureaucrats tend to talk to each other, you know? With the upcoming sports betting legislation, Illinois and other states will impose regulations and restrictions. Of course, government influence is a part of that. WagerEasy will need licenses to operate here and elsewhere. There will be favors. And I can't compromise all that over a little criminal case. You see that don't you?"

I saw it perfectly. How Walsh had used me when we shook hands at Saturday's cocktail party. How he'd played the embarrassed liberal, eager to do his duty before his elitist friends, while he planned to squirm out of the whole thing. To gain control of me, he'd offered me a plum PI job at WagerEasy.

I was tempted to tell Walsh that I'd track down the judge and each of the cocktail guests and tell them about their spineless host and how he decided to shirk his duty. Inform them they'd be required to testify as witnesses to what Walsh had admitted at the party for Yuri's sake.

Or, maybe I could tell Walsh a little of what I'd learned yesterday. That Yuri and Blick were the least of Walsh's worries because Burrascano theorized that WagerEasy and its local chief, namely Walsh, might have orchestrated a frame-up of the Outfit's gambling czar to obtain their high-roller clients for free.

I could also explain to Walsh that there were guys in the Outfit like DiNatale who didn't have the patience for the kind of investigations Uncle Mike and I did. Maybe Walsh would like to experience DiNatale's means of interrogation, one in which Walsh hung out of a window head-first to gain a new perspective on the street sixteen stories below.

Or, I could let Yuri and her boys convince Walsh to do the right thing. Give him the full Blick ass-kicking experience. So many options, so little time.

Jimmy's murder had nothing to do with drugs as rumored in the papers. How much did Walsh know about the deal Jimmy was working with Burrascano? Maybe Walsh knew nothing, and maybe he knew everything. But my guess was that he wouldn't tell me outright forcing me to wait and watch. It would be my little secret, my edge.

But I said none of this. Instead, I repressed my anger, shrugged, and said, "I'm sorry, Garrett, it's out of my hands."

Walsh folded his arms. "What the hell do you mean?"

"I spoke with Ms. St. Clair. I told her everything and how you confirmed that it was self-defense. She's even been on the phone with that friend of yours from the local news—Stuart something? They've got an interview lined up this afternoon." Of course, that was a lie, but Walsh needed to squirm.

"Damnit." Walsh pointed a finger at me. "Eddie, you better think of something. Blick is one of the most vengeful characters out there. Plus, he's got lots of connections. He's also got anger issues. WagerEasy will be toast."

I avoided talk of connections, anger issues, vengeance, and options, and shook my head in a show of sympathy. "You know, you might be worried about nothing."

"What? Why's that?"

"I think I can stall the interview between Stuart and St. Clair. If you sign the court papers, St. Clair thinks she can convince the DA to drop the charges to avoid publicity. The whole thing will blow over. Blick might not be happy with you, but it won't be as bad as confronting him face to face in the courtroom. Plus, if there is other evidence, Blick will hardly be able to throw the whole blame on you." More lies. The chance the DA would drop charges against a hardened, sought after scourge such as Yuri Provost was as likely as me hitting one of Oscar's four-game parlays.

"What other evidence?" Walsh said.

"You said yourself Blick has anger issues. I've already gathered evidence on his history of violence. All of that will be used to bolster a claim of self-defense." I had no such evidence but knew firsthand the kind of evidence needed in a case of self-defense based on my criminal battery charges with the

Bears linebacker. The victim's prior violent behavior could be admissible.

"I better not be held responsible." Walsh began to pace behind the desk. "It will ruin everything."

"It will take a lot of work, but St. Clair is one of the best in the business. You heard what the judge said at the party about her. I've seen her work magic on these cases time and again."

Walsh listened, but I could see the wheels of his weasel mind shifting gears. "This is a critical time. We're trying to gain a competitive edge. I'm paying you to keep a lid on this."

"Okay, in addition to my other duties filling in for James Golding, I'll run interference for you with Blick. If he squawks or starts to spread rumors, I'll be the third party that tells everyone in the business how righteous you are. Once they know the real facts, nobody will blame you. In fact, you'll be a hero."

Walsh sat down at his desk and rubbed the back of his neck. "Maybe you're the kind of guy we need. Let me take another look at those papers." He pulled out a pen and glanced up at me. "You don't know how much is going on around here, but you'll find out fast."

15

WALSH ESCORTED ME DOWN THE FAR END OF THE HALL TO
an empty office with a blank nameplate posted outside.

"This was Golding's office," Walsh said, pointing the way
but not stepping inside as if the office might be contaminated.
"Make yourself at home and I'll send in your coworker. She'll
give you the orientation and introduce you to the team. I'd do
it, but I've got a conference call." He looked at his watch.

I nodded and stepped into the office as Walsh sprinted
away. It was located at the polar opposite end from Walsh, low
on the ladder, reserved for a misfit with no chance to advance.
On the walk down the hall, Walsh had said, "Golding would
go his own way. Don't blame me for what you hear about
him." A ringing endorsement if I ever heard one.

Could Walsh and Jimmy Golding have been in competition
for the same corporate brass ring? Perhaps it was Walsh's lack
of sympathy for a murder victim or maybe Walsh was only

worried about his own skin, but I pictured him on that conference call right now informing home office that he'd hired a detective to work undercover to get to the bottom of the drug problem in the office. He probably encouraged the ugly rumors in the media about a drug deal gone awry and relished Jimmy's reputation being dragged through the mud.

Of course, that was assuming the "office drug problem" could be a concern for Walsh and home office. It was my bet they knew it was a ruse, and that Jimmy had a deal going down with Burrascano. Yet, for the sake of publicity, they'd let the "office drug problem" ruse fester in the media. I was now a part of that cover-up.

Uncle Mike and I had questioned Burrascano about his deal with WagerEasy which was intended to be finalized at the vacant factory by Jimmy and his coworkers, but the gambling boss had provided scant details. We wanted to know the amount of money, the names of the high rollers, and the structure, but insight into the Outfit's business had been withheld. It was Burrascano's custom to give us just enough information to keep us going, making it critical for me to learn whatever I could at WagerEasy.

The court papers Walsh signed had reached St. Clair's office with only minutes to spare, and Ms. Spiegleman confirmed they would be e-filed. Mission accomplished. When the DA got a look at them and with the short time frame before next week's trial, fireworks could be expected.

Since Walsh the weasel had swallowed my fib that it was likely the DA would roll over, and a deal could be hammered out, my quick expulsion from the premises would probably follow. It meant I'd have to learn as much as possible in a very short time.

The view from Jimmy's leather chair didn't offer any hint of the view Walsh's office provided. No glimpse of Lake Michigan and its clouds or choppy waves. Just a mirror image skyscraper, where office workers sat like zombies before their computer screens. It gave me the shakes. Jimmy had been confronted with this perspective, a million miles from the soothing view offered by the track bleachers.

There was nothing on Jimmy's desk or on the shelves. Behind the shelf-unit was a stack of harness programs from last year's meeting at Thornton Racetrack. The person or persons who had sanitized the office had failed to find them. The old programs confirmed what I already knew from Jimmy's notebooks—his gambling had continued.

If Jimmy had bet through the WagerEasy software, I could try to get a look at his account and review his recent wagers. Was Jimmy on a losing streak at the track that forced him to scavenge for a corporate job, or was the track bum on the trail of something else he'd uncovered in his research?

The desk drawers were scrubbed clean as were the cabinets beneath the empty shelves. Nothing to tell me about Jimmy's role and what I would be expected to do. How did I possibly think I could play the imposter? The staff would immediately finger me as a corporate spy.

There was a knock on the door jamb and a woman poked her head in and said, "Hello, sorry about the wait." Her face broke into a smile. "Eddie?"

"I'll be damned," I said.

It was Tara Reilly, the blonde with the home-run swing. She'd stepped up her fashion statement since I last saw her. The jeans and sweatshirt were replaced by black slacks and a red sweater with a gold chain necklace.

She closed the door behind her and sat down in a chair that fronted the desk, and a look of astonishment graced her movie star features. "What are you doing here? You're Golding's replacement?"

"That's right. You were Golding's coworker?"

"I just transferred," she said. "I took the place of one of those guys who was murdered. You're the talk of the office. Everyone is asking. 'Where did he come from? What's his experience?'"

She had directed the conversation back to me. A smooth transition. I'd formulated a story, and I might as well put it to the test. "I've spent time at the track. Walsh thought I was a perfect fit."

"Yes, the regulars at O'Connell's not only told me you could fight, but that you had a thing for the horses." The way she shook her head told me that it didn't appear likely a horseplayer could expect to live up to the high expectations at WagerEasy. "But Golding had an MBA. Work experience."

Jimmy had a graduate degree? The track virus could infect anyone. What else didn't I know about my old track buddy? "Golding was a track bum before he went to work here."

"You knew him from the racetrack?"

Now it was my turn to transition. "I don't think WagerEasy had candidates anxious to take Golding's position after what happened. How about Kubala?"

She brushed back her lush, shoulder-length blond hair. A slight hesitation and nod of her head told me the abrupt change of subject had raised a red flag. She was smart and able to handle herself. She just transferred? It struck me as too convenient. "Haven't seen any sign of him lately, thank God. I still feel bad about the whole thing. Kubala said he knew you. That's why we let him come with us. Then the guys started talking about how good they were at pool, and the goon starts a fight."

"He's a psycho."

"My mother sure was scared. She won't let me go back to O'Connell's."

"Not that you'll listen to her."

She smiled, the full, bright, Hollywood smile of a star. "Well, that's true, but don't tell her." I couldn't help but study her features and appreciate her beauty. A perfect complexion, high cheekbones, and upturned nose would probably allow her to get a high-priced job modeling if she chose it.

"Sorry, your mother was dragged into this mess with Kubala. But he hasn't quit. He followed my uncle today. He might be trying to bait me."

"Get you to do something stupid?"

"Exactly. Be sure to use the police officer posted outside your house if you go anywhere."

She studied me. "Kubala is out to get you, right? That was plain to see. But you don't seem all that worried."

"I just don't want anyone else to get hurt." I also wanted to tell her not to fight my battles, but that ship had sailed when she swung the pool cue. "If Kubala followed my uncle, he might go after one of those two guys you were with the other night. Are you seeing one of them?" I needed to cover all the bases.

"No, they're just friends from school. I told them about Kubala trying to run me off the road, but I'll call them again and warn them."

"Good. What about you? How did you end up here at WagerEasy?" I needed to steer the conversation back to WagerEasy. I had to get an idea of my duties to convince the other employees I was for real.

"I started in the WagerEasy legal department. Before that, I was a glorified paralegal for a small firm that did contract work on WagerEasy's office lease. I heard the company was hiring and paid well so I called my uncle."

"Your uncle? What do you mean?"

"If there is one person in Illinois who is, at this moment, the most important person in the entire sports betting industry, it's not the mayor or the coach of the Bears, or the manager of the Cubs, it's Uncle Sean."

"Why is that?" I liked the way her eyes lit up with a hint of mischief when she brought up her uncle.

"State Senator Brennan—the man in charge of the sports betting bill? I'm sure you've read about him in the sports pages."

I laughed. "We may need your connections. Walsh seems like a tough boss." Tara probably carried extra clout in the office because of her uncle, and as my team member, maybe some of it would rub off on me.

"And I may need your connections," she said.

"Really?"

"Look," she said, "I'm going to need help on the gambling part of this job."

"Sure. Did you get to know Golding before the murders?"

"Not as well as I would've liked. I've got to warn you, people around here are putting up a good front, but they're hurting. The headlines and social media about the murders— such bullshit. But why *was* Golding in that shithole? I keep asking myself that."

"You don't think it was a drug deal gone bad?"

"I don't know if it was a drug deal." She looked over my shoulder out the window. "I just transferred but people still ask me what I know—why were they there, if they were on business—and I have to tell them I don't know. They look at me like I'm another dumb blonde. Drives me crazy. Like everyone else in the office, I did know them. I saw them in the break room and at inter-departmental meetings. I'm hurting like everyone else. I'll tell you, Eddie, it makes it tough to get up and come into the office."

Her hands gripped the arms of the chair and her lips tightened. "It's tough to feel safe. Murders and that madman Kubala. Get another job, I tell myself." An embarrassed smile took the place of an expression of fear. "But you came to our house. My mom counts on me to help pay expenses. Whenever you're forced to hunt for another job, you wonder if your timing is right. This is your first day. You probably don't want to hear my tale of woe. But you need to worry, too, and not just about Kubala."

"Why's that?"

"WagerEasy merged with another company. There's talk of layoffs. All that and we're under pressure to make WagerEasy number one in every bettor's head."

I'd read up on the deal with StatsRUs. Making WagerEasy number one sounded like fun. I knew what gamblers wanted. "Piece of cake."

"It's no joke. I'll need your help on the gambling part of the job if I hope to survive. Uncle Sean is no guarantee of a job."

"It's a bargain," I said. "Maybe we can find some of those answers. I guess we should get started." I had dozens of questions about procedures, the technology, and who the key people were besides Walsh, and how things worked with home office, but tried to act as if today was just another day at the office.

"I forgot to tell you. Golding had set appointments for this morning. I thought you could sit in. It'll give you a chance to learn on the job."

"When?"

She walked over and opened my office door. "Starting right now."

"What's it about?"

"Just follow my lead."

Walk into a meeting cold? It was the dumbest move an imposter could make. "Let's go," I said.

"One more thing," she said. "Ditch the tie."

16

TARA LED ME TO A SMALL, NO-FRILLS, WINDOWLESS conference room near the WagerEasy office entrance. A plump woman with short hair wearing a dark purple suit sat at the table with her back to the door.

The woman turned her head when we walked in and exchanged an icy nod with Tara. The woman in purple looked me over and then her lip curled upward as if bile had welled up in the back of her throat. She asked if I was Walsh's new hire. When I told her I was and introduced myself and extended my hand, she turned away and shook her head.

She returned to the file and the papers she'd laid out on the table. "Fine," she snorted, "You can call me Ms. Larsen, Legal Department."

Tara side-stepped around the table, not taking her eyes off Larsen, giving her a wide berth the way one might circumvent an angry crocodile. I took the same path.

"Call me Mr. O'Connell," I said. The walk-in cooler at O'Connell's was a spa compared to the chill in the room.

After a long minute flipping pages of the file, Larsen scratched at her short, brown hair and looked up at me. I expected questions about my qualifications or lack thereof, but instead, she picked up the phone and told Nancy, the receptionist, to send in Mr. Johnson.

Tara maintained silence and, out of caution, I followed suit. A few moments later, the receptionist opened the door of the conference room and escorted Mr. Johnson inside. He was in his early fifties, average height, dressed in jeans and a dark blue wool shirt, and he smelled of cigarettes. He carried a sheaf of papers in one hand.

Larsen pointed to the chair at the end of the table. "Take a seat, Mr. uh . . . Johnson."

Johnson looked at Tara and me and Larsen as if we were inquisitors and sat down.

"This is the first one of these I've been to," he said. "I haven't been downtown in a while. Didn't know if I'd make it on time. The traffic is—"

"I'll take your paperwork." Larsen perused them and then slid them across the table to Tara. "Ms. Reilly is quite familiar with the inner workings in my department."

"I transferred out last week," Tara told Mr. Johnson. Under her breath, she whispered, "Thank, God."

Now I understood why Tara transferred from the legal department. I resisted the urge to apologize to Johnson for Larsen's rude behavior and introduced myself and Tara to Johnson.

A furtive look at the papers revealed a standard non-disclosure agreement and financials.

"Mr. Johnson, why don't we start off with a bit of information?" Larsen said, holding a pen over a legal pad. "You know who we are. WagerEasy is an international sports betting operator providing legal online and retail betting services to millions and technology to its partners. Tell us a little about your operation."

"The wife didn't want me to come down," Johnson said, looking first at me and then the others.

"Your financials have not been fully completed," Larsen said.

"The Leech—Mr. Golding—was working on a solution for everybody. He was someone we could talk to," Johnson said. "Someone we could *all* talk to. From the guys at the top to the little guys like me."

What would Johnson say if he knew that Jimmy had bypassed all the little guys and gone to Burrascano to sign up all the high rollers? I wasn't going to tell him.

"Well, as you know, he's no longer with us," Larsen dropped the pen and folded her arms. "If you want us to open the channels of communication, we need your full cooperation. Unless we get all your information, we can't proceed with talk of numbers."

Johnson licked his lips and shook his head. "This is my paycheck. I still got kids in college."

"WagerEasy is not a welfare agency, Mr. Johnson. We're here to commence good faith negotiations. Now is a critical time in the industry. Offers you might receive today will be gone tomorrow. If you don't want to submit full financial—"

"Just a minute, Ms. Larsen," I said. I didn't care if she was from the in-house legal department, I wouldn't sit by and let her bully the guy. My full-time job might be bartender, but I'd played the imposter before on jobs for Burrascano and had gotten used to the corporate shuffle. Once you cut through their bullshit terminology, they were just like anybody else, except they had more money. "Mr. Johnson, you said Mr. Golding had a solution?"

Larsen grunted. "You're totally out of bounds, Mr. O'Connell."

Johnson pulled a toothpick from his shirt pocket and slid it between his lips. "Yeah. He promised everything would be secret. Now that he's gone, I don't know what to think."

"I assure you, Mr. Johnson, that the paperwork provides for mutual confidentiality," Larsen said.

"Whatever the hell that means." Johnson's voice rose in anger. "I've been doing business for twenty-plus years out of the same joint on the far south side the way my father did, and we never had one single signed scrap of paper. So why the hell am I doing it now? The Leech is gone. I don't know you guys. You play soccer for fuck sake."

Larsen rose in her seat. "Profanity won't be allowed—"

"Wait a minute," I said. "Let's start over. I think Mr. Johnson—"

"Sam," Johnson said.

"Sam, call me Eddie. I think Sam has a point, Ms. Larsen. These might be critical times in the industry, but they're also difficult times." I now had a handle on why we were here and what the meeting was about.

WagerEasy had brought in Sam Johnson, if that was his real name, to consider buying his bookmaking business, which probably consisted of nothing more than his list of customers, and would make any seller uneasy. Jimmy had been WagerEasy's connection to the high rollers WagerEasy craved in order to gain that competitive edge, and now that Jimmy was gone, where would these bookies turn?

"You know it," Johnson said. "It sucks. Right now, if the casinos or racetracks get a license and open a sportsbook, I've still got an edge. My customers can't always find the time to drive across town and stand in some fucking line, but once everything goes full mobile like New Jersey, I won't be able to compete. These new computer platforms—"

"That's not our concern," Larsen said.

"In-play wagering?" I asked. It was what Oscar had been afraid of.

"You got that right," Johnson said.

Larsen looked at me as if that bile had popped back up her throat. "Mr. O'Connell here just joined the company this morning and—"

"Maybe he just joined this morning, but I'd rather talk to him than you," Johnson said, standing up.

"Ms. Larsen is in charge of the in-house legal department, Mr. Johnson, and has final decision-making power," Tara said. She spoke with a hint of despair as if there was no way to escape the wrath of Ms. Larsen.

For the sake of Johnson's potential deal, I tried a diversionary tactic and waved at Johnson to sit back down. "Have you heard of Oscar Colasso? He's the bookie at our neighborhood bar."

A genuine smile lit up Johnson's face for the first time that morning. "Sure, I know that fat fuck. He's got a sweet deal with those taverns on the near north side. You won't be meeting with him. He can afford to lose customers and subs, but not me. I hear he's with that Sloan Group. They're signing up all the big-time guys. They're smart. There's power in numbers. But they're linked to organized crime and, except for the mob tax, I refuse to make a deal with the devil." He kept his gaze trained on me and didn't turn toward Larsen. "Like I said, I'm small-time."

Johnson remained an independent bookie and paid the mob tax, but I'd known bookies who'd joined the mob's network and regretted it later. "How small-time is that, Mr. Johnson?"

"Our customers support my wife and me, my brother-in-law, and two clerks who have been with me for twenty years. My customers trust me. It's a two-way street, you know. They could go to the police with their complaints. It's not like I've got a ton of protection. But I'm in a tough spot. I've heard what happened to the small-time guys back in Jersey."

"What do you mean?" I asked.

He laughed and the toothpick bobbed in his mouth. "You *are* new. Like I said, the wife thinks I'm nuts for coming. WagerEasy and conglomerates move into the U.S. and think we don't talk, but we do. I heard how the cops busted those little guys like me." Johnson leaned in across the table toward me after stealing a glance at Larsen. "Who they can't buy, gets fucked."

Larsen almost stood. "Again, I must warn you about profanity—"

"Maybe it was another bookie network. Or organized crime," I said.

He shook his head. "They don't rat to the cops. They take you out into an alley and kick your head in for fun. If you pay the tax, you're fine. I know better than to screw that up."

I couldn't argue with the analysis.

"We've gotten far off the subject of today's meeting and our time here at WagerEasy is limited," Larsen said.

"Maybe if you listened to these people, you'd learn something. We'd all learn something," Tara told Larsen.

Larsen pursed her lips and her face reddened. "You should be darn glad you transferred."

"And maybe I should talk to my uncle about you," Tara said. "Maybe you don't know it, but Eddie and Walsh are drinking buddies."

Larsen sat back and looked at me with wide eyes. "I was not informed," she mumbled. She tried to cast a smile in my direction, but the overwhelming effort twisted her facial muscles into a ghoulish sneer.

I didn't flinch. Tara's lie about me and Walsh was pure genius.

"They want to call us all criminals," Johnson said. "It's been guys like me doing all the heavy lifting. I do okay, but I don't own a yacht." Again, he looked toward me and Tara, ignoring Larsen. "It sucks to sell out. My customers need me. They need me to cut them off when they get in over their heads. What's going to happen when it's all legal? They're going to max out their credit cards, take a second or third mortgage on the house and go broke. All because they think they can win. They'll lose their jobs, get a divorce. I've seen it happen."

"At least they won't get credit from a legal supplier like WagerEasy," Larsen said. "And each one of these bettors has more than one bookie because they look for the best line on a game. They all have alternatives. You cut them off, but other bookies don't. It's not so simple."

"Sure, some go elsewhere," Johnson said. "But my long-time customers appreciate me. They know if I cut them off, something's wrong. It wakes them up. It costs me, but I'd rather have them for the long haul than have them run up a huge debt I'll never collect."

Johnson was concerned about the welfare of his customers; unlike some bookies I knew. I couldn't argue with what Johnson said—a bettor had his mind made up he could win. If he didn't think that way, then why gamble in the first place?

Johnson turned from Larsen back to Tara and me. "Why'd they have to go and make it legal? We're small business, the backbone of this country. I treat my customers right. Keep them on a short leash. If they don't get their shit together, then they can't play—simple. They thank me for it later. Some of them have got a problem. Let's face it. Without me, they'd be out on the streets—doesn't help anyone."

"Very interesting, Mr. Johnson," Larsen said. "We'll be in touch." She stood up.

It was an abrupt end to what I thought had been a fruitful meeting. "I guess that's the way things go these days," I said. "Big business keeps getting bigger, screws the little guy that built the business, and nobody knows, really knows, the customer."

Larsen smiled. "It's a numbers game now."

"I'd rather deal with the mob," Johnson said, standing up. "It was a pleasure meeting you, Eddie, and you miss." He nodded at Tara and shook my hand again. "Good riddance to you, Ms. Larsen. I'll take my chances." He walked out.

Tara and I began to navigate our way around Larsen.

"I suppose you think your continuous interruptions helped, Mr. O'Connell," Larsen said.

"Do all your meetings go this well?" I asked.

"Not when Mr. Golding ran things," Tara said.

"What's that supposed to mean?" Larsen bellowed. "Neither of you have the expertise to analyze these financials. Johnson, or whatever his name is, doesn't have enough business for WagerEasy to waste one second of its time. His business will shrink and he'll soon be a memory. Everyone will be on their phone wagering as the game is played. Betting on if the team will score on the power play. Everything is about to change."

"Makes me want to puke," I said.

"Then you shouldn't have taken this job," Larsen said. "Show me something. Show me why you're here. Golding had the Midas touch. What can you do?"

To say I was pissed off at this point was an understatement. Tara stood by the door about to walk out.

"I can get you a meeting with the Sloan Group," I said.

Larsen's hands dropped to her side as if she'd been hit in the gut. The Johnson file flopped to the floor. "Holy shit."

17

AFTER A SHORT BREAK TO GRAB COFFEE IN THE LUNCHROOM, I was back in my office, or what had been Jimmy's office. Attempts to chat at the water cooler went nowhere. My coworkers had given me the same wide berth that Tara and I had given Larsen. It seemed that everyone was being cautious about me, Walsh's rumored drinking buddy.

Who could blame them? People were nervous. Tara had mentioned possible layoffs due to a recent merger. Some had probably hoped to move up out of the cubicles to Jimmy's office and then I showed up. Maybe I should check to see if my coffee was poisoned.

I sipped the coffee anyway and stared out at the building across the street. I'd seen a posting on the breakroom bulletin board. A notice of a memorial service for Jimmy and someone had written on it, "who cares." Snow flurries had begun to drift down. At O'Connell's, the graveyard shift would be calling for another round.

Tara walked into the office and shut the door. "I hope you weren't bluffing. Because if you can't set up a meeting with the Sloan Group, Larsen—the bitch from hell—will never let you live it down."

"Is she out there right now telling everyone?"

"You bet."

"Who is Ms. Larsen? It seems that WagerEasy has given her a lot of power."

"You'll learn. It's like the Wild West at WagerEasy. Each person grabs their territory and then defends it to the death. Larsen used to work for a patent law firm that represents the manufacturer of those video gaming machines and other betting devices. That firm also acts as WagerEasy's outside counsel. It allows Larsen to connect with a few worlds at WagerEasy—IT, legal, and marketing. It gives her a lot of pull. That's why you need to mark your territory or Larsen will take it."

Walsh's comment on the phone conversation I'd overheard earlier came to mind. The importance of technology to WagerEasy had become clear.

"I'll have to get busy then," I said. I had no idea if Uncle Mike could set up a meeting with the Sloan Group.

Tara sat on the arm of the chair, half sitting and half standing, her arms crossed. "I know you think I'm only a member of the team. You can tell me to go away. But don't. Hear me out."

I wasn't about to argue. I needed an ally in this place.

"I liked how you stood up to Larsen." Her lips grew taut and her chin jutted out. "I liked how you defended Mr. Johnson or Mr. Smith or whatever his name is."

"Thanks."

"You're welcome." Her voice softened. "Like anyone else who is on the job for the first day, I can understand you want to feel your way and make sure you don't screw up, right?"

"Right."

"Well, forget it." She stood and snapped her fingers. "Snap out of it. None of that applies here and now today at WagerEasy. Get all that first-day anxiety out of your head."

"You're saying what exactly?"

"You said you'd keep me informed on the gambling part of this job. Obviously, you know your shit. You knew about in-play wagering, you know other bookies, you even know the Sloan Group. My part of the bargain is to show you the ropes around the office." She stepped around to the corner of my desk. "So, I'm going to live up to my end. Either you get something working with the Sloan Group today or expect somebody else to grab it because everybody out there wants your job and your office with a window and thinks you're a dumbfuck."

If I took an active role in deals, maybe I'd solidify my position or maybe I'd anger Walsh. My job was to find out if there was a drug problem. I should've never mentioned the Sloan Group or challenged Larsen. My true purpose here was to investigate Jimmy's murder from inside WagerEasy, and how could I do that if I made a grandstand play that might cost me my job?

"Let's chill out a minute," I said. "Forget about those people out there—"

"You can't. The merger is happening and those people are fighting for their jobs. Layoffs are a potential reality for you and me too. You don't have time."

And time was what I needed. But would Walsh lay me off? He just brought me on board. Or maybe Walsh hired me simply to try and get out of signing those court papers. Another reason to keep me on board would help and the way Larsen reacted to the news I could get the Sloan Group told me I had a trump card in my pocket. "You're not doing this because you've got a grudge against Larsen, are you? I mean, I wouldn't blame you—"

"Yes, that's another reason. But not all that relevant. You said you wanted to find answers together."

I also needed to confront Sloan. He probably hated WagerEasy as a competitor. This could work. "What do you suggest, Tara?"

"Let's do an exploratory meeting. Get to Sloan tonight. Make him your 'boy.' I'll tell Walsh you will—"

"Just a minute. Hold on," I said. I didn't know what an exploratory meeting might involve and didn't know what it would mean for my job if Tara told Walsh.

"You can't just sit here. You'll be gone tomorrow. And I'll be on the sidewalk with you."

"Let's not tell Walsh. This needs to be confidential." Did she report to Walsh? Maybe I couldn't trust her.

She placed her hands on her hips. "If we don't tell Walsh, you won't accomplish a thing. We need to get credit. We're fighting for survival—"

"You've got your uncle," I said.

"And you're Walsh's drinking buddy." A sly smile crept across her lips.

"You were lying? You don't have an uncle in the state legislature?"

"How do you think I survived those months in the legal department?"

I pointed a finger at her. "You're good." She was more than good. She was on my side and she was smart.

"They believe what they want to believe. They believed I got my job through my uncle. They can't figure out why Walsh would hire you, so therefore you must be Walsh's drinking buddy. You don't have any other qualifications."

"Thanks a lot. Assuming I can get a meeting with Sloan, you're going with me."

Tara held up the palms of her hands toward me. "Oh, no, I'm not meeting this guy. I've heard some things about Travis Sloan. The guy gives me the creeps."

"What have you heard?"

"WagerEasy isn't stupid. The legal department sends out reports."

That didn't surprise me. WagerEasy had big money to invest in the United States market and needed all the background research it could muster. "How will it look if I show up to a meeting and don't have any staff along? I've got to look like an executive from WagerEasy ready to toss money around."

"Yup," she said. "You show up alone and I wouldn't even believe you."

"See? You're coming."

18

THAT NIGHT, TARA AND I MET AT THE PARKING LOT OF O'Connell's. When she heard the meeting place with Sloan would be at Thornton Racetrack, where the track was located, and that there was no racing tonight, she insisted we drive over together. Sometimes people in Chicago got worried about shootings when they drove in or near the city or into parts of Chicago they weren't familiar with, so at first, I attributed Tara's worries to that. Then I thought about Kubala. The racetrack might be the perfect spot for the bald ex-con to try something.

I secretly scouted for Kubala's vehicle on the way over. We got off the "Ike" and drove past Cicero to Thornton Racetrack. I parked up close to the clubhouse.

"What if Sloan tells us to go to hell?" I asked.

"No big deal," Tara said. "I'll call it a negotiating tactic. Don't worry. I'll dress it up when I report to Walsh."

Tara had told Walsh about our exploratory meeting. He'd been "hot" over the prospect of a deal with the gambling ringleader and set a meeting tomorrow at the office with me and Tara to go over the results. Such a meeting might give me a better idea of what WagerEasy was willing to offer. It might also give me an insider's look at what Jimmy's deal with Burrascano had included.

"Dress it up? You were a creative writing major in college?"

"Worse. An econ major." She nudged me. "That's really fiction."

We almost ran the ten yards to the entrance to escape the brutally cold weather. Inside the clubhouse, a man stood behind the counter where racing programs and tip sheets were sold on racing nights. I recognized him as one of DiNatale's men. He wore a dark overcoat and looked at me then looked outside. He was about my height but twice as wide and his face had an interesting network of scars. He recognized me and told me the meeting was upstairs at the Jockey Club.

I thanked him and led Tara to the stairway.

I'd contacted Uncle Mike earlier in the day about a proposed meeting with Travis Sloan of the Sloan Group. My uncle responded to my request with an expected string of expletives, along with objections and complaints. First, he said how he'd just gotten started and was trying his best to show Sloan that he wasn't a plant by Burrascano or the feds. That was followed by my uncle's declaration about WagerEasy and how those people were nuts. I told him that I agreed, but that it was merger mania time and if I didn't jump on board, I might get whacked in a wave of layoffs.

After more discussion, Uncle Mike decided it might be a good thing. Who didn't want to listen to a company like WagerEasy that wanted to ante up cash for a buyout? Heck, if they wanted to buy O'Connell's, he said, they could set a meeting any time.

Uncle Mike and I decided to hold the meeting at Thornton Racetrack because Burrascano was able to assure Sloan it would be a safe place—plenty of security, and no bugs or wires. I wasn't sure at what point Burrascano had gotten involved in the meeting, and he wasn't going to join us, but I had a feeling he'd be listening in. Maybe the feds didn't have the place bugged, but I'm sure Burrascano did.

Tara and I walked up the stairs to the Jockey Club on the third floor, the same place where Uncle Mike and I had met Burrascano. She wanted to find out how I knew the guy behind the counter. I told her he was a friend of my uncle.

"You're not the only one with an uncle and connections," I said.

"You mean a real uncle, not a make-believe one like my uncle, State Senator Brennan?"

"Right. He helped set up this meeting tonight with Sloan. Uncle Mike works for him."

"That's good. A friendly face at the meeting will help. I was beginning to regret the whole thing."

We walked up the last flight of stairs. I began to wish the elevator wasn't out of order. Tara told me this was simply an introductory meeting, but what if Sloan wanted to throw numbers and terms around? What would I tell Travis Sloan about a deal with WagerEasy? I must be out of my mind. I'd have to sweet talk the guy. Keep him interested enough to buy time so I could stay on Walsh's good side. My best and only strategy would be to try not to piss Sloan off.

We reached the third floor of the exclusive Jockey Club. Tara skipped across the polished wood floor to the empty stage and did a twirl. "Look at this place."

Light from the stairwell pierced the shadows. The stage and dance floor hadn't lost their luster. To the left, the unlit chandeliers in the dining area shimmered. I walked up on stage to her and pointed out the windows into the darkness. "It's all lit up on race nights."

"It's a ghost ship. Like the Titanic, something out of the past," she whispered. She did another half a twirl. "Ladies and gentlemen, for my next number . . ."

"May I have this dance?" I asked with a quick, formal bow.

She studied me then smiled. "I believe I have an opening on my dance card."

I placed my right arm around her waist and took her hand with my left. We shuffled a few steps to an imaginary orchestra and felt the old thrill.

"You dance divinely," she said.

"So do you, my dear," I said.

"Hey, let's go," a voice called out. To our right, Uncle Mike waved to us from the doorway of the private suite at the end of the long bar.

Tara's face reddened as we parted. She grabbed hold of my arm. "I'll just follow your lead," she told me.

Inside the room, Uncle Mike and DiNatale, Burrascano's right-hand man, sat at a table with Sloan. The three of them stood up and gave Tara the eye as we took off our coats and went through the introductions.

"No need to introduce Eddie," Sloan said. "I met him the other night at the club."

Tara glanced my way. Maybe she thought I'd held something back.

Sloan and DiNatale were still a mismatched pair. Sloan in his western attire and DiNatale dressed in a sharp black suit, gray shirt, and blood-red tie. Uncle Mike wore a gray, wool sweater. There was a definite chill from the winter wind streaming through the old windows. Outside, the track below was cloaked in darkness for a Monday night.

Sloan directed us to our seats and took charge. "When I heard my consultant, Mike O'Connell here, had an 'in' with WagerEasy, I said, damnit to hell, let's meet and get to know each other."

"That's my job," Uncle Mike said. "I introduce you to the right people and show you how the city works."

Sloan straightened the hunk of turquoise that held his bolo tie. "Always better to get the lay of the land through family. We go through the front door and the lawyers want a urine sample. Nobody'd get anywhere."

It wasn't the way I heard it from Uncle Mike. Sloan had been less than enthusiastic about meeting people who worked for the "enemy."

"WagerEasy wants to explore deals and asked that I set this up," I said. I went on to tell Sloan how much I appreciated the opportunity.

"And Tara is your assistant?" Sloan asked.

I had introduced Tara as one of my team, not my assistant. "She works in our department."

Sloan sat back and smiled toward DiNatale and then winked at Tara. Then he turned to Uncle Mike. "The nephew's doing all right, Mike. We're here. Let's hear what you got, Eddie. I've got places to go tonight. Hot spots downtown."

I looked to Tara.

She cleared her throat and then recited the usual opening Larsen had used. How WagerEasy was an international sports betting operator and described what they provided. Then she looked at Sloan and asked about his operation.

"Dang, that's impressive," Sloan said. "So, it's all about me giving you information?"

"That would get us started," Tara said.

"I got lots of questions. But they're about your outfit. Like this recent deal with StatsRUs," Sloan said. "It's a dumb name, but I hear it beefed up your operation."

We sat at a different kind of poker table. DiNatale's body language and facial expressions didn't convey his usual pent-up rage. Maybe he and the cowboy had become close. Sloan didn't betray a single underlying emotion. He was cold and slippery. Uncle Mike looked like a guy with a bad case of indigestion.

"It's the last piece of the puzzle, Travis," I said. "When legalization goes into effect, the stats will be streamed to the customer to provide in-play wagering. It will hurt business for local bookies."

Sloan rubbed his clean-shaven chin and his smile disappeared. "You got me there, partner."

"And what about this guy from Reno I've heard about," I asked. "He's burned a lot of your bookies, and you don't know who he is." The guy from Reno and in-play wagering were the two things that had worried Oscar and maybe it would make Sloan think about doing a deal as well.

"We'll get that son-of-a-bitch." Sloan leaned in across the table toward Tara and me. "Let me tell you where we stand if you don't know it. Sports betting ain't legal yet. Each state has to approve it, so let's stop talking like it's a done deal."

Tara edged closer to the table. "State Senator Brennan has pushed the sports betting bill—"

"And I hear they've found a couple of stumbling blocks and need more hearings," Sloan said.

DiNatale snickered.

"It's only temporary," Tara said. "WagerEasy has its lobbyists—"

"Look, darling, in Texas we don't have to worry about legalization. We know how to keep a handle on our vices. Gambling stays in the back room where it belongs. Hell, we even ran the tribal casinos out of the state to prove a point. So, if you don't think I can't get a handle on a few of these state legislators here in Illinois, you better think again. This whole state approval stuff is right in my wheelhouse."

The way Sloan said the word "wheelhouse" made what he said into a statement of fact, not a negotiating ploy.

"Illinois is on the verge of bankruptcy," I said. "If any state needed every dollar of tax revenue it can find, it's Illinois."

"I don't deal only with Illinois, son. I deal with a lot of states," Sloan said. "And so does WagerEasy. So, let's not get bottled up with the Land of Lincoln. We're seeing a number of states getting cold feet on this digital thing. You know, the in-play or mobile sports betting. The thing WagerEasy is counting on. Casinos are lobbying hard to stop it."

Sloan was implying that he'd aligned his gambling ring and growing network of bookies with casinos in certain states. It made sense. Casinos wanted to protect their turf and the entertainment dollar and would be against mobile in-play wagering. He also seemed to imply that his coalition was responsible for the "cold feet" in these states.

"Other states see the revenue in New Jersey right now. It will only get bigger with in-play wagering," I said.

"And when the sports franchises find out that gamblers can play along on their cell phone with live streaming and broadcasting fees start going through the roof, what do you think will happen?" Tara asked. "The state legislators will have no choice."

"The value of these sports franchises will quadruple," I said. "Even franchises like arena football will be gold mines. It will change the way fans watch sports. Owners with big money will lobby hard."

Sloan waved his hand at us like he was swatting a fly. "C'mon, that's a worst-case scenario. Our bookies have hard-earned customers that won't go away overnight. We can stall this thing for a long time."

"So, what are you saying?" Tara asked.

DiNatale snickered again.

"Think of all that cash WagerEasy will burn on lobbyists and paying off legislators," Sloan said. "Wouldn't it be better to go direct and pay me?"

Tara shook her head. "You can't be serious."

Sloan looked to DiNatale. "What do you think, Vic? Don't you think our honorable legislators need to look into WagerEasy and in-play wagering?"

"Sounds illegal. Lots of guys might have a problem. Get addicted. Those fuckers should appoint a committee," DiNatale chuckled.

Sloan and DiNatale would contact a few of their favorite legislators and direct them to dig up dirt on WagerEasy. It would probably bring legalization to a screeching halt and force WagerEasy to fight trumped-up charges. Walsh would point the finger at me and my termination would upend my plan to dig into Jimmy's murder.

Sloan clapped Uncle Mike on the back. "You did good, Mike. Gave us all a chance to clear the air. Now, these folks at WagerEasy know what they're up against. Gives them something to chew on." He stood. "I'll wait to hear from you all."

19

TARA AND I GOT INTO THE CAR IN THE TRACK PARKING LOT. She thought the meeting went well, and I thought it was an unmitigated disaster. I'd hoped to pressure Sloan, and he pressured me by making threats to have some sleazy legislators go after WagerEasy.

I could see why Sloan had been named as a suspect by Burrascano. Sloan's eyes and mouth telegraphed a lack of emotion, an ability to kill on reflex. And he seemed to be on good terms with DiNatale. But I had no idea how much of that was an act by DiNatale because he'd used the same bullshit charm on me in the past. When DiNatale and Sloan decided to quit acting like old buddies, I wouldn't want to be around. It made me worried for Uncle Mike.

As we drove back from the track, I thought I spotted a car behind us that matched the description of Kubala's vehicle. I didn't say anything to Tara. No reason to get her worried about it if I wasn't one-hundred percent positive.

Tara was brimming with good news she could incorporate into her report to Walsh. She dwelled on the way Sloan described our employer, "Those folks from WagerEasy," like we were all kinfolk at a barn dance.

She also harped on the fact that Sloan had left the door open. "I'll wait to hear from you all." According to the optimism of merger mania, in Tara's view, this meant another meeting would be welcomed and expected.

"We made great strides," Tara said.

"What about the threats to get state legislators to question WagerEasy and stop legalization?"

"That's just sales talk. Posturing. Don't give it another thought."

I began to see what Jimmy had been caught up in. Maybe he'd also drunk from the well. With this strange brew coursing through his system, a deal with Burrascano would make sense. And the deal with Burrascano almost did come to fruition.

Under the influence of merger mania, Jimmy failed to ask one more question. Failed to see what could happen. How murder could enter into the equation.

The car I thought could be Kubala's car turned off before we pulled into the parking lot of O'Connell's. If it was Kubala, he was in no mood for a rematch tonight.

I found a spot in the back of the lot to park. "Why don't we get a beer?" I asked. "I'll buy."

"Good idea," Tara said. "I'm too wound up to go home. You made some good arguments tonight."

"So did you."

She pulled on my arm, and I bent down toward her. She edged across the seat near me and ran her hand up to my shoulder. Her lips parted, and I kissed her. A brief kiss, then one that was longer and deeper. She pulled away then pulled me close, her cheek against mine.

"I wondered when we'd get around to this," she whispered.

"Not something I planned." But it was something I'd thought about. Tara wasn't easy to resist, and we'd been together most of the day.

We kissed again and things became heated. My hand ended up in her hair. Her hand pulled on the back of my neck. I lost count of the kisses, but that's the idea.

She whacked me in the chest. "C'mon, let's get the beer. The windows are fogging up."

After the necking session, I probably needed something stronger than beer but agreed to go inside the bar.

Outside, the temperature flirted with zero and the wind chill made my nose run. Snow crunched underfoot. "We pay a guy to plow this lot," I said, throwing my arm over her shoulder and trying not to slip on the layer of new-fallen snow hiding a layer of ice.

The lights of the tavern promised warmth. Voices and music from the back patio, where smokers braved the conditions, caused us to quicken our stride. From what I could tell, it was a good crowd. We could always count on Monday night football.

I stopped. "Wait a minute."

"What?"

"That's Oscar's car." It was a late model, gold caddie with bumper stickers plastered all over the back bumper and trunk—Rotary Club, Elk's Club, VFW, all the places he frequented. "He shouldn't be here on a Monday. Thursday is his night."

Tara bent down near the car. "Is there someone inside?"

I scraped off a layer of snow. Through the darkened windows, I could make out something. "Maybe he's on the phone." I rapped on the driver's side window.

"The car's not running. He'll freeze," Tara said. "Maybe he passed out."

I pulled on the door handle. It opened. Inside, Oscar sat upright, his shoulders strapped in by the seatbelt, but his head had drooped forward. I nudged him. His eyes open. His face lifeless.

Then I saw the bullet hole in his forehead.

20

AFTER I'D MADE THE CALL TO THE POLICE AND UNCLE MIKE, we stood outside with the O'Connell's crowd. Several squad cars and an ambulance were now at work around Oscar's caddie.

The corpse appeared to be a plant by Oscar's killer. From the lack of blood splatter in the car, I figured that Oscar had been killed elsewhere and then placed in the driver's seat. Oscar's car had probably been driven here as part of the scheme. Dead men don't have the wits to turn off the car engine before they expire.

By leaving Oscar in his car at O'Connell's, the killer made it personal to me, Uncle Mike, and all the patrons of O'Connell's. But my time as an investigator had taught me to bury all that. Maybe it came from watching Liz and Uncle Mike bury their emotions.

"Who would do this?" Tara asked, standing beside me.

I couldn't give her an answer. It was a surreal scene. The cops secured the area around Oscar's caddie and kept the crowd back. The detectives had questioned Tara and me and received little to go on. Uncle Mike talked with one of the detectives.

The O'Connell's crowd huddled outside in silent reverence, their collective breath streaming into the brutally cold night and the bright lights of the emergency vehicles. Someone had turned off the music inside. Several customers wept.

Everyone asked why Oscar would be here on a Monday night. He hadn't come into the bar. Where were his bodyguards?

There was no turning back now. No way Uncle Mike or I would give the killer's warning message a second thought. We must be in the right places—Uncle Mike as Sloan's consultant and me at WagerEasy—to get this reaction from the killer. And now we needed to keep pushing, keep playing our roles to the hilt.

"Do you think it was Kubala?" Tara whispered.

"I don't know."

Kubala and I had a grudge match that involved our fists. I didn't think he'd resort to murder. A move like this one with Oscar didn't seem to fit his character flaws.

My thoughts and theories gravitated toward Sloan. Maybe he wanted us to know what we were really up against. He and DiNatale were acting like old friends. What kind of game were they playing?

Oscar had said he planned to meet with Sloan. Maybe Oscar didn't like Sloan's proposal and, when Oscar refused to join up, Sloan had him killed.

I thought about guys like the small-time bookie I'd met at WagerEasy earlier today. Maybe now he'd have no choice but to make a deal with the devil.

For Sloan and the Sloan Group, maybe it wasn't only a fight in the state legislature, but a fight in the streets.

21

At WagerEasy the next morning, Nancy, the receptionist, didn't smile or say good morning the way she'd done yesterday. I walked around the perimeter of the cubicle maze and noticed that a stony silence had replaced the steady hum of employee chatter.

I met with Tara in my office. She told me the office had become a morgue. The layoffs had begun.

Tara had turned in our report of the exploratory meeting with Sloan and hoped that would save us. "I knew it was coming but didn't expect it this soon," she said.

"Walsh left me a message. He wants to meet with me first thing," I said.

"You alone?" she said. "That's not good. If everything was fine, he'd want to meet with both of us about the Sloan meeting. He's in the large conference room with people from HR calling people in one by one."

It didn't make sense. I wasn't a real employee. I was an imposter looking into the supposed drug problem in the office. Why would Walsh put me on the list of layoffs?

It was the last thing I needed. My plan with Uncle Mike required that we stay in our present positions and continue to push our agendas. We'd gotten the killer's attention and we couldn't let up on the gas pedal.

Tara decided to check with her friends in the legal department who always seemed to be the first to know what home office might do next. I had let Walsh know I'd arrived and asked when he wanted to meet. He emailed back that he'd let me know.

After Tara left, my cell buzzed. The call was from St. Clair's office.

"Eddie O'Connell," I answered.

"It's Pam." Pam Ferguson was the senior associate at St. Clair's office and managed the staff with an iron fist. "We've got an emergency hearing tomorrow with Judge Andropolous, Eddie. He's reconsidering our motion to allow Garrett Walsh to testify. Ms. St. Clair needs to have Walsh present at court tomorrow."

"What? You're kidding."

"No, I'm not kidding. I'll be up all night preparing for this damn thing with Helen even though my husband planned to take me to dinner. Let me know if you have any trouble getting Walsh to court tomorrow."

"And if I do have trouble?"

"Just let me know."

She hung up. I had a million other questions. Would the subpoena Walsh signed be enough to force him to appear tomorrow? Why had the judge decided to reconsider, and what did this mean for Yuri Provost? I needed that law degree, but I'd been too damn busy playing the ponies.

Walsh's secretary poked her head in the doorway. "He wants to see you in his office." She looked down at her shoes.

———

Walsh didn't look up when I entered his office. His head was buried in paperwork while he made me sweat for a few minutes.

"Tell me about Travis Sloan," Walsh said.

"It's in Tara's report."

"I want to hear it from you."

I told Tara her fictionalized version wouldn't get us anywhere. "Sloan is crafty. He knows his business is doomed, but he believes legalization will take time."

"Time?"

"That he can drag things out in the state legislature here in Illinois and other states."

Walsh leaned back in his chair and looked down through his glasses at a piece of paper. "Is that what Tara refers to as a 'negotiating tactic' in this report?"

I should've told Tara that twisting the facts wouldn't help us. "I guess."

"You read the report?"

"Sure, I read it." What was this high school? "If you want it in black and white, Sloan is going to bribe our state legislators to delay the sports betting bill."

"What? I never heard of such a thing."

I had to remind myself that Walsh lived in Winnetka, an island of rich elitists on the north side where life was good. "This is Illinois, the Land of Corruption. Sloan is open to further talks. He's coming from a position of strength."

"Damnit," Walsh said. "I'll be frank with you, Eddie . . ." He stood and turned his back to me and stared out through the buildings at the lake.

I squirmed. When people were "frank," it meant you were fucked.

"WagerEasy is in a tough spot," Walsh said with his back to me. "The company has invested millions, and right now we have only seven states. We did the deal with StatsRUs. More millions. Unless you're a moron, you've heard about the layoffs."

If he was going to call me a moron, maybe I could ruin his day. "Another thing you won't like."

"What?"

"You have to appear at an emergency hearing tomorrow on Yuri Provost's case."

Walsh twisted around and cringed like a guy who'd been punched in the kidneys. "I thought you told me that case would settle. I don't have time to go over there."

"You signed the papers. The judge has ordered you to appear in court tomorrow on that subpoena."

He slapped the top of the desk with the flat of his hand. "Damnit."

I explained about the emergency hearing on the DA's motion to reconsider.

"This is bullshit. Good God, I can't get away. The judge can't do this. That trial is not until next week. I've got a schedule to maintain and these StatsRUs people are only here for one more day. Plus, we've got a human resource specialist and an in-house attorney from home office. Where the hell is that subpoena?"

"St. Clair's office told me the subpoena is broadly worded. You're compelled to appear, and I hear Judge Andropolous has a short fuse."

"What are you saying?" Walsh paced behind the desk.

I could see that Walsh was under a lot of pressure. Maybe WagerEasy no longer wanted Walsh at the helm.

"St. Clair told me if you aren't there at nine a.m., in court, the sheriff will fetch you." It was another lie, but I wasn't feeling real charitable.

"Great. I suppose Blick will be there. He's been making things tough for WagerEasy to get a license in those states that legalized. He's killing us. I thought you were going to run interference?"

I stayed calm. "Give me a name, and I'll call." Today was my second day on the job. Give me a break. But I kept all that inside.

His voice rose several notches. "I need you to be proactive, Eddie."

How many people could hear Walsh down the hall? He picked up the newspaper off the desk, the one with a picture of Oscar slumped over in the front seat of his Cadillac and waved it in my face. "We simply can't have this kind of publicity. You work for WagerEasy and a bookie is found dead at your family's place of business?"

"These things happen in Chicago. Nobody will connect it to WagerEasy."

"Social media will be all over WagerEasy's connection to you, and O'Connell's, and a murdered bookie. I've also gotten poor reports from Ms. Larsen about you."

I almost laughed. "When did you get a *good* report from Ms. Larsen about anybody?" If I was going down, I'd get in my shots.

"Other than Sloan fucking with us in the legislature, what else have you got? You got anything on this so-called office drug investigation you're supposed to be working on?" Walsh leaned over the desk, the newspaper in one hand and his other balled into a fist. "Tell me why I shouldn't put you at the top of the list of layoffs."

"I was hired to cover WagerEasy's ass on the drug thing. Don't expect me to give you answers after one day."

"You're a liability, Eddie."

I had to stay in the game. "I've got another contact."

"Great. I'm waiting. It's going to be a long day."

"I heard that Sloan wants to do a deal with Thornton Racetrack to put a sportsbook into the old grandstands." It was something Sloan had asked Uncle Mike to set up. "If we can screw him over by doing the deal instead, it will give us leverage. Plus, a sportsbook at the track will be good for WagerEasy."

Walsh sat back down. He took a deep breath. "I'm listening."

"The track will get an automatic license in any sports betting bill that gets passed. That's been part of every proposed bill I've seen. A physical site will also allow WagerEasy to sign up new customers for its mobile app."

"Like our competitor did in New Jersey?"

"Right."

"I got news for you Eddie, we tried to contact the track and didn't get anywhere. Golding tried and failed several times. And I assume you're able to get us in contact with the owner of Thornton Racetrack?"

"I can. I've got a call into them now." Uncle Mike said he'd call Burrascano and that it should be a slam dunk. If we could force our two suspects, WagerEasy and Sloan, into a head-to-head matchup over the track, our chances of getting the killer or killers to expose themselves would multiply.

"You're sure?"

"My contacts say I can get it set up this week." I decided to add one more shot. "I've been proactive."

Walsh frowned at my comment, then swiveled in his chair and leaned back to give it the once-over in his executive mind. After a long minute with me on the hot seat, he swiveled back. "Eddie, you've signed your ticket. You're off the list of layoffs. The track deal is what we need. It will give WagerEasy the edge. Get us out there in the public eye. If we can beat our competitors to a sportsbook at the track, it will be a real feather in our cap and bring the Sloan Group to us. Do it. You've got until Friday to set up a meeting."

———

I strolled back through the tomb. People worked in silence, their heads down. Back in my office, Tara was pacing.

"I'm still here for the moment," I said.

"Thank God. How about me?"

"I need you. I've got another lead to tell you about. What did you find out in legal?"

"Larsen is livid. People are crying in her department." She sat down on one of the chairs that fronted my desk and dropped her head in her hands. For a second I thought she might cry but then she looked up at me, her lips a tight line and face red.

"One of my best friends was laid off. I should just fucking quit this place. We'll be inundated with techies from StatsRUs." She stood back up and paced again as she slammed one fist into an open palm.

"I was about to quit because of Larsen," she said, "and then I was able to transfer over to your department, and I told myself to give it one more try." She was talking to herself more than to me. I let her talk it out. I was just happy her anger wasn't directed at me and glad there were no pool cues around.

"It's not easy to find another job," she continued. "I finally got out from under Larsen's thumb. Yes, Ms. Larsen, no, Ms. Larsen, you're a bitch, Ms. Larsen." I tried not to laugh. "Give it another try, Tara. Sure, you're going to work in a department where Golding and two others were just gruesomely murdered, but have fun. Learn the ropes, and it'll look good on your resume."

She sat back down again. "Poor Vivian. She's slaved over there for five years, five long, miserable years for that witch

Larsen. Vivian is in her forties and lives alone. At least Larsen stood up for her. But what can Larsen do? She's trying to save her own butt. So, Vivian has to pack a box. Goodbye and good luck, Vivian. You were one of the first ones hired, and you're one of the first to get the boot. These greedy corporations and their hunger for profits. Hiding behind their 'cost-cutting.' It's a crime."

She stopped and looked at me. I tried to read her, but that task had become more complicated since we'd gotten romantically involved last night. We were no longer coworkers, we were on the road to being lovers, and I wondered if she wanted me as much as I wanted her right at this moment.

A sweet smile lit up her face. "Tell me, did Walsh like my report?"

No need to sugarcoat Walsh's reaction. We needed to do everything we could to make the track deal work and stay employed. "He hated it."

22

THAT NIGHT, A MEMORIAL SERVICE HAD BEEN SCHEDULED for Jimmy in the basement of a small church off Austin Boulevard in Oak Park. Some people talked about how the boulevard had been known as the dividing line between Chicago's near west side and the high-income area of Oak Park. Then there were people who alleged the street was the line between being safe and taking your life into your hands. Other people, the truly righteous, said that this kind of talk stoked fear and reinforced segregation.

No one knew how to talk about race. If you tried, you'd find yourself labeled a racist or a softheaded liberal. At O'Connell's, the regulars tried to avoid the subject. How do you ever solve a problem if you can't find the right words to talk about it?

Traffic out of downtown and on Austin made me late for the service. Inside the church, a narrow stairway led down to a vacant kitchen area with several long tables. A large banner proclaimed, "Knights of Columbus Pancake Breakfast Every First Sunday of the Month." Another, smaller sign with white letters on a magnetic blackboard said, "Goldin Memorial" with an arrow pointed to the open chapel at the east end of the basement. They couldn't even spell Jimmy's last name right. I crossed the concrete floor and ducked beneath dripping water pipes and found a folding chair at the end of the last row.

There was no casket and no crowd, but there were candles and a picture of Jimmy up on the makeshift altar. I took a seat. Besides the priest, there was only one other person present, a man in the front row. Uncle Mike must've been running late.

The priest nodded in my direction and continued. "I didn't know James Golding, but his wonderful brother, who set up this memorial, tells me he was a fine man." He nodded toward the man in front. I didn't know Jimmy had a brother. Maybe the brother could shed some light on Jimmy. "James will be in our prayers and mentioned at the mass scheduled to be held in his name this Sunday. Although James and his brother are not official members of the parish, the church welcomes the entire Golding family to participate and join us in the future."

The priest went on with more remarks and offered up prayers, and I did the sign of the cross when required and stood when we needed to stand and echoed those prayers that were meant to be said aloud. Most of the time, I couldn't take my eyes off the picture of Jimmy up near the altar. A small desk lamp illuminated the photo.

He was a young man, only about five years older than me with dark features and a sly smile. His eyes weren't sad. His mischievous expression made him seem alive. As if he wanted to ask me a question this very minute. As if there was something he didn't know, some information he needed. The Leech always wanted to know more. What question was on the tip of his tongue?

Did he want to know what was happening at WagerEasy today? No, that wouldn't be it. Maybe he wanted to ask about my investigation and if I was getting any closer to his killer. No, that couldn't be it. He was up there flipping through racing programs and jotting down notes. He might want to ask me something about tonight's races. Something in those notebooks of his. Most days he was in his own zone, but some days he valued my opinion and allowed me to contribute.

I always thought we'd come full circle and one day I'd be back at the track with him doing what we were meant to do. Because the races were meant to be played.

At the end of the brief service, someone tapped me on the shoulder. It was Detective Saboski, Liz's new partner. It was part of an investigator's job to go to funerals just to see who showed up and who didn't.

Saboski told me to move over and took a seat beside me. "Where are all Golding's track buddies?"

I'd thought about the people from the track too. All those horseplayers were dedicated lifers. What excuse did they have for not showing up at Jimmy's funeral? Who would be around when and if I showed up to build a sportsbook inside Thornton Racetrack on behalf of WagerEasy?

"Nobody at the track knew his real name," I said. The priest and Jimmy's brother walked past us toward the back. I turned around. Uncle Mike had arrived and stood off by the vacant kitchen with Liz, the two of them trying hard to remain reverent but unable to keep from laughing since the service had ended.

"I had an uncle who played the ponies," Saboski said. "He died broke. Fell over dead at the finish line with losing tickets in his pocket."

"At least he died with some action," I said.

Saboski looked at me as if I was from Planet Trifecta. "You're kidding, right? His kids couldn't afford college. When he wasn't playing the horses, he was talking about the horses down at the local tavern."

"Sounds like a fun guy." I wondered if I'd met him at the track.

"Golding didn't have any friends. None of his coworkers are here. Liz and I have talked to several of them and they blame Golding for the other two that got killed. They feel Golding led them astray. Got them into drugs."

Had Saboski bought into the theory that the reason for the Blowtorch Murders was a drug deal gone bad? Or was the guy trying to trip me up? Maybe he'd heard that I'd gone to work at WagerEasy and wanted to find out what I was up to. In any case, I didn't like his attitude or his comments about Jimmy. Sometimes the only persons a victim had in his corner were the detectives handling the case.

"You uncover evidence of drug use by Golding or the other two?" I asked.

"You know I can't talk to you about the investigation. But I do wonder why you and your uncle are here. Still playing cops and robbers? The old guy should stay retired and go fishing. You should get a real job."

Maybe Liz and Saboski were using the rumored drug deal to allow the killer to grow complacent and careless. They wanted to interview Burrascano. Why would they want to do that if they thought the murders were due to a drug deal? If Saboski wanted to make a game out of it, then I'd play along.

"I thought the feds would take over, and you could go fishing," I said.

"The feds don't tell us shit. They've got organized crime on the brain and want to take over but so far Liz and me—"

"Liz and you? Give me a break. Liz is the one with all the pull."

Saboski hunched forward. "Funny man. We've got an interview lined up with Burrascano. Do you know who he is?"

Liz hadn't told her partner about Uncle Mike's connection to Burrascano. A sign of loyalty I could appreciate. "Sure. Everyone knows who he is."

"That kept the feds happy for the moment."

"No forensics? There must be something. It had to be a small crew to pull off those murders. String up Golding." Jimmy caught in the ropes. Suspended between the routine world of the track and the tsunami change of sports betting.

Jimmy's brother walked past us and went up to the altar and lit one of the candles.

Saboski stood. "I'm not going to talk with you. I've told you more than I should already. Maybe you should know." A wicked smile played on his lips as he looked at Jimmy's photo then back at me. "You might have a problem with the murder of Oscar Colasso. I'm just saying." He clapped me on the shoulder.

"What do you mean?" I asked.

"See you around, Eddie. Maybe Liz and I will get to O'Connell's one of these nights for a beer."

"Don't be a stranger." Why would I have a problem with Oscar's murder? Then I thought things through. I cussed under my breath. The detectives must've found Oscar's records. Maybe they found out I owed Oscar money.

After Saboski left, I walked up to Jimmy's brother and introduced myself. He didn't look at all like Jimmy. He wore a suit made with thin material and sported a deep tan.

His name was John and had flown in yesterday from California. "Our mother passed away a few months ago. I'm glad she wasn't around to find out about all this." He took a deep breath. "James didn't leave a will. The cops seized his bank account in a damn forfeiture action. I got an attorney fighting it. James looked out for me and mom. He paid for her stay in the rest home, and he helped me with my business. I'm having a tough time financially lately."

It was like Jimmy to take care of people. He'd loaned me money a couple of times. "He was a good man."

"Face it," the brother said. "He never cared about anything but the horses or a sports bet. Look around. Nobody showed. Nobody from that job he took to help out family. First real job he's had in years. He had so much potential. He could've done anything. What's your connection?"

I couldn't let him know I was Jimmy's friend. Not with Liz and Saboski around. "I work at the same place James worked. Where are you from?"

"At least one of his coworkers showed up. Thanks. It means a lot. I moved away from Chicago years ago. I got a chain of tanning salons in San Diego, thanks to James. No way the girls will flaunt it at the beach all milky-white. I always tried to get James out there. I told him how great it is at Del Mar Racetrack—where 'the surf meets the turf.' I got close once or twice but he always had something going on. Something at the track here in Chi-town. Don't get me wrong. He was a good brother. He gave me the money to start my business, but he was distant. Always focused on his gambling."

Jimmy had, in fact, won money at the track over the years, enough to bankroll his brother. Jimmy took the job at WagerEasy to pay for his mother's stay in a rest home. "You talk to James recently?"

"No, that's what pisses me off. I should've called. Look, I've got to talk to the cops and then catch the redeye." The brother shook his head. "Sometimes things get so messed up. Here's my card. If you hear anything, let me know, will you? It's not easy to trust the cops after this seizure mess."

"Sure." Maybe if he'd spent time with Jimmy at the track, he would've known his brother the way I did.

He walked toward the other end of the church basement where I saw two other latecomers. One of the women was Tara. My breath caught in my throat when I saw her.

Tara and the other woman came over.

"Eddie, what are you doing here?" Tara asked in a low voice out of reverence for the surroundings. She slipped her arm around my waist.

"I wanted to find out what I could about James Golding, the guy I replaced. What are you doing here?"

"I'm sorry." Tara pulled on the other woman's coat sleeve and introduced us. "I took Vivian out for a few drinks to celebrate her separation from WagerEasy and Ms. Larsen."

Tara had told me that she was in her forties but I would've never guessed. Vivian was a tall, slim woman who conveyed a confident smile. A curled strand of her black hair fell across sad eyes. I told her how sorry I was that she'd been laid off.

Vivian shrugged. "Your first couple days at WagerEasy and my last. Oh, well, at least I'm not the only one." Vivian glanced toward the makeshift altar. "Poor James. That's such a good picture of him. A handsome man. Such a tragedy." Then she shook her head and looked around. "Where is everyone? I didn't think we were that late, but the traffic—"

"Not much of a crowd," I said.

"Vivian lives near here so we took a cab together," Tara said. "We're a bit under the weather."

Vivian giggled and swayed back and forth. "He is hot, Tara."

I put my arm around Tara's shoulder and pulled her close.

"Want to sit down?" Tara asked Vivian.

"I don't have anyone to hold me up. No," Vivian fumbled through her purse and pulled out a cigarette. "I'll be outside." She turned and weaved her way across the open cement floor.

"I'm not in much better shape," Tara said. "We needed to blow off steam. I bought her a couple of drinks, and I didn't think she should go home alone. You know the stories you hear about a drunken single woman on her way home? Vivian was the one who wanted to be here. She had a bit of a thing for Golding, not that he ever did anything about it."

That sounded like Jimmy, but he missed an opportunity. From what I could tell, Vivian would've been good for him.

I bent down and kissed Tara. Right here in front of Jimmy and the world.

"There were other people at the bar," Tara said when we parted. "Let me tell you, you're not exactly Mr. Popular around the office. But I stuck up for you."

I couldn't blame the staff. I was a recent hire and had dodged the layoff. "That's too bad. But I'm not in a popularity contest. No one showed for the service. I guess people blame Golding for the murders of his assistants. That's why no one's here." I recalled the note scribbled by someone on the breakroom notice of the memorial service, "who cares?"

"You have to blame somebody, right?" Tara said. "The media says it was a drug deal, but I'm not buying it. Nobody can figure that out. But there's money in coke, meth, or whatever. Maybe they had a harebrained scheme to resell it and make a score. All three of them gambled. They played the horses on WagerEasy's simulcast site whenever they weren't putting deals together. Betting sports, too."

"You didn't tell me that." Since I'd had trouble getting into Jimmy's computer, maybe I could get into the WagerEasy accounts of one of the other two employees who had been killed and see what kind of wagers they made under Jimmy's tutelage.

Tara's phone buzzed. She pulled the cell from her purse. "Vivian is spilling her cookies out on the church steps. Could this day get any weirder?" She stood up. "See you in the office tomorrow, Eddie."

"No, I'll give you a hand. Let me drive you both home." I thought of Kubala.

"Okay. I'm staying at Vivian's house and that's not far." She stopped and pulled her hair back then looked up at me. There were tears in her eyes. "That's nice. After last night—"

"No problem." I hadn't thought of Oscar's murder and maybe I should have.

I walked out with her and told Uncle Mike where I was going. Uncle Mike and I had another appointment tonight.

23

Uncle Mike and I had planned to meet at Jimmy's memorial service and then drive downtown to meet with Irv, the accountant. On our jobs for Burrascano, we had to have someone who could follow the money, and Irv and his team had proven invaluable.

It meant another trip downtown. We headed back down Austin to the Eisenhower Expressway. Oh well, sometimes when you're on a job, you get so caught up in the details, you tend to lose track of time anyway.

I'd reminded Tara about security and to watch for Kubala, since she'd arranged to stay at Vivian's place. As added insurance, Uncle Mike called in a favor and requested that a patrol car sit outside. Again, I was impressed by my uncle's degree of pull within the department.

Once that was settled, I wanted to know if Uncle Mike had gotten any more details than I did from Saboski or Liz about Jimmy's or Oscar's murder.

"Liz is still not saying anything. Just that she's got a meeting set up with Burrascano and she only told me that because I got Burrascano to call her back. Won't tell me where or when."

"You two looked like you were sharing a few laughs."

Uncle Mike pulled out a cigar and cracked the window. A cold breeze sucked the hot air out of the truck. "Laughter is still the best medicine. Wayne will be gone any day. Damnit, poor guy. She was running back over to hospice."

"That's awful." I thought of Liz and all her worries. How did she handle it?

"I've been working with my contacts in the department. Seems that Liz has possible evidence that someone was at the scene other than the killers."

"And she suspects Burrascano or members of the Outfit?" Burrascano had told us he was there but came late to the party.

"Yeah. I saw you and Saboski talking. What did he have to say?"

I told Uncle Mike about our conversation. How the meeting with Burrascano kept the feds from taking over the case. I didn't mention what Saboski told me about Oscar. That I might be a person of interest in Oscar's murder. I'd kept my gambling debt from Uncle Mike and he'd blow a gasket if he found out. Maybe Saboski was just trying to get under my skin.

"If the feds want to take over the case, they must know something." Uncle Mike flicked his lighter, and I was enveloped in second-hand smoke from the cigar before it formed a stream that flowed out the window. "Liz talked to the detectives who were assigned to Oscar's murder. I guess Oscar was killed elsewhere and then driven over to our parking lot."

"That's what I figured. The killer could be sending us a message." The mechanics of moving Oscar's rotund body must've required a team.

"Bastards."

"I'm still playing the waiting game with Walsh," I said. "He hasn't mentioned anything about Jimmy's deal with Burrascano for the high-roller list. It's as if he didn't know about it. Walsh had this competitive thing going with Jimmy and continues to blame a drug problem in the office for the murders."

"Yeah, how's that drug investigation going?"

I laughed. In our opinion, the Blowtorch Murders had nothing to do with drugs. "Well, I asked Saboski about a drug deal, and he dodged the question. Jimmy's brother says the cops seized Jimmy's bank account in a forfeiture case." Any gambler would call that the ultimate insult. Another reason for me to pursue justice for Jimmy.

"This drug thing is nice cover for everybody. How did things go today at the office?"

I told Uncle Mike about the layoffs. The fact I'd been able to promise talks with Thornton Racetrack had paid off for me and Tara with Walsh.

"I wanted to say hello to Tara, but she ran right past me. You and her have hit it off?"

I wondered when Uncle Mike would get to the subject. "She's terrific."

He gave me a sidelong glance. "Don't let it jeopardize your job at WagerEasy. We need you where you are."

Easier said than done. I didn't tell my uncle how tough it had been for us all day long. We both wanted to take up where we'd left off the night before.

I drove on in silence for a minute. I'd been thinking all day of my impression of Walsh in the office and everything that happened at WagerEasy over the last two days. "First, Walsh hires me. Then he sticks me in an office at the end of the hall and then Tara shows up."

"Why hire you in the first place?"

"That was made clear yesterday. He used the job as a bribe to try to get out of the subpoena. It turns out Blick, the guy Yuri beat to a pulp, has some connections that give him leverage over WagerEasy. Walsh needs to stay on everybody's good side. These political hacks all talk to each other. Probably trying to figure out who they can squeeze for a bribe and who they can't. Yet, it's as if Walsh wants to keep me close. To remind me of his power, he threatens to add me to the list of layoffs. I think he suspects me of something."

"Only the guilty suspect people."

I jammed on the brakes as traffic came to a momentary standstill. It was part of the challenge of Chicago traffic. The "Ike" was a lot better headed back into the city than the west-bound lanes during rush hour, but it was still bad. Traffic in Chicago got worse every year.

At this time of night, there was only one way to tell if you were being followed and Kubala continued to concern me. When traffic started to move again, I told Uncle Mike of my concerns. He agreed we should take precautions.

At the last second without signaling, I cut across three lanes to an exit, pulled into a convenience store parking lot, and turned around in the lot to face the oncoming traffic with my lights on.

Uncle Mike puffed on the stogie. "See anybody?"

"Not yet." I observed each car that exited for signs they were tailing us. Kubala had been driving a green Dodge when he tried to run Tara off the road, but he might've switched vehicles. "Did Sloan say anything to you about last night's meeting with me and Tara? WagerEasy still wants that deal with the Sloan Group."

"No. And he didn't say anything about Oscar's murder. I'm not sure he trusts me yet. He's got me setting up meetings with legislators. The politicians can't wait to line up and meet with Sloan and get their packet of cash. Makes me want to puke."

"Did Burrascano get back to you about a meeting between the track owners and WagerEasy? I have until Friday."

"I should hear tomorrow."

"Did Burrascano say anything about Oscar's murder?"

"Damnit. Poor Oscar. It sucks to be on the wrong end of change." Uncle Mike belched. "Damn stomach of mine. What Burrascano says is gospel. Burrascano told me he didn't give the order to murder Oscar, so if Sloan had Oscar killed, he'll be in big trouble with Burrascano. No wonder Sloan doesn't talk to me much. He can't afford to let anything get back to Burrascano."

"Sloan has to report to Burrascano?"

"Yeah. Sloan knows his place in Chicago but he's pushing the boundaries and it pisses off Burrascano." Uncle Mike put the cigar in the ashtray and put his stocking cap on. "Damn winter. As you know, Burrascano is in bad shape. I've heard rumors about his health. It's one reason the feds backed off and let Liz do the interview. Burrascano doesn't have much time and that means we don't have much time."

"If he dies then what will Sloan and DiNatale do?"

"If we don't have any results by then, look out. We might need to take a vacation. Burrascano suspects DiNatale. What better way for DiNatale to put succession on the fast track than to have Burrascano framed for murder? Burrascano would've looked like a fool if the cops caught him leaving the scene of the Blowtorch Murders. So far I haven't been able to find out anything concrete to implicate DiNatale."

"Maybe DiNatale is getting chummy with Sloan in anticipation of Burrascano's death." It was what I'd seen at the club and at last night's meeting.

"Yeah. Burrascano is under pressure on this whole legalization mess and he's sick. A great combination, but he's tough. He likes the idea of WagerEasy trying to fuck Sloan on the sportsbook deal with the track. He wants to see how Sloan reacts."

"I'll push WagerEasy to set up a meeting with the track about the sportsbook once you get the green light from Burrascano."

"Be careful. Keep Sloan on your radar." The slight inflection in Uncle Mike's voice revealed the true degree of danger Sloan could mean for us.

The umbrella of protection Burrascano provided could disappear at any moment. DiNatale had never liked us and might want to make a statement. That doubled the danger level.

What it added up to was a simple matter of time—we had very little of it.

I told Uncle Mike about the merger deal WagerEasy concluded with StatsRUs as I got back on the expressway.

"I guess you'll need to get chummy with Larsen and find out what she knows," Uncle Mike said.

"Great. That's not all. Tomorrow I've got to be sure Walsh shows up in court for an emergency hearing on Yuri's case."

"The DA is trying to get the judge to reconsider?"

"Yeah. If things don't go right, Walsh might fire my ass." Every move we made reverberated somewhere else, and the more complicated it became, the higher the risk. I loved the action.

"I hope not," Uncle Mike said. "I still get a kick out of you buying Thornton Racetrack."

Only Uncle Mike, the hardened retired homicide detective could find humor in all this. I had to match his deft touch. "Yeah. If I totaled up all my losing tickets over the years, I'd already own the place."

24

Irv's firm was located on the top three floors of one of the tallest buildings in the Loop. According to Uncle Mike, at one time, there were only ten accountants in the firm and each one did their own thing. Then they picked up a batch of accountants from the firm that imploded from the Enron scandal, each with an attitude that would make any aggressive CFO beg and drool, and Irv's firm became the place to go if you got in hot water with one of the Big Eight. They took pride in their maverick image. Irv's firm had become the Oakland Raiders of accounting.

Uncle Mike and I checked in with security on the main level and headed toward the elevators. "Irv has really moved up in the world," I said.

"It's been a while since you've seen him. I had that busted leg from the New Orleans job when you went solo in Denver and then there was Vegas."

Uncle Mike hit the button for the eighty-sixth floor. "I'm glad you started the PI business. Be patient and let it grow. When DiNatale takes over, we won't be doing any more of these jobs."

It was one of those modern express elevators that smoothly shoots you up into the sky and doesn't cause your stomach to do a backflip. "That's fine with me. I wouldn't work for him no matter what he paid me."

Outside the lobby, I stopped and took in the view before we walked through the glass doors. Luxurious leather furniture filled the space with fine artwork on the walls. Beyond, a crowd of people occupied a glass-enclosed conference room despite the late hour.

"Impressive isn't it? The firm has offices now in Houston."

"That's in addition to New York, Washington, Los Angeles, and Atlanta? You did it for him. You gave him—what did he call it—a second chance?"

"A second lease on life. Leave it to an accountant to talk about leases."

We stepped inside and were immediately met by the receptionist. She kept the small talk to a minimum and led us past the conference room where at least twenty or twenty-five people were milling about. It was a strange fishbowl scene. Through the conference room windows was a view of Chicagoland—the suburbs and beyond to Naperville or West Chicago or whatever was out there twinkling in the far reaches of the night—while the people inside the soundproof space seemed immune to the view, engaged in about ten separate conversations, sipping coffee, walking about, and eating sandwiches.

We followed the receptionist, and when we were almost past the conference room, I happened to glance back for one more look. Everyone in the conference room had stopped talking and stood staring out at me and Uncle Mike. Some lined the window and pointed at us. I thought they were the ones in the fishbowl when instead it was me and my uncle.

Irv met us in his oversized, corner office. He had been partially bald before and now was completely bald. He shook my hand and then held Uncle Mike's hand in both of his. "Mike, good to see you again. Glad to get your call. Did I tell you I'm now a proud grandfather?"

Uncle Mike, a bit red-faced, but smiling broadly, said, "That's great, Irv."

He let go of Uncle Mike's hand and ran over to his desk to grab his phone. "Here are some pictures."

Irv and Uncle Mike admired the baby. I'd always thought if you've seen one baby, you've seen them all, but I joined in. I knew what it meant to Irv.

His only child, Tommy Turnquist, had gotten into serious trouble about fifteen or twenty years ago when he was about twenty-one. He was charged as an accessory to murder and armed robbery. Uncle Mike took over the case from detectives who at the time seemed legit, but rumors had begun to circulate through the department. Years later, it would be publicly revealed how the routine of the detectives included forced confessions and extorting money from suspects.

The day after Tommy was sentenced, Uncle Mike and Liz found the actual perpetrators. If not for Uncle Mike and Liz, Irv's son would still be in prison, instead of practicing general medicine for the Red Cross in Nigeria. Irv liked to say how the judge had scared Tommy right off the continent.

Once we dispensed with the family stuff, we took our places around Irv's desk and Irv tried to sit as well. His limitless energy kept him from staying too long in one place.

Uncle Mike gave Irv a sketchy outline of our current job. Enough to highlight why we needed an accountant, yet not enough to provide information on certain persons of interest that "will remain nameless." He did mention that I was working at WagerEasy as a PI to uncover a drug problem that didn't exist and how certain parties might figure in the Blowtorch Murders.

Irv's eyes widened. He took off his glasses and rubbed his forehead. "Jeesus Christ, Mike. The Blowtorch Murders? That's not just Chicago, that's national news. This is so goddamn cool." Irv bounced up from his seat. "I've got the picture. You need hard numbers." He began to pace around the room. "There's the merger between StatsRUs and WagerEasy. We'll get all over that."

"What bookie deals have been done and the terms," I said.

"Right. That means WagerEasy and their competitors. I'll talk to our people who handle business brokers. Of course, any deal with bookies probably involves a shell company to funnel the money, but we can get those with some digging."

It seemed that Uncle Mike's willingness to cross established ethical lines encouraged others to take the plunge.

"I also need information on Thornton Racetrack," I said. "What it's worth, that sort of thing."

"Right. Got it." Irv snapped his fingers. "WagerEasy needs a physical site to sign up new customers on the mobile app."

We hadn't mentioned WagerEasy's need for a physical site, yet Irv seemed to grasp the issues as he mentally followed the money.

"And don't forget about Walsh and these other guys," Uncle Mike said.

"And Jimmy Golding. I need everything on him," I said.

"Eddie, you brought those papers?" Uncle Mike asked. "Might be worth looking at, Irv."

I pulled out the financial documents I'd found in Jimmy's box and handed them to Irv.

Irv set them down on his desk. He never took notes. He had some sort of photographic memory because he never missed an item we discussed. Sometimes I had to call and ask him to condense stuff into laymen's language because he'd provided too much material.

"Fine. But you guys are a legend around here. Those people in the conference room? They're all volunteers. They can't wait to get their marching orders."

"They maintain secrecy, right?" Irv prided himself on confidentiality, but I had to ask.

"Don't worry," Irv said, talking fast. "How do you think Coke maintains their trade secret formula? We make these people sign a packet of documents an inch thick with every penalty we can think of, and accountants know them all, let me tell you."

Uncle Mike sighed and stood up. "Okay, Irv. Appreciate it. We're under the usual time constraints."

"Sure, you need it yesterday. Done. We're a team."

25

THE NEXT MORNING, WALSH AND I SAT IN THE HALL OUTSIDE
the courtroom on a wood bench and watched the flow of
humanity. Walsh was St. Clair's trump card, our Exhibit "A,"
the one blight on an otherwise airtight case for the state. It
hadn't been easy. Only the threat of the sheriff got him to come
to court.

We waited in the hallway of the Leighton Criminal Courts
Building, while St. Clair argued last-minute pretrial motions
before Judge Andropolous in the courtroom. I'd slipped into
the courtroom once or twice and the prosecution team of three
young attorneys and a squad of paralegals seemed intent on
annihilating St. Clair, the old pro, and her associate, Pam
Ferguson. The prosecution had asked the court to reconsider
its objection to the late disclosure of the witness and St. Clair
argued just as vehemently against it. Yuri's fate depended on
the judge standing by his previous order.

The way the prosecution team stole glances at Walsh when they walked back and forth to the courtroom during several recesses told me they were worried. Walsh was adorned in his finest Winnetka threads, a custom black suit with delicate stripes, a starched white shirt with cufflinks, and a striped, silk, gray and red tie that stood out like a racing stripe. I thought some of the court personnel who drifted past might ask for his autograph.

Fate seemed determined to play dirty tricks on me. What better joke to pull than to send me back to the one place I hated more than anywhere else? The venue of my most miserable days on the planet.

I got to relive those days when I had fought my own charges of aggravated battery. Another chance to put my tailbone into traction on the hardwood benches and check out the zombie people who straggled through the halls looking for lost relatives. All the great memories came streaming back, while I tried to pretend the legal process inside the courtroom wouldn't cost me my job at WagerEasy and blow up my investigation.

The wood bench reminded me how I'd spent endless hours thinking that I'd do serious time. What must Yuri be going through? She'd walked into court and stared through me with dead eyes. No smile, no nod of the head. As if we'd never met. I knew why. The brain synapses don't connect, chances are even-money your life is about to change and your future will be seen through vertical bars, and there's nothing you can do but plead for mercy you probably don't deserve.

I shifted gears. "I've sat in on a few of these deals Golding had been working on with these bookies."

Walsh acted as if he hadn't heard me. "What the hell am I doing here, O'Connell? I thought you said this damn case would settle."

"Give it time. If the court doesn't wimp out and reconsider its order, the DA will have to give a deal serious thought." Ever since we'd met up outside the courthouse this morning, Walsh had kept asking me this same question. I was getting tired of answering it.

"I'm here, but Blick isn't? He's the victim. Where is he?"

I didn't think Walsh wanted to meet face to face with the bureaucrat who could make life a living hell for WagerEasy, but now Walsh wanted Blick to share the misery of a court appearance. "I don't know. The DA probably has him under wraps." I'd never met Blick, but from the way Walsh and Yuri had talked about him, I expected him to dress up in a neck brace for his grand entrance to the courtroom.

Reynolds Blick, Ph.D., was a board member of the Alliance to Prevent Gambling Addiction, a nonprofit funded by a public relations group that listed casinos throughout the country as clients. Blick had the kind of clout that could make life hell for a company like WagerEasy. I assumed big money contacts connected to each state's casinos could hold up a sports betting license for years.

"A fine investigator you turned out to be. What have you done at the office—anything?" Walsh asked.

Clearly, Walsh was frustrated. I'd wanted to accompany Walsh to the courtroom to get the Winnetka exec out of his comfort zone and into a place under the hot lights where the pressure might loosen his jaw. The Walsh at home had been compliant, the liberal elite—whatever that meant. The Walsh in the office had been the boss who could evade questions. Here in the courthouse hallway, where seedy pimp lawyers checked out his suit and asked if he needed representation, I got another version of Walsh.

"I'm working on the Sloan Group deal. I'm waiting for Thornton Racetrack to call back," I said.

"You won't get anywhere on those deals with that fat cow, Larsen."

Walsh would never talk this way around the office. It was a good sign. But I didn't agree with his cheap shot about Larsen. She had the best interests of WagerEasy in mind at all times. "What if it wasn't drugs that got Golding and the other two killed in that hellhole? What if it was one of these deals?"

"That's impossible."

Either Walsh had no knowledge of the deal Jimmy had made with Burrascano or he did a good job of hiding it. "You and Golding didn't get along, did you."

"That's an understatement. Golding wasn't a people person."

"You said yourself how competitive things are. Everyone wants a piece of that one-hundred-and-fifty-billion wagered each year. It's possible, isn't it, that Golding was killed over some deal?"

Walsh stood and stretched. His weasel mind seemed to work through the angles.

"Why were you in that restaurant with Blick when the fight occurred?" I asked.

"Schmoozing those execs from StatsRUs," Walsh said. "Why am I wasting my time here? What the hell is taking so long?"

I felt sorry for the Winnetka refugee. No caterer with a cheese tray. No heiress wife to take him sailing. Just raw civic duty bullshit. He never mentioned one word about Yuri and what she was going through.

"They make you wait and grind you down," I said.

"My old man used to end up in places like this." Walsh looked up at the entrance to the courtroom. "He smoked and drank and swore. He told these stories about his escapades on the air. He had a ton of friends. You know who my old man was, don't you?"

"No." The court had beaten Walsh down. He was opening up, and I didn't want to stop him.

"I'm not surprised. My mom and dad got divorced when I was in first grade. She got remarried and I got stuck with 'Walsh,' my stepfather's name. It was a relief. Then I wouldn't have to fill the shoes of the legendary sportscaster Ivan Novitzky."

"Ivan the Terrible?" I'd heard him broadcast games when I was a kid. He moved around a lot and did the White Sox one year. In the late innings, he'd slur his words. He was a Chicago favorite, and it got him a national job doing football until he passed away.

Walsh shook his head. The sad, sentimental way he shook his head and the way he spoke about his real father told me that he did, in fact, try to fill those shoes.

"My dad always made fun of those guys who married into money." Walsh chuckled. "Couldn't make it on their own, he'd say. They were afraid to drink or fight or womanize. Would never bet everything they had. They weren't real men. He was a big-time gambler—you knew that right?"

"No." I listened for any nuance in Walsh's voice that might echo the past voice of the sportscaster Ivan Novitzky. There was something there in the way he pronounced "real men" as if anything less would be the worst creature on earth. I could hear Novitzky say the same kind of thing about a player who whined and didn't show guts on the field.

Walsh talked while he paced in a small semi-circle. "My old man never got in trouble like this. A case of assault and battery? Shit. People looked out for him because the fans loved him. His ratings were astronomical even when his team was out of it. Lawyers got him off. Judges gave him a lecture and let him go. He hung out with gangsters and would've appreciated a deal with the mob. Hell, one time a guy who he'd beat the crap out of apologized for making him mad. He was larger than life."

"He always talked up stories and players during his play-by-play," I said.

Walsh smiled and kept up the pacing. "Dad always said how the years changed the way he viewed the game. The players had become interchangeable parts of a machine. Superstars were bound to fade and then be pushed into retirement or traded away. The one thing that didn't change? He'd grin and chuckle the way he did on air. The owners, he said, they don't change. They're the ones behind the machine.

Dad looked at me straight in the eyes and told me, 'Son, be an owner. Don't get pushed around.' My old man had smarts. He'd been around."

A familiar face passed in the hall. A guy wearing a Cub's hat pulled down low and a cheap brown suit, but I recognized him.

Kubala.

I jumped off the wood bench and stepped into his direct path. "You clean up well, Kubala. Time to fool the judge?"

He looked up, genuine surprise in his expression. It was clear he wasn't stalking me today. "O'Connell, what the fuck?"

"I like the hat. I hope that pool cue didn't leave a permanent scar."

"Fuck you."

"Maybe I should fill in the judge about your driving and running people off the road."

I'd pulled Kubala's criminal record and talked to some of Uncle Mike's connections at the department. He'd spent more time in juvenile detention and prison than on the outside. In confinement, he joined up with a gang of neo-Nazi skinheads. An informant had testified against several members of the gang on armed robbery and felony murder charges, but Kubala got off easy with probation after four years. When Kubala got out, the informant had been killed. It was still under investigation.

"Let's try it again outside court," Kubala said. "Or when you least expect it."

"Too bad it can't be here and now." I was tempted, but the wood bench had reminded me of the consequences.

"The blonde saved you before." The look of pure hate on his face could not be denied. "Not again. I'll take care of her, too."

"You'll pay for it if you do anything."

Kubala took several steps down the hall then glanced back at me. "What about the track the other night?" He kept walking and disappeared into the crowd.

So Kubala had followed me and Tara to the track Monday night. What did he know about Oscar's murder? Maybe he had raised the stakes on his grudge against me to murder.

Walsh, who was close enough to hear the exchange with Kubala, scratched the back of his finely-groomed scalp. "Nice playmate."

"Nice when he's unconscious." The image of Kubala out cold after Tara leveled him with the pool cue flashed. I took several deep breaths. My adrenaline had spiked.

"What is he, one of those cage fighters? He's big enough."

"He belongs in a cage." Maybe I should follow Kubala and talk to the judge on his case. Then I realized I couldn't tell him anything concrete. Other than the disorderly conduct charge when he broke the kid's jaw last Thursday at O'Connell's, no police report on Kubala had been filed.

"What can Blick do against a big company like WagerEasy?" I asked Walsh after we had taken our seats back on the wood bench.

"His addiction nonprofit can be a pain in the backside. He's got a lot of followers on social media, and he's always on a rant. One of those do-gooders."

I maneuvered Walsh back to that happy place, spilling his guts. "I know what you mean."

"If he launches a campaign against a company, you're screwed. He can hold up a sports betting license with the snap of his fingers."

"Stuck in hearings forever?" Reynolds Blick, Ph.D. I could picture him in state legislative committee hearings presenting statistics on gambling addiction and its costs to the taxpayer.

"Political power. He's got a mix of nuts. Ministers, bankruptcy attorneys, conservative windbags, and widows. You should see him when he talks at these conferences."

"That's right," I said. "He gave a talk at that sports betting conference you attended." It was why Blick happened to be in that bar.

Walsh stood and began pacing again. "You should see the guy. He talks and even the hard-nosed bookies and gambling executives are transfixed. He's like one of those southern preachers who scream hellfire and damnation. I'm telling you, he's really something."

"Sort of larger than life?"

"Right," Walsh laughed. "My old man would laugh his head off. 'Fuck 'em,' he would've said. Even though dad had a gambling problem. No doubt about it."

"What did Blick think of the recent merger with StatsRUs?"

"The key is information. What is a player's record in previous situations or what happened the last time these two teams met? Bettors are suckers for every possible statistic and will pay real money to get it."

"What do you mean?"

"StatsRUs has got the info every bettor craves. To be first-in-class, we need it."

"Like what?"

"You know…" Walsh stopped in mid-sentence.

I turned to look. A man in a wheelchair came toward us. He was being pushed by another man. The man in the wheelchair pointed at us and the wheelchair picked up speed.

"I heard it was you, you turncoat," the man in the wheelchair called out when he got within shouting range.

I nudged Walsh with an elbow. "Is that—"

"That's him," Walsh said.

Blick was an older man with long gray hair and a beard. He had all the victim accessories. The neck brace, the wheelchair, a cast that extended from his hand up to his elbow, held by a sling around his neck, and facial bandages. One look at him and the jury would stamp "guilty" on the Yuri Provost verdict form and with her record she'd be sent straight to prison for the rest of her natural life.

The young man who was pushing the wheelchair had a wry smile as if there was a joke tucked away in the medical paraphernalia. It had been months since the battery took place. He pushed the wheelchair up to us.

"You look good," Walsh said to Blick.

"Lucky I'm out of the hospital, you bastard." Blick's speech was garbled by a dental appliance between his teeth. I thought of Yuri's army boots shined to a high gloss administering an education. "After I gave you Coach Fitz."

"Don't blame Mr. Walsh," I said. "The defendant's attorney served him with a subpoena." I didn't know Coach Fitz but the name was familiar. Then I remembered. That was the name in one of the sets of employment records in Jimmy's box.

Blick looked up at me through thick glasses. "Fuck off." He turned to Walsh. "You're going to wish you kept your mouth shut."

Blick reminded me of someone I had seen recently. Maybe yesterday. Was it on the street? If it was, he didn't have a wheelchair or any of the paraphernalia. Maybe on Monday when I walked over from St. Clair's office to start work at WagerEasy. I tried to picture Blick hunched over with a scarf and stocking cap fighting that icy wind off the lake.

Walsh smirked. "You'll need to learn how to talk first. I can still picture you squirming on the bar floor like a fat nightcrawler—"

"When I get out of this chair, I'll see you crawl," Blick said.

"Not easy to defend yourself when you're rolling around holding your nuts," Walsh said.

This was another side of Walsh. I thought he might suck up to Blick, the bureaucrat with all the leverage within the gambling industry.

"Your company will be dead on arrival," Blick said.

It was my chance to run interference and earn my pay. "People will find out about you. Those racial taunts. You got what you deserved."

"Who the fuck—"

"My name's Eddie O'Connell," I said, "and I work for Mr. Walsh and he doesn't appreciate threats." I looked down the hall over Blick's shoulder and noticed a small crowd approaching.

"Nobody gives a shit about what I said to that woman, that ghetto criminal. Look at me," Blick said. One of the men in the approaching crowd waved in my direction.

"You might want to think about your job," I said. The small crowd included a television camera and Stuart from the local news channel. The crowd stopped and the man began to film behind Blick. I wanted to keep Blick's full attention. "When people back home hear what you said—"

"Nobody will hear," Blick said. "Plus, they'd appreciate it."

"All the facts will come out," I tried not to look up at the camera and stayed focused on Blick. St. Clair knew how to pull last-minute tricks. Maybe I could help. "The courtroom is the place where the truth comes out, Mr. Blick. Everybody will hear about your lover's quarrel with Yuri Provost."

Blick's arm slipped out of the sling to flip me off. "You can't railroad me with that—"

"Yuri said you liked her on top."

Blick came out of his chair and tripped. A string of expletives and racial slurs spewed forth from Blick's mouth in a steady stream and were recorded for posterity by the film crew.

The man who pushed the wheelchair tried to help Blick back into the chair.

"Get away," Blick stood and faced the camera behind him. No need for the wheelchair.

The expression on Blick's face was worth the long morning in court.

"What's the problem, Blick?" Walsh asked. "Worried that a lot of people will send this video to their state legislator?"

I was getting more than a small profit from my day in court. Not only did Blick get what he deserved, Walsh had leaked more to me than he probably meant to. His old man would've "appreciated a deal with the mob," a comment I hadn't prompted with a question. The thought of Jimmy's deal with Burrascano was probably brewing beneath the surface for Walsh. The deal should be on Walsh's mind since it had resulted in murder. Nothing had been mentioned or rumored in the media about a deal with Burrascano. Hell, Saboski and Liz never mentioned it. I could only conclude that Walsh knew about Jimmy's deal with Burrascano on behalf of WagerEasy.

The question was how I'd use the information.

26

I WAS ON A MINI-HIGH. VIDEO OF AN ENRAGED BLICK spouting racist talk had been relayed to the DA's cell phone. St. Clair had Stuart, the news guy, forward it as a private preview of coming attractions. If the DA didn't do "the right thing" and shit-can the entire case against Yuri Provost, then it would be a segment on the nightly news. St. Clair was using the current powder keg of race within the city to attempt to free her client.

It took an hour or two of back and forth, and things "looked promising" when St. Clair cut me and Walsh loose. Only a few seconds earlier, in the elevator riding up to the WagerEasy offices, I received a text from Pam, St. Clair's associate, that they "made it go away." I'd called Walsh with the news and he was thrilled.

Did I condone St. Clair's methods? Tough to say. I hadn't fully switched to St. Clair's team and, due to my mother's case, continued to think a lot of vomit seeped out of those law books. Blick had received a beating from Yuri so maybe the racist deserved some form of justice despite the obvious fact that he'd exaggerated his injuries. But did Yuri deserve a long prison sentence for her reaction to Blick's racial slurs?

Pam told me that hard facts make bad law. Maybe that's why Yuri's case cried out to be dumped—it was a case with rotten, stinking facts, and a jury trial could only result in law at its worst.

It was late afternoon by the time I got off the elevator and walked to my office. The cubicle maze generated more chatter than the morgue atmosphere yesterday afternoon. Without Walsh, the layoffs had been interrupted and people probably thought they were in the clear.

I was golden for the moment at WagerEasy, but now I had a whole new set of worries. I'd talked up a deal with Thornton Racetrack and the Sloan Group and knew next to nothing about how WagerEasy could move forward with serious talks. Instead of playing the ponies, I should've gotten that MBA.

I knew one thing. I wanted to do a deal with Thornton Racetrack. I couldn't think of a more fitting memorial for Jimmy.

Before I could sit down on the chair inside Jimmy's old office, Tara came in.

"Where have you been all day?" She slumped into one of the chairs. Strands of her blond hair hung down across her bloodshot eyes. "Not only do I have to deal with my hangover,

I have to cover for you with Larsen. You know what kind of hell that is?"

Someone knocked on my office door. Larsen.

"I think I'm about to find out," I told Tara.

"Find out what?" Larsen stepped into my office with a clipboard in hand and a pen behind one ear as if she was a high school hall monitor.

"Mr. O'Connell," Larsen said. "Your third day on the job and you're A-W-O-L. What's your story? You know we have a lot of new people here today and we could use this office for someone who actually puts in a full day's work."

Tara massaged her temples with both hands.

"I didn't know I had to report to you, Ms. Larsen. I report to Walsh. What new people?" I asked.

"I suppose you don't bother to read your interoffice memos? They're right there on your desk." Larsen pointed at the stack of papers. "I had them delivered to you since you don't bother to check your email."

Tara sat up straight and winced as if she hoped a new position might help her hangover. "I didn't get the chance to tell you. The new people are from StatsRUs."

"Really?" I asked. "They don't waste any time around here. Out with the old crop and in with the new."

"Corporations do that kind of thing." Larsen smiled at what she probably considered a clever remark.

Tara turned to Larsen. "Why do you care? Eddie's not in your department. You're just a busy-body."

Larsen's face turned red and she leaned down to confront Tara face to face. "I should've fired you right away, Tara. I knew you'd be trouble. You thought you'd slide right through doing as little as possible because of your uncle and your good looks."

"Please, God," Tara said.

I'd heard enough and from the looks of Tara's hangover, she might be ready to do something crazy.

"Let's stop the in-fighting. We've got a job to do. Tara is a member of our team and very good at what she does," I said.

"And what is that?" Larsen said.

I looked at Tara. Did Larsen have reason to suspect our romantic relationship?

"Whether you like it or not, Ms. Larsen, we've got to work together," I said. "We've got big deals in the works." Uncle Mike said to get chummy with Larsen. He had it easy. All he had to do was deal with a killer like Sloan.

"Okay," Larsen nodded. "Tell me about these big deals. You said you can get a meeting with the Sloan Group but it's all been a lot of hot air."

"We met them on Monday night," Tara said. "An exploratory meeting."

"What?" Larsen bellowed. "Why wasn't I informed?"

"Walsh also gave me the green light on Thornton Racetrack," I said.

"I haven't even heard of this deal," Larsen said. "They wouldn't return calls."

"When did you talk to Walsh?" Tara asked me.

Larsen said, "Walsh has been out of the office all day—"

"I was at an off-site meeting," I said. "With Walsh."

Larsen swallowed hard, her facial muscles frozen in stunned silence.

"No shit?" Tara said.

"You know that's something I can check out," Larsen said.

"Check it out if you want. It was confidential," I said. "Now, let's move on. I want to close these deals instead of ending up in a shouting match. I don't want what happened to Golding to happen to my deals." Tara had told me about the in-fighting between Jimmy and Larsen.

Larsen's mouth opened and closed several times as if she was hyperventilating. "Your deals? And how do you know about those arguments?" She turned to Tara. "Someone has a loose mouth."

"I transferred out of your gulag," Tara said.

"How can we get any work done when your able team member has been running around all morning talking to people instead of doing any work?" Larsen asked.

"Damn. I need info on that severance package," Tara said.

Someone knocked on the door. "It's open," I called.

Walsh poked his head into my office. "The attorney from Thornton Racetrack called. Thanks to Eddie's contacts, they want to meet tomorrow."

"Oh, my God, we're not ready." Larsen's clipboard slipped from her hands and she caught it in midair. "We've done preliminary work, but it's not near enough."

"Pull an all-nighter, people." Walsh clapped his hands. "Let's go. We need this one."

27

I GOT A CALL FROM IRV THAT HE HAD THOSE PAST TAX returns for me to sign and that someone would meet me at Shultz's Alehouse. "I love their Old Fashioned with a slice of lemon. I could drink two at a time," he said.

It was a code. It meant that the person with the documents would be at the bar with two Old Fashioneds with lemon instead of the usual orange slice. Irv's team must've pulled their own all-nighter.

At one time, I thought this cloak and dagger stuff was over the top. Then Uncle Mike set me straight. Financial documents of the type that Irv managed to obtain could be the lifeblood of an investigation. It didn't matter if we were focused upon a large corporation, a small start-up, a simple partnership, or an individual. What mattered was the degree of risk and the amount at stake.

If the perpetrator had bet their entire bankroll then they might do whatever it took and sometimes that included murder. They didn't want to end up with nothing but losing tickets in their pocket like Saboski's uncle.

Financial maneuvers and supporting documents could be crucial to the perpetrators of crime. They depended on secrecy. Talks with the accountant were privileged and confidential to a certain extent. Any accounting firm caught giving such documents to the wrong person could wave goodbye to their profession. Uncle Mike and I didn't want that to happen to Irv or his firm.

At WagerEasy, we had agreed to work late on the Thornton Racetrack deal, but both Larsen and Tara needed to run some errands around quitting time at five o'clock. Tara made some excuse so she could grab a bit of "the hair of the dog" at the office watering hole around the corner, and Larsen needed to run to the bank.

I notified Irv and ran out to meet his delivery person at the alehouse, fully aware that I'd probably pick up a load of dynamite.

When you join the cattle drive at rush hour out on the city's sidewalks and you're not headed to the train, you're like the one guy in a marching band who's a half-step behind. I tried to get in rhythm but was out of sync at first. They all moved as an organism, and if I wanted to be absorbed into the anonymous flow, I had to abide by the rules. Remain silent, cheerless, driven to make the pace demanded by traffic lights, and train schedules, and daycare pickup. Don't let the brisk winter wind off the lake slow you down. I did my best to keep up, get absorbed, in case someone was following me.

I'd become the topic of conversation around the office. Walsh had asked some suspicious questions this morning. There were people in the underworld who knew about Uncle Mike and his nephew and the jobs we'd done first for Joey L and then Burrascano. DiNatale had had me followed on prior jobs. This morning in court, Kubala promised a rematch soon. I had to stay on my game.

Shultz's Alehouse was packed with a happy hour crowd that needed fortification before it stepped into the rush hour stampede. I shoved my way through the five-deep crowd that encircled the bar acting like a guy in need of a quick toddy. The noise level made it tough to think. Everyone was shouting over everyone else. Raucous laughter exploded after a day in the trenches. I spotted my contact in a crowd near the end of the bar, two Old Fashioneds with lemon placed before him, studying his phone.

I walked up. A carryall bag hung over the back of the bar chair. "Is this seat taken?" I recognized him from Irv's office.

The man glanced up at me. "No, I'm moving. It's all yours."

I threw my coat over the back of the chair and the carryall bag, sat down, and ordered a beer. The man took the Old Fashioneds and walked into the crowd. In the mirror behind the bar, I followed his progress. It also gave me the chance to see if anyone was watching his progress.

The dark microbrew came, and I downed half of it in one gulp. It hit that sweet spot where all you want is another one.

After court today, I could've used several. Instead, I had to get back to a brawl with Larsen over the Thornton Racetrack deal.

I resisted the urge to fling the bag open and spread documents across the bar and dive into it all. I told myself to try and take a breather, stay in control. Enjoy the beer.

I tried not to be too obvious but kept up my surveillance of the bar crowd. It must've been more than a hundred people. Then I saw a familiar face.

It wasn't easy to recognize him without his sling or bandages. There at one of the booths with the high backs that afforded a sense of enclosure and secrecy was Blick. He stood and put on a dark purple coat.

My first impulse was to confront him, get in an argument and give him a few real injuries to complain about. Of course, I rejected that primitive urge. Control—hadn't I just reminded myself of that?

What had Blick been drinking? Maybe he was trying to wash away the embarrassment of being exposed as a bigot and the deeper revelation that the law wasn't on his side today. He should feel lucky that the DA's deal would keep Blick's sorry ass off the evening news. The dismissal had been a way for the DA to quell racial animosity that had a tendency to spring up daily through every crack in the city's busted pavement.

Blick edged away from the table. I wanted to see who he was drinking with and where he was going. I turned to keep my face out of the mirror and bent down to stay hidden by the bar crowd. After I threw some cash on the bar, I slipped one arm through the carryall and then the sleeve of my coat. Irv's bag would remain inside my coat as I walked out.

It wasn't easy to push through the crowd, plus I had to veer towards the back to get a look inside that booth. Blick had gotten a good head start outside but I was able to see that he was headed toward the lake and maybe the "L" platform at Adams and Wabash. I pushed past a couple of tables. The guy in the booth who had been with Blick looked familiar, an older gentleman with a bushy mustache, but I couldn't place him.

Back into the frigid weather, the wind off the lake in my face, I got into the flow. Blick wore a Bears stocking cap but so did half the commuters rushing toward the "L" stop. I spotted the purple coat at a red light when the stampede halted.

He didn't go up the stairs to the "L" platform. Instead, he took a right on Wabash. Hunched over to conserve body heat, he kept up a fast pace. To make up ground on the ex-cripple, I ran past a few people, Irv's bag flopping against my chest. A guy cussed me out. "What if everyone ran, buddy?"

Blick made another right at the next block. He was doubling back. This little jaunt was getting interesting.

I didn't make a quick turn—afraid he might be watching—I crossed the street. Since the street wasn't a direct link to the trains, there weren't many commuters and Blick was halfway down the block. I sprinted ahead and saw him duck into a parking garage. I jaywalked across the middle of the street, a common practice. Daredevils in Chicago were to be admired.

Should I follow Blick into the garage? There was a flow of cars exiting and people walking up the ramp. It wouldn't provide the best cover, but I didn't want to lose him.

I ducked behind a group walking up the entrance ramp. It wasn't one of those garages with an attendant to retrieve your car. Everyone was on their own.

Blick stood near a limo parked in one of the reserved spots that bordered the exit ramp across from me. He was talking through an open window and smiling. The smile made me hate him more than ever. Then Blick got into the limo, and it drove out of the garage.

I couldn't see through the tinted windows, but I noted the license plate number.

———

I decided to drop by Vern's to catch up with Tara. We needed to discuss a strategy to handle Larsen. Tomorrow's meeting with the owner of Thornton Racetrack meant a lot to me, and I didn't want Larsen to ruin it with her bully act.

Maybe I'd gotten sentimental over the old track and a possible deal for a sportsbook. But the major reason to make the deal work, and take the next step to serious talks, would be to pressure Sloan. He also wanted to set up a sportsbook inside the track. It would be excellent cover for his illegal bookie network.

I rounded the corner, a block from Vern's, and saw a couple pushing and screaming at each other at the end of the block. It wasn't a route to the trains or the "L" and a nearby construction site made the sidewalk into an obstacle course so the area remained free of commuters. The woman's hair was familiar and then I recognized her voice. It was Tara.

The man pushed Tara toward a building, and she fell backward into a snowbank. I sprinted then broke into a full run. The man had something in his hand.

"Hold it," I yelled.

Tara reached into her purse. Probably for pepper spray. The man turned in my direction. It was Kubala and the thing in his hand was a switchblade.

"Eddie," Kubala said. "Is now a good time?"

"Drop it." I stopped several yards from him.

He brandished the knife. "After you, her pretty face." The way he smiled and set his feet told me I'd be bringing my fists to a knife fight. Not my preferred choice. I'd done it before and even when you won, you'd need stitches.

We faced off on the sidewalk. Kubala edged closer and waved the knife. My fists were up, and I sent out a couple of jabs. I bobbed and weaved and got him moving to his right in a short semi-circle. We had an area of ten square feet. Plenty of room to maneuver.

He held the knife with his thumb on top of the blade. It wasn't the hammer grip, a grip that would allow him to thrust underhand to stab at an artery in my thigh or overhand to stab at my chest. With the grip he used, the knife did him more harm than good.

Maybe Kubala had missed the prison class on knife fights. If he got a hold of me from behind, he could cut my throat, but that wasn't going to happen.

"I don't like the knife." I acted fearful so he wouldn't drop it or change his grip.

"This time you're on your own. The blonde won't help." He lunged at me. I glided away and danced to my right. His bulky winter coat slowed him down. I had Irv's bag over my shoulder to slow me down as well.

Kubala mirrored my move by side-stepping to his right and waved the knife around. He seemed to be enjoying himself. He lunged several times just to watch me dodge the blade.

"What's wrong, Eddie?" Kubala asked. "You afraid of a little steel?"

A head fake got him to lash out. He wanted to avoid my right hand which had caught him before. I kept him moving in one direction.

A woman on the corner screamed for the police. Tara echoed her call.

I threw a couple of jabs into the air and kept moving. Kubala, in a crouch, looked for an opening. He caught my forearm and slashed my coat.

"Like that?" he said.

"Drop the knife. Fight like a man," I said.

"Fuck off."

I threw more jabs into the air to keep him moving. Near his feet, I spotted the shimmer of black ice in the shade. It would be a longshot, but the way Kubala shuffled his feet like a guy who couldn't dance told me to give it a try.

I took a chance and stepped close and faked a big right hand with my shoulder.

He took a clumsy stride back and his right foot caught the shiny edge of the ice. When he slipped, his knife hand dropped. I pounced. Two quick steps added to the force of a full right hand.

He might've groaned, but I remember his wide eyes staring at me at that split second before my right hand connected. His eyes seemed to beg for mercy, and like any fighter going in for the knockout, I probably licked my chops and smiled.

I caught him flush in the side of the head. That sweet home-run connection. No need to follow up with a combination. He dropped to his knees then his head plopped on the pavement with the hollow sound of a punctured basketball.

"Eddie, the police," Tara said.

The woman on the corner screamed like King Kong had her in his massive paw.

I wanted to pummel Kubala, but he was out. Blood leaking out onto the sidewalk. I went to Tara. She hadn't been cut. I helped her up.

"We don't have time for the cops," she said.

"C'mon." I didn't need them either. Maybe they'd find a way to charge me for defending myself. It'd happened before.

Tara pointed to Kubala. "You saved him, not me."

Then I saw the gun. She slid it back into her purse.

———

Tara and I had slipped back into the lobby of the WagerEasy building. Police vehicles and an ambulance sped past.

Most of the building's workers were on the way home, so we were alone in the elevator on the way up.

"What the hell?" I asked. "A gun?"

Tara looked at me, hurt in her eyes. "You don't want me to walk around this city defenseless, do you?"

"No, of course not. Would you have shot him?"

"Hell, yes."

"Have you fired it before?"

Her shoulders sagged. "I'm not thinking. I could've missed and he would've cut me up. Thank God, I didn't have to use it. Thank God, you were there."

I put my arm around her. "Sorry."

We embraced and then kissed.

"I don't know about going back," she said. "Larsen drives me mad."

"I'll mediate. I know she tries to push all your buttons. But we need this deal." I hadn't told her why the Thornton Racetrack deal was important to me. How it might pressure Sloan and flush the killer. It seemed so damn complicated at the moment, it almost seemed nuts.

"Really?" She looked up. Her arms tightened around my chest. "Fuck WagerEasy. They'll lay us off after they get what they want."

I needed her help. She knew the corporate stuff. Tara and Larsen could get things done. But not if Tara walked in there with a short fuse.

"I think Kubala could've been involved in Oscar's murder," I said.

"You do?"

"He's served time in prison." I didn't mention that Kubala had stalked us Monday night when we met Sloan at the track.

The question of Kubala's involvement seemed to settle her down. I needed the same prescription. My adrenaline was still off the charts. I might go ballistic with Larsen, too. Maybe somebody recognized us during the fight and would tell the cops. The cops could walk into the office any minute, and I didn't look good in a set of handcuffs. Plus, I thought of that rock-hard bench in the courthouse.

"The folks at O'Connell's really want Oscar's killer," I said. "Like any bookie, he screwed us on the point spread most of the time, but he was *our* bookie. We don't like it when he shows up dead in the parking lot."

She looked up at me, and we kissed again. She seemed to like the idea we would be working on something more than WagerEasy's bottom line.

We stepped off the elevator and went back into the office with fake smiles on our faces. Tara seemed to enjoy the fact we shared another secret.

———

Later that night, after even Larsen admitted to exhaustion, I drove Tara back to her house. No way I'd let her take the "L" with Kubala out there. I'd checked in with Uncle Mike, and he called the precinct. Maybe Kubala had been thrown behind bars for a probation violation on a weapons charge. No such luck. Kubala probably gave the cops a story and maybe the woman screaming her lungs out didn't give a statement.

On the way, Tara and I discussed the need for a nightcap at O'Connell's. Instead, we ended up at my place. Whoever said a knife fight could be a turn off? Just the opposite.

We barely had the door shut behind us before we kissed, our bodies entwined in a mutual bear hug. Then, she pulled away.

"I wanted to see your place." She walked from the back door into the kitchen and opened a few cupboards. All she'd find were a few stacks of canned food and boxes of cereal. I ate most of my meals out.

"Not much to see in a two-bedroom," I said. Except for the dirty laundry I'd left in the bedroom and coffee cups stacked in the sink. I hadn't expected a guest. "I spend off-hours at the gym."

"I can tell. I'm glad. You have a habit of rescuing me, and I'm beginning to depend on it." She draped an arm up around my neck and we kissed. Then she pushed me away and went into the living room.

"Want anything? Wine?"

"No. I overdid it last night." She studied the books on the bookshelf.

I pulled out a vinyl by Billie Holiday and placed it on the turntable. "You like jazz?"

"Love it." She wandered over to the dining table. "What's all this?"

I joined her. Strewn about on the table were a half-dozen open spiral notebooks. Jimmy's notebooks. "They're handicapping notes." I'd left Irv's bag in the trunk of my car. I'd never share those.

"What?"

"Notes on trainers and horses from the racetrack. Thornton and other tracks."

"I don't get it."

"A trainer finds what works and then tends to do it again and again."

"To win a race?" She bent down and examined the page. Could she recognize Jimmy's writing? I couldn't tell her these were Jimmy's notebooks or that I knew Jimmy. It might jeopardize our investigation. I had to think of Uncle Mike as well.

"The trainers who give you a good payoff are the ones who get your attention."

She flipped the page. "There's a lot here. Scribbling and numbers. Math. Another language."

"Some fire their horses when a meet opens. Others run their horses into shape and then ship them to another track. You need to identify a trainer's signature move."

"What's this one?" She flipped open another notebook.

"College football. There's a late game tomorrow night with Gypsum University."

She laughed. "Never heard of them."

"I'd be surprised if you did. They're in a little conference out west."

"Are you going to bet?"

"Not much." I planned to bet a lot. Since Oscar was no longer around to take bets, I'd place it on the WagerEasy website. As an employee, I could access the legal site in New Jersey. A nice perk.

"Do you bet often?"

"Not really." Lies flowed when it came to my gambling. I owned a couple of recliners, an old couch, a stereo, and a flat screen. Gamblers groomed their bankroll; they didn't buy furniture. I could tell her about my gambling debt with Oscar, a debt now floating out there in the bookie's estate, but I didn't. One of Oscar's long lost relatives would find the list of receivables and eventually it would end up in the hands of a guy who knew what it was and how to collect. The debt wouldn't go away.

Billie sang the first line of "Solitude," and I thought of Jimmy in that storage cage. At least his work wouldn't go to waste. I'd place those bets he'd planned to make.

She hummed along. "You'll need to explain all this to me. Remember our deal. You promised to keep me informed about the gambling part of the job."

She spent a surprising amount of time on those notebooks. From behind, I pulled back her hair and kissed her neck below her ear. Took liberties and inhaled her perfume.

She twisted around and looked at me. I wished I could read her thoughts. Maybe she was trying to read my thoughts as well. An attempt to figure out who I was.

I wasn't who I pretended to be. At WagerEasy, I wanted answers about Jimmy's murder. Deals were devices to flush a killer.

Tara was a puzzle. She lived with her mother. She had a fake uncle. A gun in her purse. I pulled her close. What else was she hiding? I didn't really want to know. Not at this moment.

She went limp in my arms. Then, she yanked me close, her lips tight against mine. All caution about our identities and secrets had been deemed irrelevant.

We knocked one of Jimmy's notebooks off the table. She pulled at my shirt and ran her hands across my chest. Our tongues probed, my hands in her hair. When we parted for air, she pulled off her sweater and threw it on the table. I followed her cue. She grabbed my belt buckle and took a second to smile up at me.

She stripped off the rest of my clothes. I handed her a condom and she did the honors. Part of an exploratory mission that required time.

When she stood up, I followed suit with her bra. I was clumsy, but she let me fumble. Then it was my turn to explore. Kisses followed the contour of her neck. My tongue found her breasts. I pulled off her slacks.

I stood and ran my hands across her shoulders and down her back to her hips and pulled her close. She locked her arms around my neck and wrapped her legs around my hips.

We made it to the couch.

28

THE NEXT DAY, LARSEN, TARA, AND I GOT OUT OF MY CAR IN
the near-empty west parking lot of Thornton Racetrack for our
appointment. The first post for the evening's harness races
wouldn't start until seven, but our meeting with the racetrack's
owner was scheduled for three o'clock. Scattered snow flurries
and a brisk wind hit me in the face when I got out of the car.

I helped Larsen with her carryall bag and other items
needed for the presentation. Larsen marched ahead toward the
track entrance while Tara walked with me.

Tara nudged me. "You think Larsen has a clue?" Tara
offered a sly smile.

Last night had seemed inevitable and unexpected at the
same time. Tara and I eventually had made it from the couch
to the bedroom, and she'd spent the night as if we'd been living
together for years. Larsen didn't seem to notice any changes

today in the two of us. She was too focused on preparations for the presentation.

We trudged behind Larsen to the grandstand entrance. Jimmy's notebooks followed a number of horses at Thornton but none of them were running tonight. I'd placed my bet on Gypsum University in tonight's college matchup out west using the WagerEasy website. Jimmy's notes didn't include comments on the moneyline or the point spread he'd want, which struck me as odd. He liked to set his own line on the game.

Today's meeting would be held in the upper level of the grandstands where WagerEasy hoped to construct the sportsbook. Within its walls, WagerEasy would be able to indoctrinate players on the wonders of the WagerEasy online betting site, together with the fun and camaraderie available at the old track when you "wagered the WagerEasy way."

Although Jimmy the Leech sometimes visited with others in the clubhouse to gather information, Jimmy and I had preferred the grandstands. The grandstands extended from mid-stretch to a short distance past the finish line, while the clubhouse extended from that point toward the first turn. Those in the more luxurious clubhouse didn't have the view one could obtain from the pedestrian grandstands.

Jimmy and I liked to witness the turn, the stretch, and the finish. Not only was it the most exciting part of the race, it told us about the development and the talent of certain horses. We wanted to know if they could handle the distance, how they reacted to competition or responded to traffic, and their basic will to win. We had a monetary interest in gauging at what stage a horse might be in the learning process or if the young horse would ever learn. The talent of the jockeys or harness drivers would play out at this critical juncture, and we needed to stay on top of those who took chances and those who'd lost their nerve. These were the kinds of things a video replay couldn't always tell you.

We were met by one of the racetrack's security guards at the entrance. He guided us past the main floor, where a few simulcast players were busy placing bets on tracks around the country, to a wide stairway. The "closed" sign had been removed. The chain and padlock hung from the handle of the heavy doors.

The guard led us up a long, wide stairway to the fourth floor. The escalators that bordered the stairway were out of order. It had been years since I'd been up to the wide, open area tucked beneath the grandstands that were approximately the size of two basketball courts. The doors to the outside grandstands were to the right, and the ticket seller windows lined the opposite wall to our left. It was the expanse a race fan must traverse in those last urgent minutes before post time. The air was stagnant, and the place had the look and feel of Uncle Mike's attic. Around the perimeter were concession stands, and bars, and seating areas.

Of course, the concessions and bars were vacant, and most hadn't been opened in years. The ticket seller windows were shuttered and in warm weather, I imagined bats hanging from the rafters above.

The smell of stale beer lingered. I marveled at the clean floor, painted in a bright checkerboard design. When I played the races here long ago, a mosaic of losing tickets had always littered the space.

Jimmy and I used to hang out at the bar along the far end. I could almost hear him ask one of the sharp players what he thought of the current workout by the favorite. The laughter and click of glasses of the winners and losers seemed to echo. During the races, the track announcer would force me to make a decision. "Only five minutes to post. Better hurry." The silence and absence of my old routine left me feeling disorientated in this forgotten place.

We were led toward an alcove where a long table was set up with chairs lined up on either side. It was one of three alcoves that led to double doors, each of which provided access to the grandstands outside. The double doors were locked with chains and padlocks.

Larsen took a seat at the end of the table nearest the double doors and began unloading stuff from her bag.

"Want any help?" I asked

Larsen shook her head. "No thanks."

Larsen had refused to share certain "internal research" about the proposed deal with Tara and me. She probably wanted to do whatever she could to show she was indispensable. Lucky for me, I had Irv's facts and figures in addition to my local knowledge of the track, none of which I shared with Larsen either.

The primary owner of the racetrack was the old movie star and sitcom star, Arlene Adams. After five husbands, she'd managed to collect a wide range of assets, including a number of old run-down racetracks like Thornton from hubby number three, a minor gangster. I wondered what Burrascano could tell me about the chain of ownership. It might increase my importance to WagerEasy if I could provide that backstory.

I couldn't afford to become expendable to my employer at this point in our investigation. I'd just uncovered a connection between Walsh and Blick. The license number of the limo Blick met last night in that parking garage led me to an obscure company in which Walsh's wife held a majority interest. What kind of game were the two of them playing? Maybe Walsh had handed over cash to Blick. Why else would the racist be smiling?

Was Walsh bribing Blick to get the guy to go easy on WagerEasy or did the two of them have another agenda? I thought about the act they'd put on in court. They were covering up something.

I dug out the employee records on Coach Fitz from Jimmy's box. Somer Fitzhugh, known as Coach Fitz, had been a defensive specialist taking his talents to various college powerhouses and the pros and changed jobs every year before going to work at StatsRUs. The notes in his performance reviews from StatsRUs showed the coach was absent on a regular basis and failed to provide timely reports. My internet digging revealed a recent photo of the coach with a bushy mustache and bulbous nose—the same man who occupied the booth at the alehouse with Blick. Why was he so important to StatsRUs that Blick would mention his name to Walsh yesterday? And why had Jimmy taken a copy of his employment records?

"Okay, Eddie. I'm ready to set up the PowerPoint screen," Larsen said.

I picked up the screen and set it up at the end of the table. When I extended the screen to its full height, I noticed one of the many television monitors mounted around the chamber that provided live video of the races to those who didn't have the energy to go outside and watch the race from the grandstands. On one of the braces of the long beams that ran at a forty-five-degree angle to the apex, where it met the opposite wall, I spotted a camera.

"Tara, why don't you place these folders at each seat," Larsen said.

Tara stood at attention and saluted. "Yes, el capitain."

"Don't get smart. I suppose you've both heard." Larsen looked at each of us with a smug smile. It was one of the endearing qualities Larsen used to grate on my nerves.

"What?" I asked.

"State Senator Brennan announced another round of hearings," Larsen said. "We're going backward again. It's probably why Walsh is late. Home office will go nuts."

Tara groaned. "More political games? Maybe my number will come up with the next round of layoffs."

"Maybe you could talk to your uncle, Tara," Larsen said. "Our entire presentation will be worthless unless the state gets its act together and goes ahead with legalization."

"You think I run things in Springfield?" Tara asked.

I caught a smile from Tara. She continued to get mileage with the phantom uncle.

Political games meant Sloan had done what he'd threatened. He'd stalled the legislation. Uncle Mike and I were playing a dangerous game.

We heard voices coming up the stairs. It was show time.

29

ARLENE ADAMS WALKED INTO THE MEETING WITH A BALD man in a gray suit. She stopped before the table, held out her arms, palms up, gave us a big smile, and said, "Hello, everyone." The man in the suit held a briefcase and gave us a forced smile.

Her blond hair was piled high on her head in an early sixties fashion. She wore a long flowing blood-red skirt and matching jacket. The mink stole with the animal's head clipped to the tail caught my attention as did the string of pearls. A pillbox hat with matching mink trim completed the ensemble.

Now in her seventies, the sitcom and movie days were long over, but I did remember her sitting in a box on a game show before she settled into seclusion in the Hollywood hills. Her face and eyes held a heavy layer of makeup, yet the years had been kind, and she'd retained some of her beauty. Her lipstick matched the dress.

Larsen stood and gave a polite bow of the head as we began the process of formal introductions.

"I've seen all your movies," Tara said.

Arlene held out her arms to Tara and Tara responded by stepping forward to give her a hug.

"You're very kind," Arlene said. "There were a couple of clunkers. You're gorgeous. Are you married?"

"No," Tara said.

"Oh, you must. It's wonderful to wake up beside a man and grab hold of strong shoulders."

Tara looked at me with lifted eyebrows to confirm she'd done just that this morning.

"Arlene, can we get started?" the suit said, sitting down at the table, and clicking his ballpoint pen like a stopwatch.

"WagerEasy is such a fine company," Arlene said, allowing Tara to escape her grasp. "I'm thankful you could make it out here in this dreadful weather." She turned to the suit. "I thought I told them to turn up the heat in this rat trap. Jeesus Christ."

He nodded and pulled out his cell. "I'll text them."

Arlene finally sat in the folding chair and looked around. "Aren't we waiting for one more? Didn't we specify—"

"Yes," Larsen said. "Mr. Walsh should be here shortly."

"That's right," I said, not wanting things to fail before they even got started. "We got here early to get set up but the traffic…"

Larsen and Tara both chimed in on the traffic.

Arlene pulled her coat around her shoulders. "You should see it in L.A. Lots of traffic, but always beautiful. Always sunny. Okay, let's try it."

Larsen cleared her throat and stood. She clicked the PowerPoint to change screens while she rattled off statistics in a monotone. She referred us to certain pages within the folder in case someone wanted a closer look. Larsen began with flow charts and graphs that detailed estimated wager volume at WagerEasy both nationwide and statewide versus expected revenues, and I got worried I might fall asleep.

Larsen followed that with more charts and graphs of the handle for tracks owned by Arlene's company. Compared to the WagerEasy data where everything was expected to increase, these charts for Arlene's tracks were all headed straight into the toilet.

A voice called out from the stairway. "Sorry, I'm late." Walsh sprinted across the floor like a bettor who needed to make a last-minute wager. "Sorry, everyone."

The suit looked at his watch and shook his bald head.

Arlene smiled. "Here's the man we've been waiting for."

Walsh went through another round of introductions and then sat down. I still didn't catch the name of the anonymous suit, and I didn't want to ask him to repeat it.

Arlene asked about the traffic, and Walsh told her it wasn't too bad.

"Great," Tara said to me under her breath.

Larsen's face turned red, and I thought she'd apologize for the lack of traffic.

"Go ahead, honey," Arlene said. "These are the most colorful graphs I've seen in a while."

Larsen skipped ahead to a video that illustrated how a bettor could wager online with WagerEasy. It was space-age type stuff. The bettor could cash out a bet during the game at market odds calculated by demand like a stock exchange for gamblers. You could bet on if the kicker would make the field goal or which team would score the next goal. This was the interactive in-play wagering that was the crack cocaine WagerEasy wanted to sell across the country. Continuous play, one bet after the next like a slot machine. No one would watch a game again the same way. You were now a part of the action, and you could do it on your phone while you chugged a beer and gnawed on chicken wings.

"Let's see the rendering," Walsh said.

Larsen clicked forward. Maybe she'd been saving this one for her grand conclusion because she seemed a bit put out, her lips tight and jaw moving.

It was an architect's video rendering that provided different perspectives of the proposed sportsbook. The interior and exterior of the space we now occupied would be completely remodeled. The old grandstands would be razed and replaced by an elongated set of glistening windows that made it appear as if a space ship had spun out of control and crash-landed into the old track.

Inside the glass-enclosed sportsbook, the video showed digital human bodies standing in lines to place sports bets. Digital waitresses carried trays of drinks through the crowded premises. Armchairs in a theater setting looked out upon rows of oversized flat screens televising games from everywhere. Another wall held an array of red neon lights on a black background, flashing odds and information on upcoming wagers, in a display that would make NORAD jealous.

The patrons would be able to view the horse races without being forced out into the weather and, at the same time, allow WagerEasy to maintain a captive audience for the current games that featured in-play wagering.

It was enough to warm the cockles of any gambler. I began to picture a name etched into the glass doors, "The Jimmy Golding Sports Book."

"I love this," Walsh said. "It will transform the Thornton gambling experience."

"It's the future," Tara said. "Cool."

I hated to think of the old grandstands demolished and replaced by the WagerEasy three-ring circus. But at least the one-hundred-year-old track would survive.

Larsen broke into a smile for the first time since we left the office.

The suit came to life. "Interesting."

"Excuse me, honey," Arlene said to Larsen. "As you know, the fancy track on the north side of town has all the prime racing dates and stakes races while little old Thornton gets all the dregs including a fall meeting. How the hell am I going to get these sports bettors to play the horses while they're ogling these football games in control central?"

Larsen shrugged as if she didn't have a clue then bent down to her laptop and tried to find another relevant video to save us.

Walsh looked at Larsen. "Well…"

While Larsen searched, the digital people on the video screen began jumping around, screaming, and doing high-fives. We missed the reason for the in-house celebration. Maybe it had been a last-second touchdown. We stared at the mass hysteria of the digital people as if they were monkeys in a monkey house.

Tara dropped her head into her hands. Maybe she tried to squelch a laugh.

I stood up and stepped toward the screen. "Let me answer your question, Ms. Adams. I've been to your fall meeting. Every year the crowd shrinks. I'm not sure if your fans took up casino betting or lotto or illegal sports betting or ended up in a rest home because every one of your horseplayers has gray hair. Most of the time I'm the youngest guy there."

"Uh, Eddie," Walsh murmured.

"No, Garret," Arlene said, "let him continue."

I walked over to the end of the table beside Larsen to block the view of the digital bettors in the throes of sports betting ecstasy. "It's the older generation that plays the horses. I think there's a sign that says 'only people sixty and older allowed.' And I'm fed up. My generation needs a second chance to discover the races. I don't know why they didn't connect. Maybe it was the Great Recession and lack of good jobs or cell phones and social media addiction or simply a lack of patience."

I turned and gestured to the digital people. "But what if they have a chance to visit the racetrack because everyone else is doing it? Because everyone wants to try something new and sports betting will be new to most of them—legal sports betting that is. I've seen them in Vegas. Sports betting will draw them in."

Arlene's face remained frozen. Larsen's mouth hung open.

"Eddie, that's enough." Walsh had his arms folded. To him, I was the PI, not the salesman. What was I trying to pull with WagerEasy's most important deal? Tara seemed to shake her head as if she questioned my sanity.

I didn't flinch. "Sorry, Mr. Walsh. I can't help it, Ms. Adams. I have to talk about it. I know that it's a chicken-egg problem. The track needs revenue from another source to increase its purses, and unless the purses are increased, the races will be crap. And it is crap that you've got running out there right now. Short fields. Stables with old broken-down nags that can't compete with any of the racinos—racetracks coupled with casinos in other states. You tried and tried to get slots in here, and you know how that turned out."

"Eddie has a good point," Walsh said.

"Thanks to those north side people and the state's casinos who want us to disappear," Arlene said.

I kept going. "With WagerEasy's investment, you'll be able to promise higher purses. Start getting back those stables you've lost. It's my guess they'll want to come back. There's money here in Chicago. People want to own horses and see them run."

Arlene shifted in her seat, leaned forward, and placed one elbow on the table.

"It's my bet," I said. "My bet that once people of my generation are exposed to horse racing and its excitement, they'll become fans. They have to. Each race can be the most exciting two minutes a gambler can ask for. They don't have to wait to see if the kicker makes the field goal or what team will win. We need to save horse racing."

"My friends would definitely take another look," Tara said.

"Thanks, Tara," I said. "Sure, there are people who say the only real horse racing is at the big-time tracks with their Triple Crown and Breeder's Cup. But I think you can get just as much of a jolt out of a cheap claiming race. And where do those top stables and trainers come from? Do they fall from the sky? No. They come up from these small tracks like the ones you own. It's about time the top people remember where they came from, and I think they might start to figure it out when purses increase and interest through social media takes off."

Walsh stood. "Ms. Larsen, don't you have data on how Thornton's revenue share from the WagerEasy sportsbook can be used to increase purse sizes?"

Arlene raised one hand toward Walsh to indicate "stop."

I didn't have any stats or graphs or studies. All I had was what I felt in my gut. "What we're talking about is a bet on horse racing itself, Ms. Adams. You owe it to yourself and you owe it to the industry to make that bet."

"Who is this young man, Garrett?" Arlene asked. "Horse racing needs a pep talk. Sometimes after you've tried everything and get shut down, again and again, you get tired and give up. Yes, I can believe in it one more time. He believes it, I can tell. And that's what counts. I can place that bet on horse racing. Garrett, if we decide to go with WagerEasy, I want this young man handling things for us."

Arlene beamed a smile my way. One minute each side was out to exploit the other over high tech, and the next, we'd found a common love of something old.

Walsh didn't seem overjoyed that I'd taken over the meeting but, by the way he now smiled, he wasn't going to let that stand in the way of taking credit. "I saw Eddie's potential when we first met."

30

THE CONVERSATION BEGAN TO FLOW. ARLENE HAD BECOME interested in what WagerEasy could offer. She didn't mind the proposed joint venture if she could reinvest in the track.

"Have you seen the parking lot?" Arlene asked. "I'm not sure if those are potholes or bomb craters. If I'm going to attract people to this location, we have to put some lipstick on this pig. Porter would've liked that."

Porter "the Pastor" Pearson was her late husband, a mobster, and hitman. Supposedly, he'd made the sign of the cross before he sent his victim to the afterlife. Irv's report mentioned that he'd owned a small casino in Vegas that got swallowed up by corporate America.

Walsh seemed to have answers for all of Arlene's concerns. How WagerEasy could help with the sports betting license, legal costs, and remodeling, and how its lobbyists could turn up the heat against the Illinois casinos who always felt Thornton Racetrack was a threat.

"I don't want to end up a year from now with a fancy sportsbook and ten fans in the seats because everyone is placing wagers on their phone at home," Arlene said.

"Don't worry," Walsh said. "Thornton will be entitled to annuity-like payments from those who sign up at the track sportsbook for their online wagers. We'll do promotions. We'll make it worth their while to come out to the track. And, if they've become fans like Eddie said they will, then it will be easy."

I began to see the downside of my speech. What if sports betting didn't mean a new life for horse racing? What if it was all a pipe dream? I didn't care. It was a good dream, and I liked the odds.

Larsen jotted notes like a stenographer on steroids. Arlene Adams seemed ready to deal. Tara nudged me. Even the anonymous suit was smiling.

Another side of Walsh had emerged, that of the dealmaker. He seemed to have a personal stake in WagerEasy's success that reached well beyond his company job in Chicago. Be an owner, Walsh's old man had said. The legendary sportscaster had faded in the public's mind like any other forgotten superstar put out to pasture.

According to Irv's documents, Thornton Racetrack was only worth the price of the raw land, minus the demolition costs to tear the place down. Revenue from the races had decreased year over year. Stuck in the city's armpit between a sewage plant and an oil refinery, the old track property would sit vacant for years if not for the sudden gift of sports betting. It was the track's only hope and the reason Arlene seemed thrilled.

Irv had noted that several other parties were interested in a sportsbook deal with the track, including a fantasy site. The track would be awarded an automatic sports betting license, and that alone gave it value. I wanted to save the track and its way of life. None of it would bring Jimmy back, but the chance to experience old thrills got my adrenaline up. Some days I'd run through the parking lot to catch the first race to get my wager down. Now another brand of excitement, one of cutting-edge uncertainty and change, reared its head, and I wanted to see it enter the starting gate and run.

"Howdy, y'all," a voice shouted.

We all looked up from our intense exchange toward the stairwell. Three men approached. It was Uncle Mike, DiNatale, and Travis Sloan. I couldn't believe it. Uncle Mike should've texted me.

Sloan took off his cowboy hat and bowed to Arlene Adams. "Hello, ma'am. My name is Travis Sloan. I heard through the O'Connell grapevine that WagerEasy wanted a follow-up meeting with me. I thought right here and now would be as good a place as any."

It was pure corn pone. What an act. He wore a brown leather winter coat with a white fur collar like the Marlboro Man or Hank Williams out on the ranch.

Walsh stood up and introduced himself. "Yes, Mr. Sloan, we have heard about you and want a formal meeting." He seemed nervous.

"Well, that's dandy," Sloan said as if the two of them might sit down and play a friendly hand of Texas Hold'em. "Let me introduce my associates. This here is Mike O'Connell and this well-dressed dude is Vic DiNatale. They know the lay of the land. I've met Eddie and…"

Tara stood and flashed her meet and greet smile. "Hello again, Mr. Sloan. Tara, Tara Reilly."

We got up and shook hands all around. After shaking Uncle Mike's hand, Walsh turned my way with a "what the fuck" look. I didn't know if the connection through my uncle would help or hinder my cause.

DiNatale shot me a wicked glance as he sat down as if warning me to remain silent about his mob connections. I didn't mind. I sat back ready to enjoy the contemporaneous farce. Sloan and Walsh in the same bull ring vying for the attention of a B movie star.

"I've already met Mr. DiNatale," Arlene said. "Mr. O'Connell, it's a pleasure. And Mr. Sloan, I've heard a lot about you."

It didn't surprise me that Arlene had met DiNatale. Porter must've known DiNatale and Burrascano.

Sloan straightened his bolo tie. "First names, please."

Irv's documents didn't have much on Travis Sloan. I assumed most of his money was cash. Other straw men probably owned his assets to avoid drawing the attention of the IRS.

Irv had an FBI contact who described an ongoing investigation by the feds into Sloan's criminal activities in addition to bookmaking. These activities included smuggling, drugs, loan sharking, and murder. A number of witnesses had disappeared and Sloan had hired an array of top lawyers. These few paragraphs were probably the most interesting portion of the four inches of documents and read like a crime novel. It confirmed what Uncle Mike had heard about Sloan.

We all sat down and Sloan got down to business with a Texas-style "aw shucks, Ma'am" smile. He seemed to enjoy the limelight almost as much as Arlene Adams.

"Well, Arlene," Sloan began. "You should know that WagerEasy is also interested in my network of bookies. We seem to add a few to the Sloan Group every day. Some of them have met with WagerEasy, but never got an offer. Imagine that—all that sales talk and nothing comes of it."

Walsh said, "Now just a minute—"

"Hold on, Garrett," Arlene said. "Let Travis talk."

Sloan had a point. Walsh, Tara, and I all looked down the table at Larsen who kept her head buried in her computer. She was the one who'd pissed off a lot of those small-time bookies, and they were all running to the Sloan Group.

"Thanks," Sloan continued, "you've got to wonder, Arlene, if you're the recipient of more of WagerEasy's hot air or if they'll actually come through. WagerEasy wants to deal with me but I don't plan to wait around and see what their home office decides to do months down the road. I'd rather do my own deal with you, Arlene, and construct the sportsbook myself, and we can split up the revenue. Then, if WagerEasy gets off the pot, we can talk about them buying the whole shebang."

I liked Sloan's approach. Until WagerEasy made a legitimate offer, Sloan would compete with them every step of the way. Of course, if Arlene did a deal with Sloan, she wouldn't see any profit, because Sloan would skim the take.

Maybe I should let Arlene take a look at that crime novel Sloan lived in the shadows.

"These are baseless allegations," Walsh said. "The small-time bookies have nothing of value and don't cooperate. You can't blame WagerEasy for that."

"Small-time to you," Sloan said, "but to me, they're kin. They hook up with me and we can't be pushed around because I've got Texas as my core base. Ain't no way sports betting will ever be legal down in the Bible Belt."

"Now hold on," Arlene said. "I hear what you're saying, Travis. But let's not plan movie distribution rights before we get a script."

Sloan smiled and nodded slightly to allow her to take the stage.

Arlene primped her hair. "Don't get me wrong, a lady likes attention, and believe me it's been a while since my string of little racetracks got any attention whatsoever. I wouldn't have these tracks if not for Porter, bless his soul. Porter was a gambler, ladies, and that was fine with me. I wouldn't have any interest in a man who didn't gamble or wasn't willing to take chances. I simply wouldn't have any respect for him."

"Never a dull moment, right?" Tara asked. Under the table, Tara squeezed my knee.

"That's right, honey," Arlene said. "It was the real thing too, me and Porter. You don't have that happen more than once or twice. My first couple of marriages were prep races for my marriage to Porter. He loved those little tracks and watched over every detail. They might have had third-rate horses but families could go and have a good time betting at the two-dollar window. Even though Thornton Racetrack is attracting attention from WagerEasy, and Mr. Sloan, and others, there are additional matters I have to take into consideration besides money. Matters for Porter."

"I'm sure we can look after what Porter may have wanted," Sloan drawled.

"It would be a priority," Walsh said.

Arlene looked down the table. "Mr. DiNatale, maybe you know what I'm talking about."

DiNatale studied a pearl cufflink on his sleeve and shook his head. "Nope. I'm afraid not."

"Well, that's too bad," Arlene said. "You know making a bet isn't like buying soap off the shelf. A bet reflects that individual. A bet is personal. Porter bet on those old tracks. They meant a lot to him. Now Eddie has asked that I make one last bet on those old tracks and horse racing."

Sloan and DiNatale stared daggers at me. Uncle Mike smiled and shook his head.

Arlene unclipped the head of the mink stole and stroked it. "We bought a house up on a hill with a pool in Vegas. Porter was a good man. Sure, he was involved in some rough stuff. I knew that. But in his heart, he cared for me and cared for people."

She caressed each word of Porter with a movie star's breathy cadence. No one interrupted her. She had the stage, and she was playing it for all it was worth.

"He always kept to the rules," she continued. "He was polite and courteous and always let me know where he was going and if he'd be late for supper. Know what I mean, girls?"

"Dependable," Tara said. "The kind who asks what *you* want to do and wants to be with you."

Larsen grimaced.

Arlene nodded. "That's right, honey. Porter hung up his clothes too. He was a gentleman. We talked about family. We had plans. Then one day he didn't come home." A bitter edge cut into her dialogue. "He didn't call. I was frantic."

She made a show of looking at DiNatale. "People should've called me and let me know." Each word drove home the accusation. "I paced around and called everyone I knew. I even called the police and they laughed at me. God, imagine what that's like."

A siren outside wailed a lonely song in the silence that followed.

Sloan didn't appear happy with DiNatale. Part of the Porter "the Pastor" Pearson story was his Jimmy Hoffa-like disappearance. Arlene Adams seemed to think that DiNatale must've had a hand in it.

A tear crawled down Arlene's cheek but the anger didn't go away. She plucked a lace handkerchief from inside her sleeve and dabbed at each eye. "People think that because you had five husbands, you're a joke." She gathered her emotions, her lips puckered and trembled. She took a deep breath. "All they had to do was call me. Let me know. That's all I asked. I wouldn't make a stink." She gripped the head of the mink, pulled it up to her lips, and kissed it. Then she glared down the table at Sloan, DiNatale, and Uncle Mike. DiNatale kept his head down and Uncle Mike remained solemn. "Just don't expect me to forget about Porter, goddamnit."

She stood. "Mr. Sloan, Mr. Walsh, we're done for now. You will hear from me."

No one dared object. We stood as Arlene and the suit got up and walked out. Except for the siren that seemed to be getting closer, everyone maintained silence until she was halfway down the stairs.

31

SLOAN AND WALSH WALKED OVER TO THE SIDE AND TALKED in a low, businesslike tone. Larsen gathered up her paperwork while Tara and I packed up the screen and laptops.

The siren screamed outside. It must've been the track ambulance. But then I heard the distinctive sound of gunshots.

DiNatale looked at his phone. "Hey, something's going on outside." Maybe he had men stationed outside.

DiNatale and Sloan raced toward the stairs. The shots seemed to be coming from the west lot.

Uncle Mike, a few steps behind me, yelled out. "Stay with them."

But he didn't need to say anything. I was right on their heels, Tara close behind me.

DiNatale, on his cell, veered off at the bottom of the stairs toward the clubhouse. The rest of us followed Sloan down another flight of stairs to the west grandstand exit where more gunfire erupted.

Outside, smoke and snowflakes drifted past. The siren blasted amidst steady rounds of gunfire. We hustled about twenty yards along a brick-walled walkway that bordered the east side of the square area which comprised the west parking lot. The south side of the lot was bordered by the back wall of the clubhouse that extended a city block, while the north side of the lot was framed by a raised set of old railroad tracks. Bordered on three sides, the only access was from the west.

To our immediate left, in the southeast corner, an ambulance crept past the clubhouse entrance. It wasn't a typical ambulance, it was a dated, white, Detroit, classic bulldozer of a vehicle reinforced with armor plates held in place by straps that ran across the roof. Holes drilled into the armor converted it into a Mad Max-type vehicle. Gun barrels protruded. The ambulance rumbled along slowly, siren blasting.

A guy near the clubhouse entrance fired back at the ambulance. Something like an AK47 opened up on the guy.

"What the fucking hell?" Sloan yelled.

"Oh, my God," Walsh shouted.

"Jeesus," Uncle Mike screamed in my ear.

Those within the lot seemed to be under attack. The west lot of Thornton Racetrack, the place I was trying to save. Where I hung out with Jimmy.

Across the lot on the north side, a boxcar covered in graffiti sat on the railroad tracks. Through the partially opened door, two men fired down on the ambulance. The ambulance fired back at the boxcar and sprayed the lot.

In the lot, a couple of police cars had joined my car and several rows of other cars. An officer got hit and fell over. The shooters in the ambulance had shot a cop.

I couldn't process it all at first. The scene came to me in bits and pieces. Hard to absorb but one thing was clear—the ambulance wasn't there to save anyone. It was there to kill anyone in its path.

Like a tank, impervious to it all, the ambulance rolled on beside the clubhouse. It began to speed up to five miles-per-hour. I grabbed for my keys. Maybe I could get to my car and block its path. But there was no way.

The men in the boxcar continued to fire on the ambulance. They weren't in uniform but could've been detectives in plain clothes. I ducked down behind the wall that lined the walkway to the grandstand entrance, but couldn't resist popping my head up to witness the action. I threw one arm over Tara's shoulders.

"Eddie, what in God's name is going on?" Tara shouted in my ear.

"I don't know."

Another burst of automatic fire and the brave guy at the clubhouse entrance stopped shooting.

The lot was a war zone. Several people were down. Two with uniforms. Windshields were shot up. My car had been riddled. Two cops behind squad cars fired back at the ambulance. How could I join them? Grab the service revolver of one of the wounded cops? No, no chance to make it through the crossfire.

At the end of the clubhouse, a maintenance crew huddled around their truck in the direct path of the armored vehicle.

No one or nothing could survive in its wake. Too much firepower.

The maintenance crew, three men dressed in denim overalls, probably there to fix those crater-like potholes, drew guns. *What the hell?* Automatic weapons. They took cover behind their truck, dropped to one knee, and blasted away as the ambulance drew closer. They'd waited, possibly in an effort to lure the ambulance toward them, and fired with the precision of a marine unit.

The scene blew me away. I cussed a blue streak, but it didn't matter, because no one could hear me. Tara did the same.

One of the maintenance crew dropped over. He'd been shot. One of the men ran to the back of the truck. The ambulance swerved off at a forty-five-degree angle toward an exit. It slowed and continued to swerve like it was drunk. Shots from the boxcar pinged against the white monster. It seemed invincible.

The ambulance picked up more speed as the engine gave off an ear-splitting, high-pitched metallic whine. It screeched into an open area of the empty parking lot. The asphalt stretched a couple hundred yards from the end of the clubhouse to the exit. Two football fields.

Then a small explosion erupted from the maintenance truck. The man who had entered the truck held a length of pipe on his shoulder. A skyrocket or something bigger sizzled in the air. A trail of white smoke twisted into a corkscrew against the steel-gray sky. In the blink of an eye, an explosion. We covered our ears. The ambulance in flames, only the wheels visible. Some sort of missile had struck it.

"Holy mother of God," Sloan screamed.

"Christ almighty," Uncle Mike yelled.

More sirens from everywhere. Police cars swooped into the lot. A fire burned in the middle of the asphalt lot, snowflakes falling like ash. Maybe it was ash. A guy leaped out of the ambulance, his coat on fire. A blistering crossfire from the maintenance crew and the shooters in the boxcar lifted him off the ground and held him in midair. Then he crumpled like a rag doll. *Fuck yes.*

A car in the third row of parked vehicles started up. The driver burned rubber as he tore out to our right and swerved erratically in an effort to escape. If he was able to get around a concrete barrier, the car could slip behind the grandstands into the east parking lot. The men in the boxcar unleashed a firestorm and the car slammed into the barrier and burst into flames.

Stunned, we waited for more fireworks.

People littered the ground. Some groaned and screamed, hidden by parked cars. Others were silent. Police jumped from their cars and ran toward them. More sirens filled the void left by the burning armored ambulance. The maintenance truck took off around the corner of the clubhouse and out of sight. The men in the boxcar jumped out and ran on foot down the tracks toward the street. Definitely not police.

"Run," I screamed to the winners.

We were a small crowd of onlookers, but a couple of old-timers and a couple of young guys with track security uniforms—shocked like the rest of us—organized a line to hold us back.

An ambulance—a regulation one—and other emergency vehicles, sirens screaming, tore into the lot from the west entrance.

More police cars, followed by a fire engine, entered the lot.

Uncle Mike stood near me and pointed. "Shit. Is that Liz's car over there?"

I looked at the parked vehicles. Liz drove an unmarked white Ford Taurus. I spotted it. It had been riddled with bullets.

"Damnit." Uncle Mike tried to push through the security personnel toward the bodies in the lot. "They must've changed the date."

It took a second for me to understand what my uncle meant. The meeting between Liz and Burrascano that Uncle Mike had set up. I didn't know when it would take place, only that it had been arranged. Liz must've told Uncle Mike, but the date was changed to today. Why today? To coincide with our meeting with Arlene? Burrascano probably spied on us the whole time through that camera I'd spotted. From his roost in the clubhouse suite, several hundred yards from our meeting place in the grandstands, he could've watched Arlene. No doubt Burrascano held a partnership interest with her.

"You can't, sir. Stay back," one of the security personnel stretched out his arms in front of my uncle.

"She's down." Uncle Mike pointed. "That's Liz. That's her coat."

Paramedics had flocked to her and worked on her. Adrenaline shot through me. One second the ambulance exploded into flames. The next, it's Liz.

Uncle Mike made a move toward her but the security officer grabbed him in a bear hug.

Other security personnel joined the scrum. Where were these guys during the shootout? I wanted to punch them out but that would be nuts. Guys doing their job, nothing more.

I tugged on Uncle Mike's arm. "C'mon, you can't do anything," I told him. "The paramedics will do it."

He swore at me and shoved me away. I held my ground and tried to explain. "Listen, Uncle Mike, there's nothing you can do—"

"Damnit. Liz." He shoved the security guard then held up his hands. "Damnit."

The security man nodded. "No problem, old man."

Liz was the first one they worked on. Then others got to an officer who was farther back among the parked cars. I recognized Saboski. He was sitting up, holding his arm, in shock.

"I can't do nothing?" Uncle Mike shouted. "Oh, yeah?" He turned and ran back toward the clubhouse entrance.

"Where are you going?" I ran after him.

"Eddie, where are you going?" Tara called after me.

Uncle Mike went through the glass doors of the clubhouse and took the stairs two at a time to the Jockey Club. I caught up to him.

"The meeting was today," Uncle Mike yelled back at me over his shoulder.

These stairs led to Burrascano's suite.

"Stop, damnit," I called out to Uncle Mike.

He was running up the stairs to confront Burrascano. Did he blame Burrascano?

I caught up to him and grabbed him by the shoulder. "Think, Uncle Mike. Don't you see? They were trying to frame Burrascano again. Those guys in the ambulance must be the same guys who killed Jimmy. They tried to frame Burrascano again today." I wasn't sure how the killer's plan crystallized in my mind. If they killed Liz on the way to her meeting with Burrascano, the sick, old mob boss would be blamed.

Uncle Mike studied me as if unable to interpret my words.

I held both his shoulders and tried to speak slowly. "Burrascano's men must've been waiting. His men waited in the boxcar and maintenance truck if the killers tried another ambush. Think. Think about our theory of the case. The person who hired those killers—those men in the ambulance—that person is still out there."

"What the fuck are you saying?" He grabbed my coat and pushed me to one side. "It's Liz out there."

"I know. But it's not your fault. I'm fucking pissed too."

"The killer is still out there? It's not Burrascano. I didn't cause this?"

"That's right."

Uncle Mike had convinced Burrascano to meet with Liz. But it had nothing to do with him.

"DiNatale ran toward the clubhouse when we left the grandstands. He's probably taken Burrascano away by now," I said.

Uncle Mike nodded. "The person who ordered these shootings and the Blowtorch Murders is still out there. The guys in the ambulance were the bastards who did it. You're right." He steadied himself against the railing and lowered himself to the steps and sat.

I sat beside him.

He shook his head. "Liz has to be okay. She has to be." He turned toward me for an answer. Words seemed to die on the tip of his tongue.

I knew how much he invested in every case. Too much. The price he paid again and again. "They're doing what they can, I'm sure of it. She has the best of care. The hospital is only a few blocks down the street."

"Burrascano is too smart. At least he got the killers. Now we need to get the fuckers in charge. You're okay? Tara is okay?" Uncle Mike asked.

He was in shock and I wasn't much better. "Yeah, we're okay."

He studied me for a long second. "Should we have seen this coming? Told Liz?"

"No, no way." Maybe I should've seen it.

He seemed to regroup and pulled himself up with every ounce of strength in his old frame. He patted my shoulder. "C'mon, let's get over to the hospital."

32

THE NEXT MORNING, I WALKED INTO THE WAGEREASY office. Half the faces in the office were strangers. The StatsRUs people had been merged into the fold.

What connection did they have to Thornton Racetrack? None. The papers gave a headcount of those shot and wounded and the number killed. Four in the ambulance and the signal car driver, plus two officers killed and several wounded, including Liz, critically, and Saboski. The guy shot near the maintenance truck and the guy at the door of the clubhouse, most likely Burrascano's men, had been taken away, I assumed and weren't included in the tally.

Another Chicagoland shooting to add to the stats. It came with the political corruption, the sports scores, weather, and the morning coffee, "Rival Gangs in Shootout at Track," gripping headlines for another day.

The shock hadn't worn off for me. The track fireworks, the realization Liz had been the target, and the long night at the hospital. Uncle Mike's pain and my own. I had to hang on here at WagerEasy. The killers, the persons who directed the murders, were getting bold and desperate. Uncle Mike and I were so close.

Tara came into my office and shut the door. "Eddie, anything new on your uncle's old partner?" She sat down.

We'd been on the phone and had texted through the night. I'd told her of the connection between Liz and Uncle Mike. "She's in a coma." At least Saboski was doing all right.

Tara winced. She wrapped her arms tight around her chest. I thought I saw a tear in her eye. I told her what the doctors said about Liz. That all anyone could do was to wait.

Tara shook her head and asked if there was anything she could do for Liz's family. Tara hadn't had a chance to talk with Liz the night of Jimmy's memorial. The thought of Liz never being able to meet Tara left an unexpected hole inside me.

"I heard the guy in the car, the one that smashed into the wall?" Tara looked past me through the window into the mirror image skyscraper across the street. Her words came out in a jumble as if to fill up the silence. "They say he was the lookout and a member of a neo-Nazi skinhead gang."

"Really? I hadn't heard." One of the frustrating things about last night was the lack of real news about the shootings. Uncle Mike wasn't in the mood to make calls to his contacts and when he did, he didn't find out much. I thought of Kubala, but he was too undisciplined. Not enough smarts to be involved in these murders. Then I thought about that group of skinheads at O'Connell's on Sunday. They'd left the bar shortly after Liz.

"What about the guys in the ambulance?" I asked.

"All part of the same gang," she said.

"Anything about the guys in the boxcar?" Uncle Mike had received a messenger at the hospital. The messenger confirmed that it was Burrascano's men in the boxcar and the maintenance truck—there to protect the gambling boss—who had laid in wait for a possible ambush and were present to greet the shooters in the ambulance. It was just as Uncle Mike and I had suspected.

I couldn't help but marvel at the firepower Burrascano's men had brought to the scene. But I couldn't tell Tara it was Burrascano's men or I'd reveal the connection Uncle Mike and I had to the Outfit's gambling boss.

"I'm not sure about the guys in the boxcar," she said. "I only heard about the skinheads through the officer from the precinct. You know one of those your uncle asked to watch over mom and me? They've all been so nice."

"Any particular cop?" There was more of an edge to my voice than I intended.

"Don't tell me you're jealous?" She came around the desk and threw her arms around my neck and gave me a peck on the cheek. "I missed you last night."

"Me, too."

"I do have some other news," she said. "I don't know if it's good news. Walsh wants to see you in his office."

Walsh wasn't doing layoffs in the conference room today but his office would work just as well if he wanted to fire me. The people at WagerEasy's home office could be scared off the deal with Thornton Racetrack due to the mass shootings in the parking lot. That alone might make me expendable.

Then there was the fact I'd decided to spout off to Arlene Adams and told her what to do. Walsh wasn't thrilled when I'd taken over the meeting.

Now that Walsh had been introduced to Travis Sloan, he didn't need me around for that anymore. By now, Walsh had probably found out about Uncle Mike and his connection to the police department. A relative of mine working for Sloan might constitute a conflict that would disqualify me from acting on WagerEasy's behalf on both the Thornton Racetrack deal and the Sloan Group deal.

My role as a PI looking into an alleged drug problem at WagerEasy was a joke.

The courtroom mess with Yuri Provost and Blick had been handled. Walsh wouldn't need me around to hold his hand.

And with Senator Brennan's decision to delay the state legislation to legalize sports betting, sitting down to do deals with small-time bookies seemed less urgent than it had before.

Walsh had cleaned up his loose ends. He didn't need me. But I still had to find the killers—the ones who gave the orders to the skinheads. I owed it to Jimmy, Oscar, and now Liz.

I walked into Walsh's office and shut the door behind me. He hung up the phone. "Have a seat, Eddie."

I took a quick look out the window at the view of the lake. It might be my last opportunity.

"Quite a day yesterday." Walsh took a deep breath. "I need you to clean out your office."

I hid any disappointment because he seemed to be studying me and maybe he wanted to see it in my face. I wouldn't give him the pleasure. "Fine."

The hint of a sly smile formed on Walsh's face. "The office next to mine has opened up. I haven't decided on your job title yet. I hope you don't mind."

I was shocked but managed to hide it. The guy was playing me. "Titles don't mean much."

"You've got that right. All they do is hold you back. I had no idea you had such strong connections to Travis Sloan."

What mattered to Walsh and to WagerEasy was the fact my uncle had sat down on the same side of the table as Travis Sloan. The foreign company had absorbed one of the most important local rules—connections mattered in Chicago.

"Those people back at home office are idiots. I always have to tell them how Chicago works." Walsh stood and began to pace behind his desk then stopped. A smile I'd never seen before lit up his face. "I'm the perfect person for the perfect job at the perfect time. I never thought I'd get where I've gotten. And now you have the chance to join me."

I'd heard similar words before. You had to be sure not to swallow the hook. I'd play along and butter him up. "Too bad your old man isn't here to see all that you've accomplished."

Walsh laughed. "That's right." He seemed to relish my reference to his old man.

"What about the sports betting bill?"

"A temporary setback. Nothing more. Our lobbyists have a handle on it." He sounded confident. He'd probably given the same spiel to home office.

"I think I mentioned this the other day. I'd like to take a look at Jimmy's gambling account with WagerEasy." My bet on Gypsum's football game had been a winner.

How much money had been in Jimmy's account before WagerEasy closed it? Over the years, Jimmy had made money. The cops had seized three-quarters of a million through the forfeiture proceeding.

How relevant was it to my investigation into the Blowtorch Murders? Tough to say. Maybe it was just one of those track life questions I needed to have answered.

"I'll ask our head of IT about it. We promise privacy on gambling accounts," Walsh said. "You know our employees really like the ability to make bets here at our Illinois location, but our in-house counsel is nervous about it. Technically, it might get the company into hot water since Illinois hasn't passed legalization yet. With the publicity over the murders, the company really wants to keep that quiet."

"I can understand." Maybe this wasn't the time to press my luck.

"I got a report that you've taken advantage of our little perk and made a sports bet yesterday," Walsh said.

Did Walsh get a report on each employee or only me? It seemed privacy was only a concern for Walsh and WagerEasy when it served their purposes. "Yeah, I thought I'd get my feet wet."

"How'd you pick that game? It's a small conference that never gets any TV coverage." Walsh studied me again. I was supposed to pump him for information, not the other way around.

Maybe Jimmy had focused on that game based on inside information and my bet had alerted people back at WagerEasy's home office. I took the cautious route. "I always think a play on these small college games offers the best value."

"I see," Walsh's Adam's apple bobbed along his scrawny turkey neck. He'd swallowed hard. I'd played enough poker to know he didn't believe me.

"There aren't a lot of games available on Thursday night."

Walsh grunted and scratched the back of his finely-groomed hair. "We'll give the drug investigation within the office a rest. Right now, we need to concentrate on these deals with Thornton Racetrack and the Sloan Group. I need you to follow up on what you said yesterday. I don't want Arlene Adams to walk around the track during the races and not see a face from WagerEasy. That means you and Tara need to attend the races nightly."

I hadn't been ordered by an employer to attend the races before. I kind of liked the idea. Maybe they'd bankroll me. I agreed to the task.

"Great." Walsh clapped his hands. "Let's keep up the pressure. Can we do these meetings with bookies out at Thornton Racetrack? That will really get under Sloan's skin."

Putting pressure on Sloan played into my hands. But Sloan was a stone-cold killer and wouldn't appreciate me trying to poach his bookies.

"The bookies aren't stupid," I said. "They know they're playing both sides of the street. They want to keep their Sloan Group option open and talk to us at the same time. They're nervous."

"Why don't we meet with the bookies in the same place we met with Arlene Adams?" Walsh said. "That will give us some privacy."

"Good idea. That way we can stay in Sloan's face but make the bookies feel comfortable." I'd also learn a lot more from the bookies if Sloan wasn't able to overhear our discussions. The chamber under the grandstands would be perfect.

"I owe Arlene a call. I'll mention the meeting place and see if it can be made available. I assume you'll set up meetings tonight and over the weekend? My wife and I will be out of town, but keep me up to date."

I didn't believe Walsh. He was probably meeting with Blick. The two of them were up to something. "Are we close to a deal with Arlene?"

"It's always day to day on these negotiations. The Stats deal took forever so I assume this deal with Thornton will go the same way."

According to Irv's financial docs, Walsh had bet what was left of his wife's inheritance on the StatsRUs deal. He'd also mortgaged that Winnetka palace. Thanks to the merger, Walsh now had a big chunk of WagerEasy stock. He could sell a portion of it after a waiting period, pay off the debt, and still have a huge equity stake. Be an owner, his old man said.

"I think we're going to do great things," Walsh said.

I stood and reached out to shake hands. He must know by now that Uncle Mike once worked homicide. I had the feeling Walsh planned to do great things with Blick. I was simply a "temporary setback" like the delay in the passage of the sports betting bill.

33

WHEN I SETTLED INTO MY NEW OFFICE BESIDE WALSH, I received a packet of non-disclosure agreements that made Irv's docs appear skimpy in comparison.

The foot-high pile that I had to sign ensured that employees kept their mouths shut about WagerEasy's affairs. When I was first hired as a PI, Walsh probably didn't think it'd be necessary for me to sign these NDAs. Did I make Walsh nervous by the idealistic way I'd talked yesterday at the meeting with Arlene Adams? Saving small racetracks might be the kind of revolutionary talk that would make a boss want a stack of non-disclosure agreements signed as insurance.

Or maybe it was that sports bet I'd made. Walsh had asked me questions and said how home office was nervous about their little in-house perk that allowed out of state employees to use the New Jersey website. Irv said these non-disclosure agreements kept their employees from talking out of school. I read a few paragraphs. My failure to abide by the promises and representations might result in the loss of my firstborn.

Many of the docs dealt with StatsRUs and provided that I could only use information for its intended purpose and not as part of any wager. Fair enough, but it did make me think about the merger.

Through Irv's digging, I'd learned that Walsh had had a large, hidden ownership stake in StatsRUs. That made sense since Walsh couldn't wait to give certain employees the ax and bring in the stats employees.

Other companies had competed for StatsRUs and the data they could stream to gamblers on a single platform for online wagering and data. Every online sports betting provider wanted that edge.

Much of the information was available through the leagues or by hiring an out of work sports junkie to sit in the crowd and keep a record of the game, but maybe there was more to it. Gamblers could never get enough information and that was why Jimmy the Leech was the Leech.

Several stacks of documents were devoted to subsidiaries of WagerEasy and StatsRUs. One was a company named LRL Corporation.

Jimmy had recently cut a personal check to LRL Corporation in the amount of forty-nine thousand-dollars. Since when did Jimmy spend that kind of money if it wasn't attached to a well-researched wager? I made a mental note to ask Irv to follow up on this obscure company.

After I'd gotten writer's cramp and finished signing the pile, I called in Tara to assure her we were still a team.

Since the office door was closed, she took a seat on the edge of my desk and smiled down at me, her hair falling around her face. "I'm grateful to avoid the ax for another week." A mischievous smile played on those lips, but I resisted the urge to take her in my arms.

"You've been ordered to attend the races nightly with me. Walsh thinks it will help convince Arlene to choose the WagerEasy way."

"Jeesh, you even talk like an executive."

I did. "Can you get me a list of the new Stats people? I need to get up to speed fast."

"Sure. A lot of bookies are calling in for appointments," Tara said. "They're now forwarding the calls to us."

The merger with StatsRUs had made headlines and made WagerEasy look like a company with deep pockets that was ready to deal. "I thought Larsen's department was fielding those calls."

Tara brushed back her hair, her lips turned downward. "I'm sorry to report that Larsen is packing a box."

I cussed. I didn't like to hear about anyone losing their job. Even Larsen. Was it the way she mishandled those deals with small-time bookies or something else? According to Tara, Larsen had plenty of connections to outside law firms used by WagerEasy. Maybe Larsen knew too much.

"She actually hugged me. Can you believe that?" Tara shook her head. "I'll miss her."

———

Tara had gotten me the list of StatsRUs employees that now occupied our office. One of them caught my attention immediately. It was Somer Fitzhugh. Coach Fitz.

Why had Blick made such a big deal to Walsh about delivering Coach Fitz? The fact that Blick had met with Coach Fitz in the alehouse just prior to Blick meeting up with Walsh's limo in the parking garage piqued my interest. Jimmy had kept the employment records of Coach Fitz in the box. Why?

It seemed too easy. I thought I'd have to dig up Coach Fitz out of the back of a college locker room. He was always an assistant coach, never the highly paid head coach. Rumors circulated that he drank and womanized and treated players like cattle, but everywhere he went a bad defense turned into the strength of the team.

One coach said, "Whenever I think our program is getting lackadaisical and going through the motions on the heels of a great year, I call in Coach Fitz. He's old-school but there's a reason old-school works. He's sort of the John Wayne of football."

Coach Fitz had been assigned my old office. The door was open. I knocked and a raspy voice shouted to come in.

I told him I wanted to introduce myself. How I had recently occupied his office and now moved up to take the office beside Walsh. Coach Fitz stood and came around the desk to shake my hand. He was a big man, close to my height, but carried almost three-hundred pounds. An All-American defensive tackle at State back in the eighties and his grip still showed strength.

"I decided to go where the real money is," Coach Fitz said, laughing, his bushy mustache twitching and bloodshot eyes gleaming. "I hear you made an impression on the owner of

Thornton Racetrack. Good. WagerEasy needs that deal and a physical site."

"Got lucky," I said.

"I hear you've also got ties to the Sloan Group. They're connected to a ton of big-money bettors. The ones we need."

"My uncle is working with Sloan as a consultant."

Coach Fitz shut the door and then walked around the desk to his seat. "It's good to have friends. I'd still be riding a blocking sled back in Jersey if not for my connections. I'm sort of a go-between like you. People in the college ranks trust me."

We'd be friends and make connections within WagerEasy. It suited me. I took a seat. "Fill me in, coach. I know StatsRUs will channel data for the bettors to access when they bet online, but what else does it offer?"

"You mean, why did the StatsRUs deal cost an arm and a leg? Hell, if I know. All I do is my job and let all these executives figure everything else out."

The coach liked to hear himself talk. I cast out a line to see if he'd bite. "Walsh told me about what you do, but I'm not sure how you—"

He waved a hand in my direction. "How we get the programs to sign up? At first, it wasn't easy but once you get one or two signed up, everybody's afraid not to do it. You see these head coaches get paid astronomical salaries and all they have to do is win to stick around. It's an easy gig if they don't screw up."

But what were they signing up for? "Is it like knocking down the dominos?"

"I didn't say that," he laughed. "But, yeah, it is. Don't tell Walsh it's easy. He'll find an intern to do my job. The coaches want to know what their players are doing. These dumb underclassmen get to school and are away from home for the first time and all they want to do is party their ass off all night. When the coach can upload the info and find out their blood alcohol level, he can address the issue. Scares the bejesus out of those punks."

That sounded like Big Brother and I found it outrageous but I acted as if I bought into it.

"The colleges are willing to pay?" I didn't have any understanding of the product Coach Fitz sold. Was it a breathalyzer or a wearable like the fitness tracker? It reminded me of those medical reports on players that Uncle Mike tossed out.

"Oh, yeah. The programs have budgets you wouldn't believe. They pay top dollar for our product—and whammo— all the player's info is right there on the coach's computer screen. All the ABD you need. It's ten times more dependable than those others."

I nodded and tried to act as if I knew what "ABD" meant. "Dependability is the key, right?"

"Any kid squawks and they threaten to take his scholarship. One of these days they'll improve the things and look out. Coaches will be swamped with data. Hell, they'll need a dozen tech nerds to stay on top of it."

I needed to know the coach's connection to Blick. "Do you know a Reynolds Blick? Walsh has mentioned him—"

Coach Fitz's eyes turned to slits. "Blick? Naw, don't know him."

I'd screwed up.

Coach Fitz talked fast before I could ask more about Blick or medical reports. "But I know Walsh's old man. He was that college football announcer, Ivan Novitzky. Did all the big games until his heart attack in the late nineties. The guy could drink me under the table. He got Walsh his job at the sports channel, but the kid didn't have the charisma of the old man, know what I mean? Say, when do we go to lunch around here?"

If Blick was simply a board member of the Alliance to Prevent Gambling Addiction with industry contacts as Walsh had claimed, then why would Coach Fitz deny he knew Blick?

Coach Fitz's demeanor changed. I asked a few more questions and he evaded each one. Maybe a few beers would restore the old coach's mood.

I said, "I haven't been there for a while, but there's an alehouse around the corner that serves decent corned beef."

That seemed to change his mood. "Great, Eddie. I could use a beer."

34

I HATED HOSPITALS LIKE EVERYONE ELSE BUT AT LEAST LATE Friday afternoon was not quite as bad as other times.

Although the staff worked eighteen-hour shifts, there was more of a laid-back vibe to Friday. The staff needed a breather as much as anyone else. Even though they remained on alert, there was a bounce to their step and a wider smile to offer as I passed them in the hall. Maybe they were thinking about the other life that awaited them outside these walls.

Uncle Mike had filled me in on the full litany of Liz's medical details.

The nurse allowed me to sit for a short while beside Liz, her breath rising in tandem with the blip of machines. Tubes ran in and out of more machines. I offered up a few prayers.

It was tough. I expected her to smile and wink at me any second as if it was a practical joke. Only a few of us knew the kind of job she did serving the public. She put herself on the line and none of those police corruption headlines could take away from her years of service. We owed public servants like Liz big time.

I thought of her at the scene of the Blowtorch Murders taking charge, deconstructing the evil art. The way she'd taken Jimmy's body into her care not only for the sake of evidence but out of respect. The way she accepted the investigation, the duty, and would do whatever it took to find Jimmy's killer despite her upcoming retirement and her husband's illness.

My mind ran down those past investigations I'd done with Liz and Uncle Mike. I was just along for the ride at first, but more and more I became a part of things and tried to provide what assistance I could.

Maybe all these thoughts were sentimental prayers, nothing more.

The police had the dead skinheads to point to as the killers. The fact the skinhead killers had been fried in the ambulance and signal car seemed like justice.

The heroes, the unknown killers of the skinheads, weren't at the top of the list for the police to capture and no one could blame them. Uncle Mike had received confirmation that the killers of the skinheads were, in fact, Burrascano's men. Uncle Mike felt that Burrascano's men had acted in self-defense but others might see it differently

Uncle Mike had tried to contact Burrascano to discuss his meetings with Sloan and DiNatale. So far, Burrascano hadn't returned my uncle's call, and during an investigation, he always returned calls promptly. It felt like we were working without a net.

I looked down at Liz, the person who had taught me so much. She'd always had time for me. "Hi, Liz. It's me, Eddie." I made the sign of the cross. "Get better. My uncle needs you. We all need you."

The nurse came by and whispered that it was time. She checked the machines and told me that other family members were in the cafeteria.

I nodded and thanked her. Instead of the cafeteria, I took the back exit.

———

Outside the hospital, I breathed in the bus fumes, listened to the traffic noise, stepped in the slush, and let the wind and snow flurries slap me in the face, and reveled in all of it. Nothing antiseptic out here. I couldn't help but see the world in a different light, and for a moment, thoughts of murder, and suspects, and all the loose ends, disappeared.

I even managed to forget about Coach Fitz and our unproductive lunch. The beers didn't loosen the coach's tongue about the products StatsRUs sold to college programs. I should've never mentioned Blick to the coach.

I had looked up ABD, or athlete biometric data. It meant the metrics of an athlete's medical characteristics during the performance of a game or workout, including a measure of the oxygen intake and heart rate. Measurements taken during peak levels could indicate if an athlete was in top shape, and according to Coach Fitz, it was what each college coach wanted.

"Eddie," a voice called.

I looked up and down the street and at the bus stop but saw no one.

"Eddie O'Connell," a voice croaked.

I turned. Twenty or thirty yards away, tucked into intersecting concrete walls beneath an overhang, stood a woman. It was the employee smoker's lair, a place provided by the hospital, out of sight of patients, passers-by, and visitors, where nurses and doctors could puff in anonymity to avoid controversy over the health effects of the smoking habit.

I recognized the person huddled against the cold. She waved me over.

"Hello, Ms. St. Clair," I said.

"You've been up to see Liz?" Her voice trembled and her eyes had lost that mischievous spark. She seemed hopeful then saw my downward glance. Every second of every day loved ones kept hope alive. St. Clair must've hoped I had miracle news about Liz.

"Yeah. Just leaving," I said.

"I hate to see her like this." St. Clair took a vengeful drag on her cigarette.

"The nurse said the family is in the cafeteria." You try to convey any information you can to be helpful. It felt lame.

"Thanks for coming. I know she'd appreciate it. It just so happens I needed to see you. I talked to your uncle earlier today. He says you two are working the case from another angle."

We stood together but looked out at the street. People stood at the bus stop within a glass-enclosed shelter and took turns stepping out into the snow to glance around the street corner to catch sight of the next bus. Some of the people waiting wore hospital scrubs beneath winter coats.

"Yeah, you know what we do." I didn't want to get her hopes up about our investigation. She'd talked to Liz on a weekly basis for years, and Uncle Mike had told me that Liz probably picked up on information off the street about the jobs we did for Burrascano. Since Liz and St. Clair were close, I assumed the criminal attorney knew.

"I just want you to know it's appreciated," St. Clair said.

She seemed smaller here huddled into the concrete crevice.

"I still talk to Liz," she said. "She's still my crutch."

She pulled out another cigarette and turned toward the blackened concrete of the adjoining walls to shield the flame from the wind. It took several flicks of the lighter before she got it lit.

"I was lucky on the Yuri Provost case the other day," she continued, exhaling smoke and putting her gloves back on. "You came through when no else could. You were the only one who thought Yuri had taken the video or maybe the only one willing to go out there and ask her for it."

"I'm not as smart as others."

She laughed then coughed. "You got Walsh to the courtroom. That subpoena would've never held up and the DA was counting on Walsh's failure to appear. Then they could argue my late motion was nothing more than a delay tactic and the witness should be excluded."

"Walsh loved doing his civic duty."

"I could tell."

"You made a great move getting the television crew to show up," I said.

"And you got Blick to blow his top." She laughed, and took a drag, and waited for a truck to churn through its gears on the busy street. "I realize things don't always go right in the courtroom. Like your mother. I'm sorry."

"No reason to be sorry," I said.

"I could've avoided bringing it up the day we met."

"At least we got justice." Joey L had ordered my mother's killer to be dragged behind a shrimp trawler off the coast of Mexico. The sharks followed and the screams of Childress were lost in the waves. I'd imagined the entire scene many times.

St. Clair smoked and wheezed. The blowing snow covered parts of her stocking cap and glistened on her eyelashes. "Yuri Provost is grateful too."

"She walked. Blick wasn't a victim, Yuri was."

St. Clair cleared her throat. "If I told you Yuri would like to thank you personally, would you go to her?"

I turned and studied St. Clair. The message was clear. Yuri Provost knew something. But St. Clair couldn't talk about privileged information.

"I'll do that. Thanks."

35

AN HOUR OR TWO LATER, UNCLE MIKE AND I DROVE TO THE offices of Yuri Provost out on the near west side. I'd told him what St. Clair had told me, and he agreed that Yuri must know something. It could be the piece of the puzzle we needed to unlock the investigation. I watched for a tail. Kubala might try something in Yuri's neighborhood. Random shootings happened there every day.

I drove Uncle Mike's truck as we inched along the Eisenhower Expressway in the Friday evening rush hour. My cell buzzed. It was a call from Irv.

"Hey, Eddie," Irv said. "I'm getting back to you with info on LRC Corporation. As you know, Golding sent them a check for 49K."

"Great. Let me put you on speaker. My uncle is in the truck with me." Last night I had a fleeting thought that LRC probably handled retirement funds for WagerEasy, and Jimmy had sent in a check for forty-nine grand as a contribution into his retirement account. Then I almost laughed myself silly. Jimmy planning retirement? The guy kept his bankroll for gambling, not the future.

"Let me get right to it," Irv said. "This is one interesting little company. If the company's officer walked into my office and asked me to do the corporate taxes, I'd kick his keister down the stairs. Holy shit. Lots of us here have looked at it. It started as a shell in Nevada then moved to Costa Rica and then back again. It has reported a lot of losses so the monies coming through now don't show a profit. The bank account is offshore and out of reach. StatsRUs was loosely run and made no mention of LRC in its latest filings. All the people connected with LRC's corporate filings are seedy Vegas lawyers. You got any real information on this company?"

"I don't know what more I can tell you." I'd asked people around the office about LRC, but nobody could tell me anything.

"We'll keep digging," Irv said. "Sometimes these shell companies have layers and we need to find the common thread. A Vegas attorney did work for both LRC and StatsRUs, and we've got a call into him. He owes a friend of mine a favor."

"How big was the StatsRUs deal for WagerEasy?" I asked. "WagerEasy had the deal with Burrascano. Could WagerEasy do two deals of that magnitude at the same time?"

"We dug into it. I don't know of a banker who would allow both those deals at least until things stabilized financially. The StatsRUs deal was too big." Irv said.

"What about those products Coach Fitz is selling?" I had called Irv earlier about them.

"We're still looking into that. StatsRUs supplies data to sports bettors," Irv said. "The fight over data is unreal. The pro leagues want each state to make it mandatory that their data be used exclusively so they can charge for it."

"Everyone wants their piece," I said.

"Those financials you gave us, Eddie. I don't know where you got them, and I won't ask. But if they're legit, somebody is in big trouble."

"What about them?" Uncle Mike asked.

"They show a much lower value for the assets of StatsRUs. If these financials are the real thing, and our initial review shows they are, then someone was cooking the books and WagerEasy overpaid for StatsRUs."

It meant Walsh profited even more from the StatsRUs sale due to his large stake in StatsRUs. If Jimmy had planned to expose Walsh, it could be another motive for murder.

I ended the call and told Uncle Mike my theory about the financials and how they implicated Walsh.

"I like it, but we need a lot more evidence to prove that kind of white-collar fraud. I also like the fact your friend's check for forty-nine thousand ends up in an offshore account. Why would Jimmy funnel money into an offshore account? Interesting."

"What about Liz?" I asked.

"What do you mean?"

"C'mon, Uncle Mike. Those medical reports on players? You read about it in a magazine—what the hell?"

I glanced over. Uncle Mike studied the tip of his cigar. "You don't let anything get by you, do you? Yeah, Liz swore me to secrecy. All that political crap going on at the department, you know. I filled her in on what we had. But as things stand right now—"

"That's right. Liz in a coma. Everything's heating up. I think Coach Fitz is selling products to coaches that provide a player's up-to-date medical information. StatsRUs is now part of WagerEasy."

Uncle Mike nodded. "Damn. That's what Liz thought. She heard the feds have an investigation going into StatsRUs but she doesn't know what it's all about."

"Nothing more on the actual product?"

"That's all she had on StatsRUs. Nothing on LRC or doctoring those financials."

"But she had something else?"

"Liz has a cop who identified Burrascano's limo leaving the scene. That's why the interview was so important."

We were the only vehicle to take the Independence Boulevard exit off the Eisenhower Expressway into the North Lawndale neighborhood. We just needed to stay alert, and we'd be fine. It was a whole lot worse in the summer when people were outside looking for trouble.

"Still no word from Burrascano?" I asked

"Nope." Uncle Mike puffed on the cigar; the window cracked open.

We continued to work without a net. I stopped at a red light near a corner bar. A couple of young men watched us and then several more men came outside. The light turned green and I accelerated slowly. I heard the muffled voice of a man calling out to us to stop.

"Keep going," Uncle Mike said.

I kept an eye on the rearview mirror. "Walsh said how important the StatsRUs deal was. How it would make WagerEasy first-in-class. He couldn't wait to get those people into the office, and according to Irv, he owns a good percentage of StatsRUs. He must've been involved in cooking the books. Maybe Walsh and Jimmy had a power struggle going at WagerEasy and that's why Walsh hired the skinheads to do the Blowtorch Murders."

"Watch these two." Uncle Mike pulled his gun from the shoulder holster.

Two men with handguns at their side studied our vehicle as we passed. I kept the same pace, both hands on the wheel in case I had to execute an evasive maneuver.

"You think Walsh knew about Jimmy's deal with Burrascano?" Uncle Mike asked.

"Yes. Walsh talked about his old man when we were waiting around Wednesday in court. He said that his old man would've appreciated a deal with the mob." Walsh had been beaten down that day waiting around at court when he let it slip.

"For the sake of argument, why does Walsh make another attempt to frame Burrascano?" Uncle Mike asked.

"Walsh found out about the meeting between Burrascano and Liz. He's probably got informants in the department. Maybe he thought Liz had evidence that would lead Burrascano to finger Walsh. Maybe Walsh began to fear for his life."

"If Burrascano comes after you, you better move to Tierra del Fuego," Uncle Mike said. "A frame would also be a way for Walsh to clean up loose ends. Then the cops chase Burrascano and that keeps Burrascano busy."

"I heard the guys in the ambulance were a skinhead gang," I said.

"Yeah. I just heard that, too. I'm spending too much time in the hospital. The feds took over the investigation as you know. The experts say the orders came from the skinhead leaders who are doing a long prison stretch downstate. So far, no one's talking."

Liz's shooting had done a number on Uncle Mike. Usually, he was on top of everything, and with his contacts, he was usually up to date every minute.

"We can't forget about Travis Sloan," Uncle Mike said. "He has motivation too. He thinks his bookie group has some good years left before legalization, and he wouldn't want the high-roller list sold. So, he'd be motivated to frame Burrascano not once but twice to get him out of the way."

"That way Sloan can deal with his buddy, DiNatale. How did Sloan take yesterday's meeting with Arlene Adams?"

"He's pissed. And he's pissed at DiNatale," Uncle Mike said. "He really wants that track deal. Not only to fuck WagerEasy but to use it as a front."

It warmed my heart to hear about DiNatale's trouble with Sloan. "This is Yuri's place up here. Looked a lot better in the daytime."

We had called ahead so one of Yuri's men checked us into the parking lot tucked behind Yuri's building. I parked, and we went inside.

Yuri's bodyguard entered the office as before. He frisked me and then turned to Uncle Mike. "I'm sorry, Mr. O'Connell."

"That's okay," Uncle Mike said, raising his arms.

The ex-cop bodyguard inspected our weapons and then handed them back to us.

"Guns are needed around here," the bodyguard said. "Ms. Provost will be out in a minute." He walked out of the office.

We settled into the chairs in front of the desk and waited.

"Quite the operation Yuri has out here," Uncle Mike said. We had passed the busy chop shop across that street. People were working overtime.

"You know that guy?" I asked referring to the ex-cop bodyguard.

"Sure, but I can't remember his name. He seemed a bit embarrassed to be doing this job. I didn't want to make a big deal."

Yuri walked in and stood beside the desk. After preliminary introductions, she said, "Thank you, gentlemen, for coming out to see me on this rotten night. I would've met you at a bar downtown, but as you know I'm not welcome or expected in those kinds of places. Also, certain people in the department still want me doing a long stretch behind bars and feel I cheated the system. You'll excuse me if I stay in my safety zone."

"No problem," I said.

Yuri leaned back against the desk and stared up at the ceiling for a moment, and then rubbed her eyes with both hands. Then she stared at Uncle Mike. "I've heard about you, Mike O'Connell. You and your partner, Liz, are well known. Mothers and fathers in the neighborhood know your names. You two worked every murder case the same way. Thanks." A smile lighted her features.

"Appreciate it," Uncle Mike said.

I wondered just how many victims she knew.

"Eddie, I didn't give you a chance in hell of finding any witness willing to come forward on my case," Yuri said.

"The cops didn't ask Walsh for a statement at the scene of your fight with Blick," I said. I couldn't help but stare at Yuri's boots. The boots that kicked Blick's ass.

"Extend my thanks to Mr. Walsh if you see him," she said. "I don't help cops. But Ms. St. Clair's childhood friend was shot, and she said I could trust you two."

I nodded. My heart thumped in my chest.

"Liz is St. Clair's oldest friend and was my partner in the department for twenty years," Uncle Mike said.

"Damn." Yuri took a deep breath. "Okay. The night of my altercation, I was there to meet someone. To do a job. I didn't know what that job would be, but I was told it would pay big money."

"That's why you went to the bar?" I asked.

"Yeah. But then nobody contacted me. Maybe because I got into that fight with the motherfucker and got arrested."

"What time were you to meet?" I asked.

"Ten o'clock. As you know from the court files, the fight happened just before ten," she said.

"How did this person hear about you?" I asked.

"The dark web, baby. It's a place for ugly stuff. One time we got paid to set up a protest. One company hitting back at their rival. I don't do murder for hire. Never," she said. "We set up a phone call. Burner phones. He called me. No names. Just agreed to meet."

"When you talked with the man on the phone, was he surprised you were a woman?" I asked.

Yuri shook her head. "Nope. I use a voice changer."

"Would you recognize the guy's voice?" Uncle Mike asked. "Or did he use a voice changer too?"

"No, no voice changer. Would I recognize his voice? That's tough. Maybe."

"Did he have an accent?" I asked. "A southern drawl?" I thought of Sloan.

"No," she said. "That I would've remembered."

"How about an eastern accent. Boston?" I asked thinking of Walsh.

"Could be," Yuri said. "I do remember something. He said the overnight change in sports betting laws meant a bonanza for certain people."

"Those were his exact words?" I asked. "He used the word 'bonanza?'"

"Yup," Yuri said. "Should've tipped me off something was fucked up."

It wasn't much. But it was something and we had to find a way to use it.

36

THE WORD "BONANZA" SOUNDED LIKE A WORD SLOAN might use, but he didn't want legalization. Uncle Mike and I rode silently down the expressway on the way back from our meeting with Yuri Provost. We'd thought we were close to breaking the case and then came up short. We hid our disappointment as I made maneuvers to see if we were being followed.

We were headed to Thornton Racetrack for my Friday night WagerEasy job that included meetings with bookies. Uncle Mike wanted to check things out and stay in the game. He sensed that Sloan had been giving him menial jobs to force him to the sidelines. Maybe Sloan began to have trust issues with Uncle Mike when I turned out to be WagerEasy's Most Valuable Player.

"Put yourself in Sloan's shoes," I said. "If not for legalization, Burrascano wouldn't let the Dallas Marlboro Man within three-hundred miles of Chicago."

"Never in a million years. Sloan is talking to bookies. Guys who pay street tax to Burrascano."

"Even though Sloan doesn't want legalization it's a bonanza for him."

Uncle Mike puffed on the cigar and filled the cab with smoke before it streamed out the crack in the window. "And if DiNatale wants to use the opportunity to put succession on the fast track—"

"He and Sloan get together to frame Burrascano."

"Yeah. But DiNatale was with Burrascano at the scene of your buddy's murder and helped Burrascano escape."

"You said Liz had a cop that identified Burrascano's limo—"

"Right."

"Burrascano's limo just happens to drive past the one cop who just happens to get a 'make' on the gambling boss's vehicle?"

"C'mon, Eddie. Not all cops on the force are on the take for Christ's sake."

"I know, I know. But if this particular cop is on DiNatale's payroll."

"I get it. DiNatale has good cover as the hero who gets Burrascano's ass out of the frame-up at the murder scene. Then one cop—out of all the cops dropping a net around the perimeter—one cop saw the limo and tells Liz. I'm liking this. If DiNatale and Sloan orchestrated things, then Yuri's dark web job wouldn't have anything to do with the Blowtorch Murders?"

"Maybe. Maybe not. Sloan could've been at the conference as well. A lot of illegal bookies were at the conference."

"The conference was in May and the murders didn't happen until last Thursday."

"Jimmy's negotiations on behalf of WagerEasy with Burrascano were on again and off again. Burrascano said he didn't know if things would come together or not, right?"

"Right."

"I can't give up on Walsh and Blick either."

"Right."

"Let's say they planned to meet Yuri, and let's say they show up to the restaurant expecting to meet with a Russian badass. Instead, a black woman is there."

"And they had no idea who Yuri Provost actually was before the meeting?"

"I didn't know when I went to meet her on the criminal case. She doesn't exactly have a website."

"Then what?"

"Blick, being a racist, tells Walsh he doesn't want to use her for the job. They argue about it. Blick says something too loud, uses a racial slur, and that gets Yuri's attention. Things escalate from there."

"Blick gets his ass kicked. Good."

"Blick and Walsh are back at square one. They've got to find somebody else to do the dirty work. Blick decides to go to the skinheads. They fit his white supremacist outlook. They're happy to take his money for a quick hour's work. They're known for their silence."

"And Sloan and his new pal, DiNatale?"

"If Sloan was at the restaurant to meet Yuri, maybe he decides to use somebody else after Yuri gets led away in handcuffs. Or maybe DiNatale tells Sloan there's been a delay. DiNatale can't use his own people for the Blowtorch Murders so he goes to the skinheads. Then he wipes out the skinheads yesterday at the track to cover things up."

"Damn. That's too good."

"Let's take another look at that video of the fight."

37

At the track, Uncle Mike and I stopped at the admission's stand and asked if we could talk to someone in the office. We explained the arrangement set up by Walsh with Arlene Adams to allow WagerEasy access to the chamber beneath the grandstands. The Thornton employee made the call, and then we explained things again. The person in the front office knew about it and said we could meet a security guard at the escalator.

I bought a racing program at the stand and walked up the stairs with Uncle Mike.

At the top of the stairs, Uncle Mike turned to me. We stood alone off to the side waiting for the guard. "What the hell, Eddie. You're going to play the horses?"

Jimmy the Leech had a couple of horses running tonight. A horse in a later race named Figure Time had caught my attention. It would be at good odds. How could I explain what

I needed to do? That I needed to make a bet for my murdered friend? Would Uncle Mike buy that? I'm not sure I did. Maybe it was just another excuse to gamble. No, it was for Jimmy. The risk I took making myself a target for the killer outweighed any risk of losing a few bucks on wagers. Gambler logic at its finest.

"I do have a couple of horses I plan to play."

Uncle Mike shot me a look of disgust. His Irish temper flared. "I've heard from the detectives on Oscar's case and you're a prime suspect."

"What the fuck?"

"The cops found Oscar's hidden ledgers and that you owed Oscar money. You made a payment to him last Sunday? Oscar doesn't extend such a fat credit line to any of the sports bettors at O'Connell's, except you. Oscar gives you special treatment and then ends up dead in our parking lot? What the fuck, Eddie? Haven't we been down this road before with your gambling? When are you going to wise up, for Christ's sake?"

How many times had I told Uncle Mike I wouldn't bet on sports again because of the previous debt I'd incurred? Uncle Mike had gone to bat for me with Joey L on that one after Oscar had turned my debt over to the mob. We'd managed to get the prior debt worked out.

"Yes, I do owe Oscar," I said. "I did it again, ran up a debt."

"Damn it, Eddie. You've got a real problem. I thought you learned your lesson."

"One of the reasons I met with Oscar last Sunday was to get information on Sloan. Oscar planned to meet with Sloan and probably refused to join his network of bookies."

"Maybe Oscar's murder is more important than we thought." Uncle Mike ignored my half-ass apology. "The detectives want a statement from you. Your time is running short. They've only agreed to wait until tomorrow as a courtesy to me. You know what the criminal lawyer costs."

"Somebody tried to frame my dumb ass. Sound familiar?" The killer's hot breath singed the back of my neck. I started out working at WagerEasy as the imposter, took a job standing in Jimmy's shoes, and had caught the killer's attention. I didn't want to end up like Jimmy.

"Yup. It's the killer." Uncle Mike gave me a sideways look. "A murder and an attempted frame-up. When they killed your friend, Jimmy, it was also a way to frame Burrascano. They like a two-for-one. They shoot Liz to try and frame Burrascano a second time. When they killed Oscar, they tried to frame you. A *twofer*—the killer's signature. The killer has you in his sights."

"It means we're getting close," I said.

Uncle Mike looked around once again to be sure no one could overhear us. "I told you Sloan plans to be at the track tonight, didn't I?"

"Yeah."

"You plan to set up shop to talk deals with bookies on behalf of WagerEasy, right? That makes you a perfect target to get killed by Sloan. Meeting with bookies will piss off Sloan. Plus, Sloan hates the fact WagerEasy wants to do a deal with Thornton Racetrack. You're Arlene's golden boy and I'll be the dumbass sitting next to you."

"The plan was to pressure these guys," I said.

"Good. It might be the only way to crack this case. I want to get the guy who shot Liz. We don't have a hell of a lot of time. I'll put in a call to a couple of friends. We might need backup."

It couldn't hurt.

38

AFTER A LONG WAIT, A WHITE-HAIRED MAN IN A TRACK
security uniform met us. He unlocked the padlock, slipped off
the chain, and led us up the four flights of stairs bordered by
the broken escalator, toward the area beneath the grandstands.

"I still can't believe it," Uncle Mike said as we walked up
the wide staircase. "This used to be filled every night. This darn
leg. I wish the escalator wasn't out of order."

I took notice of the scuff marks on the stairs. How many
horseplayers had made this trek over the years?

We followed the old security guard into the dark chamber
where we'd met with Arlene Adams the day before.

"I don't know why you want to come in here," the guard
said. "I told them to turn on the heat this afternoon, but I can't
help you with the lights. The lights over that table work, but a
fuse blew on the other bank of lights and we've got it on order.

You can't find our old electronic stuff at the hardware store. Been out of date for years."

The track announcer's voice pierced the darkness. "Ladies and gentlemen, here are the late changes for tonight's card."

We listened for a moment. The voice seemed to call out over my shoulder and echoed throughout the cavernous room. At the far end, where Jimmy the Leech once ruled, the bar dissolved into shadows, except for parts of the brass railing that reflected a shaft of light from the doorway.

"The lights were on yesterday," Uncle Mike told the security guard.

"The day of the shootings?" The old man asked. "We came in here with the police later to be sure no one was hiding and they started to flicker. I think they called in an electrician earlier today. God knows when they'll get out here."

"I guess it doesn't matter when since Thornton doesn't expect racing fans to come up here anyway." I wanted to check out the view of the track. "Can we open one of these doors to the cheap seats outside?"

"Sure." He made a show of his key ring, jangling the keys like pocket change. "I might have to try a few of these." He went to work on the padlock that secured a chain.

Uncle Mike said, "You're going to play the races?"

"These bookies I plan to meet like the action. If they're forced to run out of our meeting to watch a race, it makes our talks more difficult."

"Makes sense. You dealmakers think of everything."

"Okay," the security guard said. "I've got the key. Sorry about the televisions in here. They need to be programmed, and we only bother to do that for the thoroughbreds, not the harness races."

Uncle Mike and I stared at one of the many closed-circuit televisions mounted around the space and the dark screens as if to confirm what the guard had said. I didn't like being unable to see the odds as they fluctuated on an upcoming race but sacrifices would need to be made.

A voice crackled over the guard's walkie-talkie and he answered it. "Be right there." He turned to us. "Got to go. A drunk and disorderly out by the finish line. Some things never change. Let me know if you need anything else."

Uncle Mike waited until the guard walked out then pointed to the palm of his hand, a gesture to mimic cell phone usage so we could replay the video of the night of Yuri's altercation with Blick.

"Hold it," I said. I stepped on the chair and then onto the table to reach up to the beam running past the TV. "Somebody planted a device here before our meeting with Arlene Adams." I used my penknife to pry it loose and then dismantled what appeared to be a camera, the type you see in casinos. "I figured it was Burrascano."

"Or maybe Sloan," Uncle Mike said.

"Whoever it was, we don't want them." I hopped down off the table and examined other beams nearby. "Maybe Walsh had the same idea. I'll check around." It had been Walsh's idea for me to work here tonight. I took a mini-tour around the perimeter, glanced behind the bar and the vacant concession areas.

"Satisfied?" Uncle Mike asked. "There was a padlock on the door."

I took a seat beside Uncle Mike at the table and pulled up the security video Yuri had stolen from The Point Spread the night of the fight with Blick.

The video displayed four separate boxes. Each box showed a different part of The Point Spread Restaurant.

"Five minutes to post," the announcer said. "Don't be late."

The rhythm of the races kept us going as we studied the video. The conference crowd from last May wore jackets because of the warm weather. It wasn't like the near-zero temperatures and blowing snow of November we now enjoyed outside.

"Watch for Blick. He's an older man of medium height with gray hair, glasses, and a beard—the professor type," I said.

I hadn't focused on this part of the video—the pre-fight bar crowd.

"There is Walsh," I said. "In the lower left-hand box. He's at the table with a group."

There were a number of customers moving in and out of the camera angles and it was a lot to keep track of.

"How about that guy who is sitting down and taking his coat off?" Uncle Mike asked.

"Not easy to tell," I said, looking at a profile of a figure from some distance seated at the bar. Then the man took inventory of others in the restaurant and his face came into view. "Yes, that's Blick."

"Walsh and Blick in different spots in the restaurant." Uncle Mike shook his head. "Doesn't look promising."

We watched as customers streamed out of the place. It was past the time for dinner, but normally I'd expect people to hang out for more drinks. Then I recalled the conference agenda. A late-night hospitality function had been scheduled back in the hotel paid for by one of the conference sponsors. The promise of free booze would pull them back.

I explained this to Uncle Mike and reminded him that Blick was the executive director of the Alliance to Prevent Gambling Addiction, a nonprofit funded by a public relations and lobbying firm that represented casinos. "Maybe it wouldn't be good for WagerEasy or Walsh to be seen with a guy like Blick. I don't know."

"Turns my stomach," Uncle Mike said. "It's like cigarette companies funding a non-smoking campaign."

"Walsh's group is leaving." We followed him, picking him up through the bar as he passed from one video box to the next.

Walsh left The Point Spread, but he'd left his jacket at the table. There was still hope.

Uncle Mike chuckled. "Here he is. Walsh is running back to get his coat."

"Wait a minute. That guy who came in behind Walsh. I've seen him before." I froze the video.

"Who is he?"

It wasn't Sloan. All I could see was a profile. Maybe he was someone I'd met at WagerEasy the past week. Maybe one of the many bookies I'd interviewed. "I don't know. Something about the face."

I asked Uncle Mike if the mystery man worked for Sloan, but my uncle didn't recognize him either. Walsh passed by the bar after retrieving his coat from within the restaurant.

"There's your buddy, Walsh. Good old Blick seated at the bar. C'mon, Walsh, why don't you stop for a cold one?" I wanted to see the two of them. Confirm what I'd seen in that parking garage. What scheme did they have going?

At that moment, 9:50 according to the video, Yuri Provost and her entourage entered The Point Spread. She swaggered past Blick and then Walsh toward the far end of the bar. She didn't address either of them.

"Yuri doesn't seem to know them," I said.

Yuri and the three men with her entered another box, one of the views of the back half of the bar. They took a seat at a table.

I watched every move Walsh made. He sidled up alongside Blick and they talked back and forth. Now I had ammunition to pressure Walsh.

"They look like a couple of co-conspirators to me." Uncle Mike said.

Walsh and Blick began to argue. Blick stood up from his chair and the two of them faced off. Then Blick turned around toward the far end of the bar. Yuri Provost strutted toward them.

I wished the video had a soundtrack. Yuri and Blick were shouting back and forth. Yuri stopped halfway and didn't walk the full length of the bar to Blick.

"See how Walsh took several steps away?" I asked. "He now acts as if he doesn't know Blick. That's why I thought he was an impartial witness." I should've spent more time with the video before.

"Yuri is going back to her table," Uncle Mike said. "When does the fight break out?"

"Another five minutes or so. Look, Walsh has taken out his cell. Blick is answering. Clever."

"They've got something cooking. I'll send a snippet of them talking together to Walsh. It should make him nervous."

"If Walsh is the killer, he'll come running. C'mon," Uncle Mike said. "Keep going with the video. I want to see Yuri stomp the racist."

39

AFTER I'D SENT THE VIDEO SNIPPET OF WALSH AND BLICK talking together at The Point Spread to Walsh, we waited.

Uncle Mike stood up from the table and walked several steps, rubbing the spot above his knee. His bad leg still gave him trouble if he sat for too long. "Any response from Walsh?"

I checked again for a reply. "Nothing."

The announcer provided the crowd with last-minute changes before the next race.

I looked up at the black TV screen and across the table toward the bar at the far end of the chamber. What did I expect? A response from Walsh might be an admission. An admission that he and Blick were friends and the courtroom scene was nothing more than an act.

Walsh knew I had been working for St. Clair and the defense team. Maybe Walsh would speculate that was how I got my hands on the video, and now that the trial was over, perhaps Yuri had talked. Walsh would need to think back. What was said between him and Blick?

If Walsh and Blick were the killers, the video clip might get them real nervous. Why had I sent it? Was I out to blackmail them? What else did I know?

I had to keep the wheels in motion and that meant I had to stick with the plan for Tara and me to meet with the bookies on behalf of WagerEasy. I called Tara and she said she was at the bar downstairs waiting for me. She told me she'd been escorted to the track by one of the cops stationed to watch her house. Kubala was still a concern. We hadn't seen him since I knocked him out cold during our Wednesday rush hour fight.

"Our first bookie is sitting at a table near me with Sloan," Tara said. "I have the files, and I can escort him up after the race."

The track announcer said, "One minute." At the track, one minute usually meant about five minutes or more, but it got people running to the windows.

"Okay, fine. I'll see you after this race." I turned to Uncle Mike and told him the timeline Tara and I discussed.

"That will give me a few minutes to call the department," he said. "Let me see if we have anything on Blick or his old buddy, Coach Fitz. See if anything new has come into the department now that they're in town. I'll also check in with our boys."

We wanted to appear vulnerable inside the chamber to get the killer to show his hand, yet remain ready to counter. The "boys" were a couple of detective friends Uncle Mike had called. They knew it involved Liz and came right over.

"I'll step out to the bleachers to watch the race," I said. "Can you find out when the department first learned from the feds that the men killed in the ambulance were members of a gang of skinheads?"

"Okay. Want me to place a few trifecta bets for you on this race?"

"No thanks."

"You degenerate." He laughed to let me know he could joke about it. But he was serious, too. Uncle Mike pulled out a stogie. Downstairs, he'd go outside and smoke while he made the call and talked to the boys.

I walked over to the doors that led to the outside and slipped off the padlock the guard had unlocked earlier. Then I pulled out the chain strung through the panic bars and stepped out to the bleachers centered at the eighth pole. I shivered in the cold and zipped my winter coat. The finely-groomed white-dirt racetrack below extended down to the first turn near the clubhouse then circled around in a one-mile oval. It was a drop of more than fifty feet from the grandstand railing to the concrete. Wooden seats on a steel framework rose up behind me. An overhang kept some of the snow off the cheap seats.

The race was one of the few scheduled tonight for trotters instead of pacers. The buggies began to organize into a line and then would trot behind the mobile gate attached to the starter vehicle. I'd get a good view of the backstretch and the stretch from up here.

The finish line, below me to the right, was also the start. The track announcer alerted the crowd that the one-mile contest under the lights was about to begin. Then one of the horses trotted off to the side and the announcer informed us of a slight delay due to equipment trouble. Another way for the track to attract more last-minute action.

I felt like an intruder. I didn't have a bet on the race and hadn't even looked over the field. None of these horses were on Jimmy's "Watch List." The odds on the tote board were meaningless. A furlong or less to my right, near the finish line below, were people willing to brave the cold, bettors with action who participated on another level.

For them, the anticipation made the bet worth the money, it was a type of magic that had driven gamblers in every endeavor from slots to poker to sports.

The same sort of magic coursed through me. The video I'd sent to Walsh, the meetings with bookies to challenge Sloan tonight, each was a calculated wager. Maybe it would come together and maybe it wouldn't, but I felt like I was in the stretch. The uncertainty was addictive. A murder investigation was "action" of another type.

Action—it was what had driven Jimmy and the old crowd. The empty grandstands rose up behind me as a testament to them all. How would this "action," this driving force, work out for all those future bettors with their phones in hand? They'd get up-to-the-second algorithmic odds on whether the kicker would make the winning field goal. Each wager adrenaline-soaked. There would be lots of angles and plays, successive plays like the pulls of the lever of a slot that the gambler would become the game. Everything would change.

They'd gamble with the household bankroll, their kids' education, their retirement. DiNatale or other loan sharks ever present to offer a loan of last resort. The entire scheme pissed me off.

Time was not WagerEasy's friend. Time didn't turn high volume daily wagering dollars that added to the bottom line. Now I knew why I was pissed off. I hadn't invested the time either.

Why did Jimmy bet on that Gypsum game? Jimmy had been an artisan and I'd failed to fulfill my role as an apprentice. It wasn't just about action—it was about having the skill to unlock the unseen.

If only I would've taken the time...

I didn't even check the tote board to see which horse was the favorite. I went back inside.

————

Since Tara wouldn't come up until after the race and Uncle Mike was out having a smoke with the boys, it gave me the chance to make my bets on behalf of Jimmy's two horses in the later races.

I ran down the stairs. Uncle Mike's lecture on my gambling problem still echoed in my ears but didn't translate. Gambler logic wouldn't allow it. In my mind, the wager was crystal clear. This bet tonight on Jimmy's horse was another type of action, the purest kind of action. The kind that operates on another level, a gut level. That mystical land of hunches and luck. My wager on Jimmy's horses would provide insurance against anything that might happen tonight.

I glanced toward the simulcast area but steered clear. Rows of screens televising other racetracks attracted a hard-core crowd throughout the day. Play on other tracks around the country kept Thornton Racetrack going during these tough times. No sign of Sloan or Tara. This area of the track was once like Grand Central with people headed up to the grandstands, over to the clubhouse opposite the stairs, through glass doors to the finish line outside, or standing in long lines for food. Now only a couple of brave customers stood at the grill for a grease infusion.

The crowd was tuned into the beginning of the race so there wasn't a line at the few betting windows opened for tonight's sparse attendance. The announcer gave an update on the equipment problem bullshit, but I didn't listen.

I placed the wagers and, as I left the window, a short, thin man walked up to me. One of DiNatale's men. I recognized him from the other night when Uncle Mike and I met with Burrascano in the Jockey Club, the guy who had run up the stairs ahead of us.

The man waved to me and in a low voice said, "Mr. DiNatale wants to see you."

I had to get back before Tara and Uncle Mike returned to our table upstairs. "I can't. I don't have time."

He reached into his coat. "Make time, Eddie."

"No—"

"You going to make me pull my gun? I got a job to do. Give me a fucking break."

I didn't want to cause a scene. I nodded and followed him past the grill through glass doors and into the vacant clubhouse on the first floor at the far end of the structure. What was DiNatale's role here tonight? Then it hit me. Maybe he had horses running. DiNatale owned a large stable under several shell companies.

The short, thin guy took up a sentry position on the grandstand side of the glass doors. DiNatale stood near the closed-up betting windows and waved to me. A bottle of fine scotch and a glass placed on the counter. "Hey, Eddie."

So, we'd pretend to be old friends. "Hi, Vic." I took a quick look around. If other members of his gang were nearby, he might try to grab me and sweat answers out of me. It wouldn't be the first time.

"Arlene is out of her fucking mind. Okay?" DiNatale's arms waved and his feet danced. "Blaming us for the disappearance of Porter. Give me a break. I don't know who did it, but it sure as hell wasn't us. Porter had title to these little tracks for Burrascano. We could care less. Whatever Porter got, he probably deserved it."

I was about to put all this to a logic test but DiNatale continued, his face close to mine, spit hitting me in the face.

"Now she thinks she's in control. Can hang this shit over our head. C'mon. The thing you should know is that dumbfuck Sloan asked me to fuck off. Can you believe that? Well, fuck him. Me, stay the fuck away from one of our tracks so he can kiss Arlene's ass? It's fucking stupid."

DiNatale was wound up, and I let him go.

"I'm the only friend Sloan has got. Burrascano? If not for the delicate situation we got with legalization, Sloan would be whistling 'Home on the Range' through his goddamn asshole."

This was DiNatale at his most explosive, and I didn't want to stumble into the crosshairs by saying something to piss him off.

"I know what you and Mike are doing, and you know I don't approve," DiNatale said. "Who gives a fuck? I'm not in charge. Not yet. This Sloan asshole acts like he already owns Thornton. Like he's in charge of our city. He's getting bookies that pay *us* street tax to pay *him*. Tells people he's got the inside track to what City Hall will do. He's full of shit."

"What are you telling me, Vic?"

"I'm telling you—don't stand too close to the fucker. Something's going on with him, and I'm the one he's fucked over. You know I'd never admit it either, and if you tell anyone you can kiss your ass goodbye."

Threats were nothing new but DiNatale's colorful tirade was. During the meeting with Arlene Adams and others, just before the carnage in the parking lot, DiNatale had shown massive amounts of self-discipline. I'd been impressed.

DiNatale's jaw worked as he stared off toward the wall lined with a dozen framed photographs of past Thornton Derby winners. "Burrascano might be getting old but he's still sound as shit. I was ready to dump the Blowtorch Murders on WagerEasy. Now I don't know. Pisses me off." His feet stopped their little dance. "Burrascano cut me some slack over it. He saw how complicated this bullshit was from the beginning. Fucking skinheads crawling out of the woodwork like termites. Blasted to shit all over the parking lot. I'm telling you—did you ever see such crazy shit in your life?"

I shook my head.

"Burrascano has got patience. He sees things the rest of us can't. Pure fucking genius. He knows how to keep his mouth shut and listen. You learn things that way." He stared at me. "Like you're doing right now."

Maybe the pressure of succession was getting to him. He didn't act as if the gambling boss had passed away, but he was starting to come unglued.

He stabbed an index finger at my chest. "Watch Sloan. That's all I got to say." He turned and waved toward his man who kept watch from the other side of the glass doors.

"Look Vic," I told DiNatale. "If you want to vent that's fine. I'm pissed about a lot of things too. But if you want more—"

"What?" If a snake could smile, DiNatale smiled.

"If you want Sloan, be ready."

"Okay." He placed his hands on his hips, exposing the gun and shoulder holster beneath his suit coat. "Fuck Sloan. This is my fucking place of business."

———

I ran back upstairs to the meeting place beneath the old grandstands. No sign of Uncle Mike or Tara. My trip to the windows wouldn't be discovered.

I took out the tickets from my shirt pocket and slipped them into my pants pocket. They were as good as gold. Inside the dark chamber, I was tempted to take my old place at the bar with the ghosts and flash the tickets around. We could talk about hunches and wagers you make to pay old debts to friends, and why I asked for DiNatale's cell number.

After a few minutes, Tara walked into the chamber alone. She was supposed to escort our first bookie appointment up the stairs and into our chamber after the race.

I stood and greeted her with a hug. She pulled me closer and we kissed. For a second, I lost track of wagers and plans.

"What happened?" I asked.

"He'll be up shortly. He didn't want to be seen with me in front of Sloan."

"Sloan is down there?" It confirmed what Uncle Mike had told me.

"He's holding court. Buying bookies drinks. Telling everyone how great it was to meet Arlene Adams, the owner of Thornton Racetrack, and how a deal is in the works to set up a sportsbook on every bookie's behalf."

The bookies were in a tough spot. They wanted to meet with WagerEasy to find out what they might get if they sold out, but maintain their option with Sloan at the same time.

She placed the WagerEasy files from the legal department on the table and sat down beside me. "What happened to all the lights?"

I explained about the ancient fuse.

"It's creepy in here." She shivered and pulled her coat tight around her shoulders.

"They said they turned up the heat but it's hard to tell."

"Here are the official payoffs for the last race, ladies and gentlemen," the track announcer said.

Tara covered her ears. "Loud enough? I guess because nobody's in here. The place needs a sportsbook."

"Yeah. It would've been jumping tonight with action on college games. Speaking of bets, did you have the winner in the last race?"

"I lost five bucks on a close photo. Took forever. Can I add that to my expense account?"

The photo delay probably saved me from being discovered running down to the windows. "Be happy we're assigned track duty." I pulled out the first WagerEasy file from the stack. "You know, Tara, I didn't like the way Sloan reacted to Arlene. Maybe it would be better if you left."

"What? I thought we were a team?"

"Yes. Just not tonight."

"I don't get it. We need to put together a report, ask questions, get financial information, and anything we can on each bookie's high rollers. Get WagerEasy to put numbers on the table. These small-time bookies deserve it. Otherwise, they'll lose out and WagerEasy will lose out on their high rollers."

"I know. But tonight might be dangerous." I explained Sloan's background.

"Shouldn't we call the police then?"

I heard clomping up the stairs. "Hear that?" I got up from my seat, out of the alcove, and began to walk over.

"Hey, Eddie, it's me," Uncle Mike called. He walked into the chamber out of breath.

"Tara is here," I said.

Tara's cell played a tune. She grabbed her purse. "Hello, Mr. O'Connell. You're not with Sloan tonight?" She studied her cell. "It's a call from my mom. I have to take it or she'll get worried." She ran off toward the stairway.

Uncle Mike sat down at the table. "Damn escalator."

I took my seat across from Uncle Mike. "What did you find out?"

"Not much. They don't have anything about Blick. It's like the guy doesn't exist. I did talk to Burrascano."

"That's a relief."

"Yeah. But he didn't sound too good. He wouldn't admit it, but the old mob boss might be in the hospital," Uncle Mike said.

"Damn. What about the other thing?" I asked.

"The department hadn't heard from the feds until this afternoon about the skinheads. I wasn't that out of touch," Uncle Mike said.

"How are the boys?"

"They're nearby. They won the last race."

Tara was still over by the stairs talking on her cell in a low voice saying stuff like "right," and "sure." It seemed her call was coming to an end.

I whispered to Uncle Mike. "I'm going to question Tara about a few things. Just go with it."

He nodded. "Always something. Jeesus."

Tara walked back to the alcove and sat down beside me. "I don't know why our bookie appointment isn't here yet. I told him we were up here. Maybe he won that race and went to collect."

"Everything okay with your mom?" I asked.

"Yes. It's not easy for her at her age. A policeman stationed out front all day and night."

"You weren't talking with someone else?" I asked.

She brushed her blond hair back from one shoulder. "What? What are you talking about?"

I wasn't buying it. "Why don't you tell me why you're really here and why you're working at WagerEasy?" I kept my voice low in case our appointment came up the stairs.

She appeared puzzled and annoyed. "What? Eddie, I don't have a clue what you're talking about." She also kept her voice low and leaned in close to me. She turned to Uncle Mike. "What's this all about?"

Uncle Mike didn't move, his stony cop face evaluating her.

"Uncle Mike checked," I said. "The feds told the department it was a group of skinheads that did the track shooting. But not until this afternoon. Yet, you told me about the skinheads this morning."

She smiled and shook her head. "Maybe the officer in front of our house heard something? A rumor? I don't know."

"I talked to the officer," Uncle Mike said. It was a bluff, but that's what good detectives do—they bluff.

Tara wasn't smiling any longer.

"You pulled a gun when Kubala assaulted you," I said.

"You can handle a vehicle," Uncle Mike said.

"The pool cue home-run swing at O'Connell's. All of it suggests you've had special training," I said.

"Special training? What do you mean?" She grabbed my arm.

"Was that really your mom on the phone?" Uncle Mike asked. "Maybe you should give me your cell, young lady."

"You're both nuts," she said. "I'm not going to give you my phone."

"You probably want to know what Jimmy and his two assistants were doing last Thursday in that vacant factory," I said.

"A drug deal," she said. "That's what the media says."

"Maybe you'd like to know why Walsh hired me. Maybe it's time we put our cards on the table," I said.

"I've got a call into the feds handling the case," Uncle Mike said. "What do you want me to tell them?"

"Go ahead," she said.

If I put my cards on the table, maybe she'd do the same. "I started at WagerEasy as an undercover detective hired by Walsh to look into the supposed drug problem that caused the murder of Golding and the other two," I said.

Her expression displayed surprise but her eyes told me the opposite.

I couldn't let up. "You were with Kubala that night at O'Connell's for a reason, weren't you?"

She hesitated. "We just happened to run into him. Me and my two friends."

"You should know this is a trap, Tara," Uncle Mike said. "We've set it to identify the killer. You don't want to be here."

"Really? Who do you plan to trap? Sloan?" With a sly smile, she looked first at Uncle Mike then me.

"We're not joking," I said.

"I'm not afraid of Sloan. This place doesn't seem dangerous to me," she said. "Just dark. What aren't you telling me?"

"Do you know a man named Blick?" I could tell her all the rest but we didn't have time. "I've discovered he's working with Walsh."

She set her cell phone down on the table. "You did? When?"

"They met up a couple of times. Just last Wednesday after work in a parking garage. Before I ran into you and Kubala fighting," I said.

She nodded and her shoulders slumped. She rubbed her face with both hands. "Last Wednesday?"

"Yeah. I've got a video showing them talking together last May."

"You do?"

She took a deep breath. "Okay, I wasn't calling my mom." She looked at me and Uncle Mike and shook her head. "I had to take the call. I'm an undercover agent." She leaned in, her elbows on the table, and dropped her head in her hands. She cussed under her breath, and I wondered what kind of trouble she'd be in for blowing her cover. She looked up. "Maybe we can help each other. Are we okay in here?"

"Yeah," Uncle Mike said. "Eddie gave it the once-over."

"That night at O'Connell's when you were with Kubala?" I asked.

"I was the closest agent. I got to him after the Blowtorch Murders. We suspected a skinhead gang and Kubala was a member. A tip from a prison inmate."

"Kubala involved in these murders? I didn't think he was smart enough for that." I was getting one surprise after another. "I've been sleeping with a fed?" I turned to Uncle Mike. "How do you like that?"

"I don't want to touch that one," Uncle Mike said. "Jeesus Christ. I've got about a million questions for you, Tara."

She turned to me with a sad expression. Then she seemed to find inner strength and threw an arm around me.

I pulled her close.

"It happens," she whispered in my ear.

I kissed her. "Sorry about the third degree," I said when we separated. "Why were you placed undercover at WagerEasy? You started work there almost a year ago."

"We've suspected Walsh and Blick but they've been careful. The fact you've seen them together—you don't know what that means to our investigation," she said.

"What is it? What do you know about Blick?" It might be the one thing that would help me connect the dots.

She pressed her fingers to my lips. Then I heard it too. Somebody else was coming up the stairs.

Uncle Mike, seated at the other side of the table, stretched to see around the alcove wall that jutted out. "Can't see the stairs from this spot."

I got up and walked over. "It's our bookie appointment."

It was lousy timing. I'd need to wait to hear what Tara knew about Blick.

40

"WE'RE UP HERE," I CALLED DOWN THE STAIRS. IT WAS SAM Johnson.

"Where are the lights? Damn," the bookie, said.

I escorted Johnson to our table in the alcove near the double doors to outside. Before he sat down with us, I suggested we move the table out of the alcove several feet into the room so Uncle Mike could see the top of the stairs. It left lights above only the lower half of the table.

I introduced Johnson to Uncle Mike. Tara didn't need any introduction since she'd met Johnson previously at our initial meeting at WagerEasy. Or, maybe I should reintroduce Tara, the federal agent. How many reports had Tara filed with the department on those bookies who had met with WagerEasy to possibly sell their business? Future indictments for breaking federal gambling laws, racketeering, wire fraud, money laundering, tax evasion, and other customary charges were probably lined up in the starting gate to be served upon the unsuspecting illegal bookies. Or, perhaps Tara worked undercover at WagerEasy for another reason? It was my news about Blick and Walsh that had broken the ice for Tara.

"Can't the track afford lights?" Johnson said.

"Thornton Racetrack is on a budget." I still suspected that "Sam Johnson" was an alias.

He looked around the dark chamber and shook his head. "Thanks for meeting with me up here. I made my bet for the next race so I'm good. I'll catch the replay later. Sloan is downstairs."

"Did you see Arlene Adams?" Tara asked.

"The old movie star?" Johnson asked. "I wish. I'd ask her for an autograph. The wife's a big fan. To answer your question, Eddie, I'm shitty. I've been on this fucking merry-go-round." He pulled a toothpick from his shirt pocket.

"Tell us," Tara said. "Maybe we can help."

Johnson shook his head. "Like I told you, my business is on the ropes. Before, I heard the Outfit had my list of high rollers—the guys who pay my bills—and they were going to sell the list. With mobile wagering and my top customers gone, I'm done. I'm still hoping WagerEasy wants to work a deal. You know how things turned out at our last meeting—Larsen and me told each other to fuck off."

Uncle Mike chuckled. "I never got to know Larsen well, but I've heard a lot about her."

"And now?" I asked Johnson.

"I got the chance to join the Sloan Group. Sloan is asking me for three-thousand down and five-hundred a month to join the group. Some of the bigger bookies pay more. It's like insurance he tells us. Pays for a lobbyist, and a sportsbook, and will keep us in business. Sloan says he's got a deal in the works with Thornton Racetrack. He says any legalization won't include the mobile interactive in-play thing. Says he's got things fixed in the legislature."

I had to admit, Sloan's scheme was brilliant. A sportsbook at the track could be a front for all the bookies. The way Sloan talked to Arlene Adams yesterday, he made it sound as if all the bookies couldn't wait to join "his network of bookies." Now, Johnson revealed that Sloan made them pay for the privilege.

"That seems like a lot of money," Tara said.

"Not really. Not if it's for real," Johnson said. "What's wrong with paying money to make a deal with the devil?" He laughed and shook his head. "Then I hear the Outfit will go ahead and sell the list of high rollers, and Sloan is just taking everybody's money before he leaves town. I'm running in circles." He looked at Uncle Mike.

Based on what DiNatale had told me, Burrascano and the Outfit might run Sloan out of town, that is if they didn't kill him first.

Uncle Mike held out the palms of his hands. "I just consulted for Sloan. I can't read his mind. He's from Texas for Christ sake."

I was surprised at the degree of intel that Johnson had. Maybe he knew more about what Burrascano had planned than me or Uncle Mike, or maybe he was guessing. There was no way to know what the rumor mill produced. "We met with Arlene yesterday before the shootings," I said. "She has her lawyers talking to WagerEasy's lawyers."

"I was there too," Tara said. "Ms. Adams wasn't happy with Sloan and the people he brought to the table." She didn't mention DiNatale's name which was a smart move. "No offense, Mr. O'Connell." She smiled toward Uncle Mike. Uncle Mike nodded in return.

"Damn," Johnson said. "I had this nice string of customers paying my bills, and now I get beat up every which way I turn." He looked at me. "I heard you moved up, Eddie."

"You're well-informed," I said.

Johnson rubbed the day-old stubble on his chin. "All I've got are my friends in the business. We know which customers to stay away from and which ones are gold. There's this new guy. Everybody's talking about him. He's from Reno. All the sportsbooks in Nevada have refused his action. But he sends different runners so nobody knows it's him and they take the action. A guy like that can cripple you. It may be time to move on."

"You know the name of this man from Reno?"

"You should know that a lot of bookies—the big-time ones in the Sloan Group—think the guy from Reno is trying to bleed the bookies dry, and that he works for WagerEasy." He looked over his shoulder and the toothpick bobbed in his mouth. "We don't know his name, but guys downstairs know what he looks like. He's fucked a lot of guys out of a big piece of cash. He just did it again on that Gypsum game. A lot of guys got hurt. At least, that's what people say. I'm small-time so I didn't get hurt."

The Gypsum game. The one I'd bet using Jimmy's notebooks. What had Jimmy learned and how had he handicapped that game?

Tara glanced my way with an insider nod of the head.

Johnson leaned across the table. "Guys are saying that this guy from Reno killed Oscar. I guess Oscar was on his tail and was getting close."

It matched what Oscar had told me. He said he'd been burned and promised to find the guy from Reno. I looked toward Uncle Mike. He was about to say something but stopped.

"Sloan has a bounty on the guy's head," Johnson said. "The Sloan Group will kill the guy from Reno on sight."

If the guy from Reno walked into the track tonight, he wouldn't walk out alive. "Why don't we try to reopen talks with you, Sam?" I asked. "No promises, but maybe we can get something done. Get you a deal with WagerEasy."

"Okay," Johnson smiled. "I hear that Larsen is gone. At least I won't be wasting my time."

A voice behind us said, "Wasting time doing what?"

We turned. It was Sloan. Two of his men stood back in the shadows and there may have been more on the stairs. He walked over to the table and placed one hand on my shoulder like we were old buddies, the tip of his bolo tie dangling on my coat and the smell of beer on his breath.

"I'll see you later, Eddie," Johnson said, getting up from the table and slipping away.

"What's going on?" Sloan asked. "Poaching my bookies? You aren't happy trying to mess with my sportsbook deal with Thornton, you want more?"

I shifted in my chair and Sloan dropped his hand from my shoulder. He walked toward the north end of the table in the same direction as the stairs. "It may seem strange to you, Travis," I said. "But I happen to play the horses. These small tracks like Thornton offer great betting opportunities."

"And Mike O'Connell," Sloan said. "What the fuck are you doing here? I thought you were in my stable."

"You want consult advice?" Uncle Mike asked. "Here's some, 'Go back to Dallas.'"

Sloan's face reddened. "You think your relationship with Burrascano makes you invincible? Gives you Superman powers? Burrascano is a sick old man. Vic DiNatale is going to be the new man in charge and we're pals."

"I notice DiNatale isn't with you. I hear you told him to get lost because he messed up your deal with Arlene," I said.

"I just talked to Burrascano," Uncle Mike said. "He's not dead yet."

Sloan's expression turned sour. "I'll be damned. This whole legalization thing has made friends into enemies. I'm in the cattle business. You got to know when to buy and when to sell. You watch the market all the time. Walsh sent you over to schmooze Arlene?"

"Are you also here to suck up to her?" I asked.

Sloan grinned. "Hell, no. I'm here to keep an eye on my investment."

"You have the beer concession? A real bonanza?" I asked.

Sloan didn't react to the key word. His grin disappeared, and I saw a different version. The one who ran a gambling ring through Texas. "I usually get what I want." He turned to Tara and allowed his eyes to run up and down her body. "What's a nice-looking filly like you doing up here in this dark place?"

"I've heard that line a million times," Tara said. "Got anything original?"

"A filly with spirit," Sloan yelped. "You got to like that. What if I did have something new?"

"It wouldn't do you any good," Tara deadpanned.

"Your team struck out with Ms. Adams," I said. "I thought you would've taken the next plane back to Dallas."

"We didn't even get in the batter's box yet, sonny," Sloan said. "You just wait."

"A new strategy?" Tara said.

"Now why would I tell you WagerEasy people anything about my strategy? A company from Europe thinks they're the world's gambling experts and can come over here and colonize us? Give me a break." Sloan shook his head. "Our sports betting may be underground but it's alive and well. People like me and my network of bookies have been toeing the line all this time, and we're not about to wander off without a fight."

"Then why do these bookies wander off to WagerEasy looking to make a deal?" I asked.

"You can't keep everybody happy," he said.

"How come DiNatale isn't here? Is it because he was a liability for you?" I had to push him. I had to force Sloan's hand. Did he order the murders?

"Vic has his own timetable. We're still friends," he said.

"You put on a tough act but you're really just working for The Man?" The Man was Burrascano.

"I do what has to be done," he said, still smiling.

"WagerEasy is here to take your business. You need to do a deal through us." I glanced at Tara. She kept a poker face, the perfect team member in a tough situation.

Sloan took a step back. "You don't want to get crossways with me, sonny. You go back to your office and tell Walsh the only way he does a deal with this track is over my dead body. And Mike, you can take a hike. I don't care who you know."

"Happy to do that," Uncle Mike said.

"There are too many dead bodies already. What do you know about it?" I asked.

Sloan took a couple more steps and pointed a finger. "You're way over the line."

"Maybe WagerEasy is a foreign company but when it comes to Chicago, you're the foreigner," Uncle Mike said.

Sloan pointed at me. "Do the smart thing and clear out of here before the next race. Nobody else does a deal with this track but me."

"Next time you come up," I said, "bring a round of beers."

Sloan cussed under his breath and walked back down the stairs with his men.

41

WHEN WE WERE SURE SLOAN AND HIS MEN HAD GONE down the stairs, we took our seats at the table.

"That appointment, the bookie, what's his name?" Uncle Mike asked.

"Sam Johnson." I looked to Tara. If Johnson knew he'd just confessed to an undercover federal agent, he'd want our scalps.

"Johnson said that Oscar was after the guy from Reno," Uncle Mike said.

"When I met with Oscar last Sunday that's what he told me," I said. "Oscar didn't plan to give the Reno dude a real warm welcome to Chicago."

"Who is the guy from Reno? That's what I want to know," Tara said, her hands clenched into fists.

I'd hoped our resident undercover agent could tell us. Instead, she was asking us questions. "The night Oscar was murdered Tara and I were followed on our way back from the track by Kubala."

"Why didn't you tell me?" Tara shot me a playful slug to the shoulder that wasn't all that playful.

"You've got your secrets, I've got mine." I tried to make a joke out of it, but Tara's surprise disclosure still hit below the belt.

"Let's put the pieces together," Uncle Mike said. He looked at me and then back at Tara as if he'd volunteered to step into the role of mediator.

"We have reason to believe that Kubala is the go-between with the skinheads who did the murders at the track. He was a member of the group in prison," Tara said.

She was smooth. If not for the fact she'd given me information about the skinheads being responsible for the shootout at the track prior to the feds informing the local police department, I wouldn't have guessed she was an undercover agent. "Kubala could be working for the guy from Reno," I said. "If he followed us to the track and back, he would've been able to notify his skinhead friends when we got near O'Connell's. That way his crew could place Oscar's body into the car."

"And the same gang of skinheads did the Blowtorch Murders and the track shootout," Uncle Mike said. "I assume they were also being paid for those jobs by the guy from Reno."

"Makes sense. Oscar's murder is the link." I wanted to follow Uncle Mike's thinking, yet I was reluctant to accept the conclusion. In my mind, Sloan remained a suspect. Sloan could've killed Oscar if he had refused to join the Sloan Group. It would've been a way for Sloan to send a message to other bookies.

"The guy from Reno is busy putting bookies out of business. Why?" Uncle Mike scratched at his chin. "Johnson thought the guy worked for WagerEasy. Any chance of that?"

"Not that I know of." I turned to Tara. The question had been eating at me. "What were you going to say about Blick? Why were you placed undercover at WagerEasy?"

Tara looked first at me and then Uncle Mike as if to confirm confidentiality. We had another bookie appointment scheduled in five minutes. The races ticked off one by one. We were in a vulnerable spot inside the chamber. Time was running out and any hedging could cost us.

Tara leaned in across the table and kept her voice low. "We believe Blick was involved in the theft of sensitive biotech information from a Swiss company."

"What the hell," Uncle Mike said.

I processed the information as best I could. Things came at me fast. The source of Walsh's investments and fancy house up in Kenilworth had been his wife. The picture in the foyer of Walsh and his wife smiling and sailing without a care in the world came to mind. "It was a Swiss company that bought Boston Bioteck, wasn't it?" It could be the connection I'd been looking for.

"Yes, it was Boston Bioteck," Tara said. "How did you know?"

"Walsh's father-in-law ran the company before he sold it," I said. "What sort of information was stolen?"

"Microchips for the military. Highly classified intellectual property." Tara's lips grew taut.

It was what Coach Fitz was selling. It had to be. Tara hadn't been placed at WagerEasy to hunt down small fry bookies like Johnson. It wasn't even about Sloan, the ruthless leader of a gambling ring, or the Outfit's deal to sell the high-roller list to WagerEasy. She was after bigger fish. "How did the feds trace the intellectual property to WagerEasy?" I asked.

"Actually, we traced the intellectual property to StatsRUs, but when we heard about the upcoming merger, we thought it'd be really clever to put somebody undercover in the acquiring company," she said.

The feds had kept abreast of Walsh on the merger. "And that's how you went to work for Larsen—"

"Right," Tara said. "Fun times."

Tara had been forced to take Larsen's dictator bullshit for a year while undercover. At the moment I wasn't all that sympathetic.

"Wait a minute," Uncle Mike said. "Why would StatsRUs want the blueprint for these microchips? What do they do?"

"It was in the Beta stage, but from my understanding, these microchips can be deployed directly into a soldier's body," Tara said, her eyes avoiding mine.

"An implant?" I asked.

"What the hell for?" Uncle Mike's face flashed a familiar shade of red. He was on the verge of losing that Irish temper he usually directed at me.

"The military needs to stay on top of technical developments." Tara talked as if she were rattling off something every school kid should know. "To build the finest force, they need to monitor not only the soldier's training but the soldier's physical capacity in the field. These microchips provide ongoing data of each soldier's capacity, including their blood pressure, sleep patterns, all kinds of stuff."

"An army of robots," Uncle Mike said.

"All the ABD a coach could want according to Coach Fitz," I said.

"It allows the coach to check on the athlete's performance. If he's training to maximum capacity and all that." Tara hesitated and her jaw clenched before she spoke. "But this microchip does even more. It will tell you with a high likelihood if the athlete can be expected to deliver a peak performance that day."

Uncle Mike slammed his fist on the table. "Bullshit. Damn tech stuff. Who is watching over this shit?"

I shook my head. "What the fuck?" What had Jimmy got himself tangled up in?

"If you can monitor these implanted microchips in athletes, you can win a shitload of sports bets," Tara said. "A sharp bettor with that kind of information would be discovered and then the bettor would be cut off. I think that's what the guy from Reno is doing. Once the bookies got wind of it, no one will take his action. Why take a chance on years in prison to win a few sports bets? All this expense. Business mergers. We assumed the blueprint for these microchips would be sold for millions to a foreign government for military use, but instead it's part of a sports betting merger."

I cussed under my breath. "It's easy to underestimate the market because it has been underground for such a long time.

Every state simply jumped on the sports betting bandwagon once the Supreme Court gave them an opening. But the market is complicated and bigger than anyone can guess."

"All that market research on sports betting has paid off for you, Eddie," Uncle Mike said with a short, satirical laugh. "Sports betting has been the cash cow for organized crime and nobody knows how much money it really generates. But what I want to know is how the hell did StatsRUs or Walsh get away with stealing sensitive military intelligence?"

"We think they stole the technology, but we have to prove it," Tara said. "StatsRUs has their own R&D department and labs. A lawsuit for patent infringement and theft has been filed by the Swiss company against StatsRUs, but that's tangled up in pretrial motions."

"Damn nightmare," Uncle Mike let out an exaggerated sigh.

"A nightmare exactly," Tara said with a wry smile. "Of course, the athletes and the schools have no idea. The schools all think the implant is a slick way to monitor an athlete's partying and fitness, but this technology could hurt the athlete. No ongoing records, no scientific record of the possible side-effects. The government unwilling to tell anyone anything because it's classified. The college kids are lab rats."

"Then, when the college kids turn pro, WagerEasy still has the implant," I said.

"What about the Gypsum game?" Tara asked me. "It was in that notebook at your apartment."

"Those were Jimmy's notebooks. He must've picked up on certain betting patterns. He was in touch with bookies and sports bettors not to mention WagerEasy's sports betting database. A sharp bettor like Jimmy didn't need much to gain an edge."

"That box of stuff from your buddy turned out to be a gold mine," Uncle Mike said.

Tara turned to me with sad eyes. "Jimmy? You mean James Golding? He was your friend?"

I nodded, a brief tip of the head, the way you nod to a stranger. I hadn't referred to James Golding as "Jimmy" to Tara until now.

"I'm sorry." Tara's eyes grew large, and she placed her hand on mine.

"If you ask me, Blick is the guy from Reno," I said. "Call it a hunch."

Tara squeezed my hand. "Eddie, how——"

"Hold it." Uncle Mike leaned over to one side. "Somebody's coming up the stairs."

Stolen microchips, implants—the case had spun in a new direction. I pulled out my gun and placed it on my lap.

42

It was Blick and Walsh. They walked from the stairway to our table inside the alcove. They wore long winter coats and they weren't smiling. Blick hid one hand inside his coat.

"Well, look who's here," I said. "Garrett, would you like to join us in an honest day's work? I thought you and the wife were going out of town this weekend."

"We expected you," Uncle Mike said.

Walsh unzipped his winter coat and drew a gun from one pocket. "Eddie, I got the video. Where did you get it?"

"I can see you guys are buddies. What happened to the act you put on in the hall outside the courtroom?" I asked.

Blick looked at Tara through the thick lenses of his glasses. "I'm afraid I haven't had the pleasure."

"You should stop by WagerEasy and we'd introduce you around," I said. "Tara is a member of our team. Tara, this is Reynolds Blick, Ph.D. Dr. Blick, this gentleman is my uncle, Mike O'Connell."

"I know about you," Tara told Blick.

Blick nodded toward Uncle Mike. "Mr. O'Connell, a pleasure."

"Nice weapon," Uncle Mike said. "Sorry we have to meet under these circumstances."

"Well, Dr. Blick," I said. "You'd meet all sorts of people at WagerEasy. You could meet your old friend, Coach Fitz."

"I have lots of friends," Blick said.

"Eddie," Walsh said. "The video means nothing."

"It must mean something or you wouldn't be here," I said. I was betting Walsh didn't know the original source of the video. "You should hear the soundtrack." It was a bluff.

Walsh's shoulders slumped. "Eddie, I knew you were trouble. At first, I thought it was strange when you showed up at my door. A witness needed for Yuri. It sounded like a scam. Now I see it was a scam and that you had another plan all along."

I didn't argue with him. "How did you and Blick cook up this plan?" I asked. "I sent my check to LRC for forty-nine grand." Another bluff.

Blick and Walsh stood silent and then they exchanged a quick glance.

"I told you," Walsh said. "He bet the Gypsum game."

"We haven't gone live," Blick said.

I adopted Uncle Mike's stone face. I wanted them to believe I knew their full scheme. What did Blick mean?

"Must've gotten the Gypsum game from Golding somehow," Walsh said.

Blick scratched at his long, bushy gray beard. "But how? Golding's dead."

Jimmy's old notebooks. Jimmy talking from the grave with the key to it all.

I nodded toward Uncle Mike and he nodded back to signal that he'd notified his boys downstairs. All we needed to do was to keep Walsh and Blick talking until our reinforcements arrived.

"He can't afford the subscription payments," Blick said. "Garrett, he's bluffing."

"I heard you're quite the gambler, Blick. Started in Reno. Blackballed at all the Nevada casinos," I said. It was another piece of information that they wouldn't expect from me.

"See? He isn't bluffing," Walsh said to Blick. "He's surprised me again and again. I knew I needed to keep him close."

"He knows about Parlay Partners?" Blick asked.

Blick just blurted it out. Parlay Partners was the last piece of the puzzle. The envelope on Jimmy's desk. It was a piece of correspondence from Parlay Partners, a tout service. Jimmy never would've taken the word of a so-called expert.

"Yeah, I know about it. And so did Jimmy Golding. He sent his check for forty-nine K. He was on to you two. I talked with Burrascano. Coach Fitz too. A real bonanza."

"You're only guessing," Walsh said.

Blick's face contorted in anger. "Yes, a bonanza for some of us."

"I know about Blick's role," I said. "Information on microchips stolen from Boston Biotech. Coach Fitz is peddling implantable microchips to colleges."

Blick laughed. "Those microchips will give us the edge over every other subscription service." He had pointed the gun.

The microchips provided the kind of information that Jimmy the Leech and others like him would scratch and dig for weeks to find. When he'd uncovered the scheme, Jimmy must've been outraged. A microchip that gave certain gamblers willing to pay big bucks an edge over everyone else was as good as a fix, and Jimmy hated a fix.

I kept up the chatter. Where were the boys? "The coaches get the million-dollar salary. The college athlete gets the shaft and a microchip. What the coaches don't know is that the info goes to LRC, a phantom corporation, and then funneled to Parlay Partners, a tout service, available only to those hedge-fund types with lots of money to pay those monthly subscription fees. That's the story isn't it, guys?"

Jimmy the Leech wasn't killed because of his deal with Burrascano. He was killed because he'd discovered the plot hatched by Walsh and Blick.

Walsh turned to Blick. "Did you hear that?"

The boys must be near the top of the stairs.

I didn't hear anything. I did wonder if Sloan and his bookies had noticed Blick when he walked up the stairs. I began to wonder if my plan might blow up in my face.

"Over there." Walsh pointed away from the stairs and toward the bar in the dark.

A man walked out from behind the bar, out of the shadows, and into the light. It was Kubala and he was holding a gun. He wore a black stocking cap over his bald head.

"About time," Blick said.

"We waited for you downstairs," Walsh said. "When you didn't show, we came up here."

"I got the opportunity and I took it," Kubala said. "Eddie left the place unattended."

My gambling had come back to haunt me again. I caught a look of disappointment from Uncle Mike. He also kept glancing toward the stairs. Where were Uncle Mike's boys?

"So, you think I'm stupid, Eddie?" Kubala said to me, then turned back to Walsh and Blick. "I could only hear some of what they said. This bitch is an FBI agent."

"I see your hired hand has shown up to do your dirty work again," I said to Walsh and Blick.

Kubala smiled and laughed. "Sorry, Eddie. I know you wished I was in that track shootout yesterday. You probably thought I was cooked in the ambulance."

"Shoot them," Blick said. "What are you waiting for?"

"Hold on," Kubala said. "I've been waiting for this moment for a long time." He gestured with his gun. "Hands on the table, folks. Where I can see them. We're going to have a little chat."

"We can fight right here," I said. "Finish what we started." Kubala probably couldn't shoot any better than he could wield a knife, but it was close range. I put my hands on the table, and Tara, and Uncle Mike followed.

"That's better," Kubala said. "We're not going to fight tonight, Eddie. You had your chance. I waited behind that damn bar because I learned a lot. I learned me and my brothers should've been getting paid a hell of a lot more, Mr. Blick.

Eddie and them know more than you and Walsh think. More than you told me. Stolen microchips?"

"Do your job," Blick said. "Then we'll talk."

"Hope you got paid for yesterday's job, Kubala," Uncle Mike said.

I had to hand it to Uncle Mike. He knew when to bluff. We needed time.

"What the fuck you talking about, old man?" Kubala asked.

"Did your friends get killed for nothing? After you shoot us, they'll shoot you. They'll point the finger at you." Uncle Mike said.

The look on Kubala's face showed he hadn't been paid for yesterday. He'd been the go-between. First, the Blowtorch Murders, then Oscar, and then the fiasco yesterday at the track.

How close had Kubala gotten to his prison buddies? I'd always heard they were like family.

It was my turn to bluff. "We talked to Burrascano," I said. "His men ambushed your buddies yesterday at the track parking lot. Payback for the frame-up when you killed Golding."

"I already heard it was Burrascano's men," Kubala said. "Tell me something I don't know." His finger worked the trigger of the gun like he couldn't wait. Maybe the sound of my voice made him think of my knockout punch. It wouldn't help our cause.

"Burrascano said he'd been tipped off," I said. "That's why he was ready for your friends." Kubala took a deep breath and stared hard at Walsh and Blick. I wanted to rub salt in his wounds. "I saw the massacre. It was a good show."

"Goddamnit, Eddie." Kubala aimed his gun at Walsh and Blick. "That sounds like something you bastards would do."

"Shit," Walsh said. "Let's talk. Eddie's lying."

Blick raised his gun and fired at Kubala. The shot hit him in the right shoulder and Kubala's gun clattered to the ground.

I grabbed my gun and fired at Blick then pulled Tara down under the table. She had her gun in hand. Uncle Mike fired as well and took cover.

A burst of gunfire erupted from the stairway. Walsh caught a burst in the chest. He collapsed with a groan. Thank God, Uncle Mike's boys had arrived.

"What are you doing with that bastard from Reno?" Someone shouted from the stairway. It was Sloan, not the boys.

I could see Blick. He was on the floor holding his knee. In the light of the stairwell, Blick had no choice but to shoot back at Sloan. Blick was greeted by a flurry of gunshots. He fell backward, spread-eagled on the floor. A cloud of fine red mist hung in the air.

I reached up and flipped off the light switch behind me that illuminated the alcove.

"Please, I'm not a part of all this," Kubala cried out, facing the light from the stairwell.

"You were with that bastard from Reno," Sloan yelled at Kubala.

"I didn't know," Kubala said. He dove for his gun.

More gunshots from the stairway but I didn't plan to wait around to check on Kubala's welfare.

"Follow me," I whispered to Tara and Uncle Mike.

43

I SCRAMBLED A FEW FEET ALONG THE FLOOR TO THE DOUBLE doors that led outside. Uncle Mike and Tara followed. Several shots were fired into the alcove by Sloan and his men and we returned fire.

In the bleachers, we might have a chance. I didn't have a plan. It was about survival. What happened to Uncle Mike's boys? The sound of gunfire had surely alerted track security. Maybe the cavalry would show up in time. Or maybe not. I'd set a trap for the killer and got us caught as well.

I opened the door a crack and it let light from the track into the alcove.

"Where the fuck you going?" Sloan called. "We detained your friends downstairs. Why don't we talk?"

Uncle Mike's boys wouldn't be able to help us. We only had seconds. Uncle Mike and Tara began to crawl through.

"I want to show you how we deal with assholes who refuse to listen in the Lone Star State," Sloan yelled.

Figures dodged and weaved through the light and shadow within the chamber. How many men did Sloan bring? Guns were fired. I shot back to provide cover from the limited protection offered by the alcove.

I slipped through last and, without cover, bullets riddled the doors. I caught one in the back of the leg when I was almost clear. I slithered through and shut the door behind me.

Outside, the cold and wind didn't faze me. Tara and Uncle Mike were running up the bleachers. Tilted at a forty-five-degree angle, at the top they'd have a strategic position. Uncle Mike had to stop midway.

"Keep going," I yelled.

I hid in one of several rows of premium bleacher seats opposite the double doors that provided an unobstructed view of the track. A race was being run. Turning my back to the horses, I waited. Once the door opened a crack, I fired. I heard a scream and the door closed fast.

"We're waiting for you, Sloan," I yelled.

Inside, a shooter fired at the padlock of Door Number 3 to my far right. Sloan didn't really want to talk. Sloan's man would be through any second and I couldn't defend both double doors with my .38.

I hobbled up the steps, the heel of my shoe soaked in blood. The back of my thigh had taken the hit. Adrenaline should've powered me up the fifty rows of bleachers but pain radiated up my spine. Maybe another bullet was lodged in my back. I made it halfway.

"C'mon, Eddie," Uncle Mike called.

I made it another few rows and heard Sloan and his men. They were shooting up those premium seats I'd just left.

The pacers were entering the backstretch and sirens wailed.

The knife-like pain pulled me down. My body gave out. My vision blurred. I felt like I might pass out.

Lying in the center aisle would make me a fat target. I dove into a row of seats and felt for the wound. My hand came away covered in blood.

Shots rang out. Sloan's men had taken up position in the premium seats. Uncle Mike and Tara returned fire from above. Intermittent shots to conserve ammunition.

I kept crawling on my belly between the rows of bleachers. If I kept moving, I'd keep from passing out.

"Figure Time has moved from the back with cover," the track announcer said over the loudspeaker. It was my horse.

Below, the shooters had left the premium seats and came at Tara and Uncle Mike the way soldiers take a hill in wartime. They shouted out to each other. One or two took the middle aisle and others moved up the outside aisles. A flurry of shots from one angle provided cover to allow others to advance a few steps then duck into a row of bleacher seats. Footsteps vibrated through the skeletal structure of the antique grandstands and transmitted locations through my torso. Row upon row of metal benches like our high school football field. Arlene promised a remodel but why pamper those in the cheap seats.

Bullets streamed overhead. The far aisle at the end of the row. Footsteps vibrated then stopped.

The track announcer described the horses in the far turn. "Figure Time has moved into fourth."

C'mon, Figure Time. I've got money on you and you'll pay boxcars. If I could make it to the end of the aisle. How far was it?

I propped myself up on my elbows and dragged my carcass a couple of feet. Blowing snow had turned the metallic aisle into a Slip and Slide. The oily stench of the refinery nearby mixed with the sulfur smell of spent ammunition.

Sirens echoed then faded. Maybe I imagined them. Maybe the cops would worry about what awaited them in the parking lot, yesterday's ambush still fresh in their minds.

I planted my elbows and held my gun with two hands. Still too far from the aisle. I needed to get closer to pick the guy off.

The shooter in the far aisle kept coming. His footsteps jostled the structure then stopped. He must've taken cover. I squirmed forward, each elbow working in combination with the toes of my boots.

"Here they come," the announcer called. "Figure Time is moving three-wide."

At odd intervals, no shots or footsteps, only the *clomp, clomp, clomp* of horses' hooves like a heartbeat.

I crept along another few feet. Pain seared my backside. I wanted to close my eyes. Deaden the pain. The call of the race added a rhythm to my breathing and movements. *Keep going, Figure Time*.

A barrage from below. The man in the aisle moved up several more rows toward me. The concession stands at the top of the bleachers where Tara and Uncle Mike hid took a battering like hail on a tin roof.

What about the main aisle behind me? Others were moving up. If only I could rise up and look around. I could check the odds on Figure Time, too. The pain held me down. Probably a good thing.

"Hey, Eddie, what the fuck?" It was a voice from below.

"We're here, Eddie." It was DiNatale. Not the cavalry I expected. He and his men must've taken the spot in the premium seats. Shots bounced around the rows of bleachers from every direction.

Someone in the aisle opposite from me screamed. "Fuck. Sloan, I'm hit."

I whispered a word of "thanks" to my old adversary.

With DiNatale below, Sloan and his men would have no choice but to take the higher ground. They had to escape the crossfire. It meant an all-out attack on Tara and Uncle Mike's position.

Don't think about how much farther you have to go. Think about the gun between your bloody hands and don't let it slip away.

"Figure Time is charging down the middle of the track."

You can do it, Figure Time. I squirmed closer to the far aisle. I've got a rendezvous with this fucker in the far aisle. Sirens drew closer. It wasn't some dream.

More hail pounded tin. Shooters on the move in a last-ditch effort. The stands shook and vibrated through me. DiNatale's men must be closing in, driving Sloan's men to the top tier. Sloan's men dove into rows of benches around me. Trench warfare.

"Figure Time takes the lead."

Someone charged a few steps up the far aisle and stole under cover. I could hear him breathing. I turned my head. He seemed to be one row below me. Tough to see with these damn blurry eyes.

I had to watch my breathing. Not give away my hiding place. There was a break in the gunfire. Noises from the aisle below. He was moving again.

A face came into view.

"Sloan?" I recognized the coat.

"Eddie?" And his voice.

His face showed shock. When I didn't fire, his shoulders pivoted toward me.

I willed my hands and fingers to squeeze the trigger.

44

I OPENED MY EYES. UNCLE MIKE WAS SITTING ON THE CHAIR beside my bed reading the newspaper. "Tell me I'm not dreaming."

He shot out of the chair, the paper fluttering into the air. "Eddie, how you feeling?"

"Good. The doctors said it was touch and go."

"You heard that? We thought you were out," Uncle Mike said.

"Maybe I dreamed it. Tara? Where's Tara?"

Uncle Mike touched my arm. "She's fine. She texted me. She'll be back soon. That woman can shoot. Hell of a woman. Got the paramedics to you—"

"When?" My mind was muddled. Wasn't there a race? I was watching a horse race.

"Yesterday," he said. "When DiNatale cut them off from below and then when you shot Sloan, the rest of Sloan's men gave up."

"Damn, I missed it." I had a horse. A bet on a horse.

"I saw DiNatale in the cafeteria. He's a believer. A convert. Thinks we can walk on water. I wish we could've turned Walsh and Blick over to the cops. This tech shit has to be stopped."

"In the cafeteria?" I wasn't processing half of what Uncle Mike said. Why would DiNatale be in the cafeteria?

"Burrascano is in the hospital. His cancer caught up with him. Everyone's here. Liz came out of it and is down the hall. St. Clair is with her. She sends her best."

What the fuck was Uncle Mike babbling about? I hope I hadn't lost my winning ticket.

"You really fucked with Kubala's head," Uncle Mike said. "That lie you told him. That Burrascano got an anonymous tip."

"Huh?" My horse was moving down the stretch. How much did I bet?

Uncle Mike leaned in close. "I told Burrascano about it and he laughed. Said 'no way.' If he'd gotten a tip, he'd have warned Liz and let the cops trap them. Never waste good men, he said. Said he wished he had young men like you. They've got him pumped up on painkillers."

"We did it for Jimmy." My throat was dry. Like a patch of sand. A horse Jimmy gave me, damnit.

Uncle Mike rubbed my arm. "I'll get the nurse. We did it for Oscar and Liz, and the others, too. The people at O'Connell's are happy. I kept our names out of the papers. We're all unidentified federal agents."

"O'Connell's? Who's tending bar?"

"You've got a new client," Uncle Mike said. "Arlene Adams wants you to find out what happened to her ex."

"Eddie." It was a woman's voice.

I looked past Uncle Mike toward the door. Tara ran over and kissed me on the cheek.

"Careful," I croaked. "Watch the tubes." There were so many tubes. Hell, I couldn't count all the damn tubes.

"Eddie." Tears welled up in her eyes.

"Hell of a woman. Can you believe she's a fed?" Uncle Mike said.

I tried to laugh. "Opposites attract. Hey, can you check my wallet? I had a ticket on a horse yesterday. I know it's a winner."

THE END

Keep reading for a sneak peek of
Wager Tough
— coming soon —

WAGER TOUGH

PREQUEL TO WAGEREASY
THE WAGER SERIES

1

August, 2014

I stood on the top concourse of the Denver baseball stadium beside the clock tower and looked down. I pictured the header Zany took over the rail in the middle of the night. His mangled body four stories below now marked by nothing more than a rust-red stain on the concrete.

"Remember, Eddie," Zany had told me one summer years ago. "Lots of handicappers want to boil everything down to a system. They want to use numbers for speed and pace. But you can't simply reduce a race to a number and hope to win on a regular basis. You have to think of the things nobody can measure with a stopwatch. You got to think about 'heart.'"

That advice had paid off over the years. But Zany showed me more heart that summer than I'd ever seen in my young life. He'd taken a spill off Uncle Mike's horse, Splendid Runner, and had suffered serious injuries as a result. At first, he came to the track in a wheelchair, then a walker and then crutches. The pain etched in his face. I'd help him back and forth to his car, place bets and fetch drinks. It surprised me that he had to count on betting the horses for income. Back then I thought all jockeys were rich.

Traffic lined the streets around the ballpark. The rooftop bars and blaring hip-hop music shook up the weeknight doldrums. Behind the squat buildings of Lo-Do loomed the center of the city, skyscrapers that provided nesting ground for high-salaried types.

Zany had left Chicago after that summer of rehab and rode at small tracks and fairs out west. Each year the number of mounts decreased, until the stats stopped ten years ago. I was surprised he could ride at all when I recalled his back problems. But what else could he do – riding and the horses was all he knew. Then I answered my own question. He also knew gambling. So he had become a bookie.

I turned and concentrated upon the crowd. A group of young people, beers in hand, pushed each other, laughed and screamed, then stumbled off the escalator. I watched for my witness, the one the police did not yet know about.

Across the vacant picnic area near the concourse railing, smokers congregated in a designated area. Rare to find a quiet spot to smoke with a view. What a lousy time I'd picked to quit.

Even as the third inning ended, fans continued to stream to the grandstands. I saw a woman break away toward me through the picnic area. She wore work clothes – an ultra-short, black cocktail dress and high heels, and talked on her pink, rhinestone-encased cell phone. She had the kind of body that forced me to do a double take.

I walked up to her.

"Are you Eddie O'Connell?" She put the cell phone away, brushed back her long, black hair and looked up at me.

"That's right," I said. "Are you Amity?"

"Do you have my money?"

I always enjoy a warm, economical greeting but I was glad she'd arrived. "Over here."

I directed her a few steps over to the clock tower, away from the flow of the crowd. No need to make things too obvious.

She snatched the five twenty-dollar bills. "What's this? My feet are killing me. It must be important for Mags to set this up. I should get double."

Mags, the head of the local crime chapter in Denver. He took orders from Burrascano back in Chicago, the man who'd hired me and Uncle Mike to find Zany's killer. Zany was connected and everyone knew it or should've known it.

Why would the mob's gambling czar hire me to do this investigation? Because my uncle was a former Chicago homicide detective and Burrascano needed answers fast. Uncle Mike's bad leg from our last job wouldn't allow him to travel so I'd gotten my first solo job by default.

I considered Amity's play for more money from her angle. The job had its demands. I noted her chipped front tooth. I wondered what the tooth might cost to fix, who slapped her around, and what she'd look like with a perfect smile. I reached for more cash.

She sighed but flipped the cash expertly between her fingers and into the black sequined evening bag strapped over her shoulder.

"Now what?" she said.

"Tell me what happened with you and Zany that night."

"What about it?"

"Look, Mags wants answers. Make it easy on yourself."

She pulled out a stick of gum and chewed. "Fine."

"Where did you meet?"

"On the first floor. Zany bought me cotton candy and we came up here. This is such bullshit. I don't know anything."

I needed to get to the place where Zany had been tortured. I took a step back from the railing. "Show me where."

She headed off into the flaming orange sunset over the Rockies to the west and the smoky haze from the grills. Besides the aroma of burgers and brats, I smelled something else. It was a pungent campfire smell. I'd heard about the forest fires burning out of control in the record drought and heat, but didn't figure the smoke could drift this far.

Amity twisted a path through the string of concession stands to a boarded-up stand farthest from the flow of traffic. It was an eight by ten-foot wooden free-standing structure.

Why Zany would have a tryst inside this closed-up stand would never be answered. The structure remained unguarded, not even a strand of yellow police ribbon.

"How often did you come here?" I asked.

Her phone rang. "A few times."

"Turn the phone off. Did you come up here with others?"

"No. Absolutely not." She took out the phone, peered at the number and turned it off. "Zany was the one with the key."

Her eyes had become childlike upon demand like actress eyes. She'd drawn her arms tight around her chest as if chilled, despite the day's record heat that still languished through the dusk. No doubt she'd heard all the rumors of what happened here. If she knew the details from the police report about the cigarette burns, the bruises, the broken fingers and gouged eye, the lacerations around the testicles, maybe she'd find a new line of work. Maybe not knowing was worse.

I took a look around. "Stand there."

Using Amity as a shield, I pulled the pick from my pocket and went to work on the padlock. I practiced on this type of lock in the dark and I jimmied it open in seconds.

I swung the door open. The few photos in the police report showed the blood stains and ripped-open boxes.

"C'mon." I touched Amity's elbow and escorted her inside. "Let's take a look."

She stood in the doorway and then followed me in. "It looks different. There were stacks of cardboard boxes all over and beer kegs there under the counter."

I liked that she volunteered information. "Tell me what you did."

"What are you, some kind of pervert?"

"Think through what happened. Where did you stand?"

She glanced around the dark chamber as if disoriented. "About here." She moved a few steps. "Against a stack of boxes."

"Then what?"

"I took off my dress."

"And."

Her lips turned into a pout as she hesitated. "We started to kiss."

"On the lips?"

"No. On his cheek. I unbuckled his pants."

"Then what?"

She looked away and blushed. This newfound modesty seemed to surprise her. Then the crowd roared, shaking the rafters of the shed like the hand of God rattling dice, and she cried out. "He didn't want to do it."

"What?"

"He wanted me to go. He paid me but then told me to leave."

"He paid for nothing?"

"Yes."

"Why would he do that?"

"You don't understand. Zany was a gentleman."

"Did someone knock on the door or cause him –"

"No."

"Did you see someone?"

"No, no one."

"Maybe one of your wacko boyfriends," I said.

"No."

"Did you bind Zany's hands?"

"No, Zany never . . ."

The Formica shell started to break apart. "What happened?"

"Nothing. Who would do this?" She covered her face with her hands and sobbed. "Why?'

The same question ran through my head. At least I could eliminate her. She didn't seem to be part of it. The killer or killers must've followed her up here, waited, and then bound Zany after she'd left. The fun started after the crowd went home and the stadium turned dark.

"You took the money and left?"

"Yes, I asked Zany to take me back but he wouldn't."

"Why not?"

"Zany had to go somewhere."

"Where?"

"I don't know. Wait. The Kelso Club."

"Did he say why?"

"No. I think he had to meet someone. That's all. Said he had to work to set things straight."

"That's it?"

"I don't know what he meant."

"This Kelso Club, is it your strip club?"

"God no. It's a fancy place. I've never been there before."

"Did he say who he planned to meet?"

"No."

Her legs began to wobble. She reached out and leaned against the wall "Let me out of here. Please."

I took a step to the side and helped her out. "You got anything else you can tell me?"

She took a big gulp of air. "No, that's all. I swear."

"Tell me if you think of anything more or if anyone contacts you." I handed her a slip of paper with a number.

"I will."

She took several unsteady steps then gained traction and ran down the concourse to the stairs.

It was probably the same direction she went that night. I looked into the lines of people at the concessions and tried to read faces. The killer had waited for Amity to leave and stood in a crowd like this one.

I inspected the concession stand once more before I closed and locked the door. The walls had done their job and broke down my one witness. It wasn't much but it was something.

How long had the torture gone on before Zany had been dragged over to the clock tower? The walls got to me too.

I gazed out over the city. What sort of monster was I looking for?

Don't miss release day—subscribe to my newsletter at www.TomFarrellBooks.com

ACKNOWLEDGMENTS

I really appreciate the support I've received from so many. I'd like to thank my critique partners who see the pages before the second or third draft. These brave readers include the Tuesday Night Mystery Critique Group: Suzanne Prouix, Chris Jorgensen, Don Beckwith, Mike McClanahan, Jedeane MacDonald, Laurie Walcott, Kay Bergstrom, Val Moses and Scott Brendel. In addition, my Thursday night critique group: Bill Brinn, Steve Reinsma, Luke Dutka, Judy Green Matheny and Jim Morris. Special thanks to my beta readers: Scott Brendel, Chris Jorgensen, Jedeane Macdonald and Sue Thomas. Many thanks to my mentors in the publishing world: Karla Jay, Wendy Terrien and Barbara Nickless. I would also like to thank my fellow writers at Rocky Mountain Fiction Writers, Pikes Peak Writers, Thrillerfest and Rocky Mountain Mystery Writers of America for the meetings and conferences they've presented over the years that have provided me with insights into the craft of writing.

To my fellow handicappers, best of luck. Stay in control and seek help, if needed.

To my editors, developmental editor Steve Parolini and copy editor Susan Brooks, thank you. To my design team, book cover by Steven Novak and Interior by Ali Cross. Thanks for your hard work.

Lastly, to my family. My wife, Kathi, and sons, Greg and Mark. You make it all worthwhile.

ABOUT THE AUTHOR

 **Tom Farrell** has worked as a golf course starter, a chemist, and clerked at City Hall in Chicago while attending law school. He has served as Vice President of Rocky Mountain Fiction Writers, a nonprofit corporation, and was a past finalist in the Pikes Peak Writer's Contest in the Mystery, Suspense and Thriller category. Now retired from practicing law, when he's not handicapping, he can be found on the golf course or at a local jazz club.

www.tomfarrellbooks.com

Printed in Great Britain
by Amazon

83818115R00212